I0685839

Asher

THE MEN OF VERSTECK VALLEY

EROSA KNOWLES

EROSA KNOWLES CREATES - USA TODAY BESTSELLING AUTHOR

Asher

MEN OF VERSTECK VALLEY BOOK 1

Mya Burch and her five-year-old son Colin, Jr. left home for a job and the start of a new life across the country in a place called Versteck Valley. It was time for her to jumpstart her career and enroll her son in a school for gifted kids. On the surface, Versteck looked like a perfect place to live in peace and raise her son. But Versteck had secrets that Mya couldn't imagine and the residents refused to share.

Asher Pendergrass had built his security company on grit and determination. He and his cousins had invested millions to make their teen-aged dream a reality. Versteck Arms was a place that accepted the best talent from around the world and they'd defend their piece of heaven against all outsiders.

Asher isn't too keen on Mya living next door and even less so when an unknown threat arrives in town harassing the single mother and her son. Strangers weren't welcome in Versteck, those who started trouble even less so. With a threat against Mya and her son rising each day, Asher and the men of Versteck have to make a decision to either band together to help the newcomer or step aside.

As always, I'd like to thank my family for their unwavering support and the women and men who write me asking for more stories. You keep me going! Thanks to Tristin, Karen, Michelle and the women who keep it real. Versteck Valley is a fictional town filled with extraordinary people. Enjoy!

Erosa

Contents

CHAPTER ONE

The gigantic gray rock broke the blue skyline in craggy peaks as the mountains rose in the distance with an interesting halo that looked like an unstarched collar around the tips. After living in Tulsa where everything was flat, seeing the mountains filled Mya with joyous pleasure. She wished she could stop the car and stare. But there would be time for that later. Still, she continued stealing glances at the majestic sight of the massive protrusions from the earth.

A sliver of excitement slid down Mya's back as the reality of what she had done hit hard. She had left home. The naysayers who predicted she would do nothing with her life could officially shut the hell up. Unbeknownst to most of her extended family and neighbors, she had returned to school, albeit an online university, and gotten delayed degrees in psychology and sociology.

Smiling with satisfaction, she thought of the members of her mom's church and the pleasure her mom would receive telling the old biddies about this new job in Colorado. Would Mama wait until Sunday? Mya doubted it.

She pressed the gas to pass the slow car in front of her on Interstate 70. Her late silver-gray model Honda moved with ease and continued traveling from Tulsa to Denver, actually northwest of Denver to Versteck Valley. She had read a little of the town's history; it was fascinating.

Versteck was built from the ashes of an old silver mining town located between a few mountains, with a town square, library, restaurants, and lots of those artsy shops with custom jewelry and artwork. She liked the idea of living in an area with old west history and today's modern facilities. After viewing pictures of her rental home and the surrounding neighborhood, it convinced her she would have all the modern conveniences she needed.

Soft jazz kept her company as she gazed straight ahead with occasional longing glances at the mountains. Half-aware of the world outside the confining comfort of the car, she glanced in the rear-view mirror at her son, Colin, smiling as he turned the page in the book he read. Books worked better than pacifiers or anything else for him, always had from the time he could focus on colors on the page. He had no problems sitting in a corner or in the middle of the room as long as the pages in the book held his interest.

Initially, it had been brightly colored picture books, and now he read elementary school level books even though he was five. Being more advanced than the rest of the class made it challenging for the three teachers whose classes he had been in to manage him. One of them suggested he get tested, not because he was so smart, but because she thought his lack of interest in sports or running on the playground was strange. At first, Mya had been offended, but after discussing it with her mother, they had him tested.

As suspected, he scored extremely high on the IQ test. Turns out, he simply wasn't interested in sports or running around with the other kids outside. She was grateful that he was an easy child. As long as he had something to read or solve, he was happy. For a five-year-old with a short attention span, she made sure he had a variety to choose from within arm's reach for this move across the country.

"How's it going, Colin?" she glanced at him again, unsurprised he hadn't answered. Chances are he didn't hear her while under the spell of whatever he read. Her mom and Jefferson, her brother, said it was unnatural in a child so young. They thought he was too old for a car seat, even though he wasn't big enough for a booster seat yet. Mya disagreed.

As she neared Denver, traffic slowed. A distant rumble made her jump and stare in the rear-view mirror. She sent an unanswered prayer that Colin hadn't heard the sound. His gray, wide-eyed stare said he did. She looked up at the clear skies and took a deep breath.

His lower lip trembled, but he hadn't panicked. Not yet. Please, please hold on until we reach this place, she prayed as the traffic eased and she started forward. The phone beeped, and she groaned. "Not now, Mom."

The GPS told her to turn off at the next exit. Thinking they were close, she took a deep breath and relaxed until she saw they had another 48 minutes to go. The map showed twisting back roads into a rural area of the state.

She glanced at Colin. He had returned to his book. The idea of being in a car with Colin in full break-down mode scared her. Should she turn around and get a hotel room in Denver? Or take her chances and continue to Versteck Valley? If the weather worsened, Colin would melt-down, unlock the car seat and climb into her lap, moving traffic or not. Few things in life bothered her resilient son, but thunderstorms spooked him to the tenth degree. He did not handle them well.

Her mom called again.

She pressed the phone button on her steering wheel. "Mom?" she answered as she came to a stop sign.

"How's the trip coming along?"

"Okay. We just drove through Denver. Versteck Valley is another 45 minutes, but I'm thinking about turning back and getting a hotel room for the night."

"What? Why? You're supposed to report to work tomorrow or something like that. That's the reason you couldn't wait for me to ride with you," her mom said, sounding suspicious.

"Orientation is tomorrow, and that's at one in the afternoon. I can make that, but it looks like a thunderstorm and I'm scared to chance it," she whispered and glanced at Colin in the rear-view mirror. Thankfully, he was reading again.

"I didn't see anything about rain in the forecast, did you?" her mom asked.

"No. But I heard some rumbling a few minutes ago that sounded like thunder." She frowned as she took a brief look up at the clear skies. "The sun's shining, and it doesn't look like rain or anything."

"If you keep going, you'll be there before dark and who knows what kind of hotel room you'll find in Denver without a reservation? You're too close to being where you're going to stop now. Call me when you get to the house."

Mya turned onto the long two-lane road heading to Versteck and said a quick prayer that the weather held. "Alright, will do. Wait. How're you feeling? How's your hip?" Her mom had surgery three days ago, which was the reason Mya didn't want her sitting in the car with them for over ten hours. It would be painful. Plus, her mom would need to make numerous stops to stretch and go to the bathroom, which would turn the 10 hour drive to 12 or 13. A flight would be easier for her mom to navigate once the doctor cleared her.

"Same as when you left early this morning, honey. It's going to take time to heal, and I'm staying off my leg. I'll be alright, don't worry about me. I'm worrying enough about you and Colin traveling alone to a new place where you don't know anybody. No need for both of us to be in the worry-house."

Mya grinned. "Worry-house? Really?" Mya's mom practically kicked her out of the house to get her to the job.

Her mom laughed, and it warmed Mya. They were close. As the oldest and only daughter, she and her mom had been through so many hills and valleys together. This separation wasn't a big deal. Once her mom healed and could travel, she would come for a long visit. If she liked it, she would consider moving.

"You like that word? I just made it up."

Mya smiled and glanced at her son again. "I could tell. Stop worrying and take care of you. I'll call once I get there and if it's late, I'll call in the morning."

"No. Call me tonight, no matter what time you get there. I won't be able to sleep if you don't."

"Alright, I'll call once we're settled." She disconnected, checked her gas, almost a full tank, and looked over her shoulder at her curly-haired son, as he turned another page. Traffic slowed to a procession of cars bumper to bumper behind an enormous piece of farm equipment that had to be moving 20 to 15 mph.

"You've got to be kidding me," she murmured while checking to see if she could pass and couldn't as cars whizzed by in the other lane. By the time the farm equipment turned onto a dirt road, 28 minutes had passed, and the GPS gave her another 39 minutes to reach her destination.

Traffic thinned, and she made decent time. With 15 minutes to go, the sky darkened and a rumble rolled across the sky.

Colin whimpered when the sound echoed in the sky again.

"No, no, no," she murmured and pressed the gas. They had to reach the house she rented before the storm. It couldn't be much further.

Raindrops hit the windshield softly at first.

Her son's eyes went wide as saucers as his gaze locked on the window. "There should be a town nearby. A place we can wait out this storm." She wasn't sure if she told Colin to prevent his breakdown or encourage herself. A police car blocked the road ahead, and she cursed.

Dressed in rain gear with water falling from his plastic covered cap, he stood outside his car with his hand up to stop her. Peeved by the delay, she hushed Colin as she rolled down her window halfway.

Without waiting for the officer to speak, she said. "I'm heading into Versteck. We're almost there and need to get out of this storm." The police officer looked into the car and nodded. "If you want to avoid the storm, make a right here and follow the road until you come to a large two-story house and go inside."

"Is it a hotel or something?" she asked.

He waved her to the right and went to the car behind her. The rain fell harder, but with the absence of thunder and lightning, they should be okay. She turned right, followed the road, and boom, crack. A double whammy of thunder and lightning. She didn't bother turning to look at Colin when he screamed and writhed in his car seat as if red ants crawled over his body. Tears ran down his creamy cheeks, now splotched red as he cried like his life was ending.

It broke her heart.

Rain fell faster, and she drove slower. Nothing she said would stop him from crying. She had to get him out of this weather and contemplated turning around. Angry because she should've followed her mind and gotten a room in Denver. She didn't know how far this hotel was or what kind of place was this far out, anyway. Dark mountains, no longer fanciful or pretty, acted as a backdrop as she drove up the street. There were no other houses or signs signaling a hotel along the long road, and she wondered if the Officer had made a mistake.

Colin's unrelenting screams gave her a headache. Just as she was about to turn around, she saw the hotel in the distance and turned onto the side road leading to the wide, columned porch. No one was outside as she pulled the car to a stop beneath the portico.

"It's alright, baby. We're here. Let's go inside, away from the noise." She hopped out with her keys and purse, ran around to the other side, and lifted him out. She'd come back for his things once they settled.

He wrapped his arms around her neck and legs around her waist as he continued to cry. Thankfully, he stopped screaming as they hurried to the door, opened it, and walked inside.

Immediately she knew something was wrong, or they handled things differently in this small town as she looked for the lobby and check-in counter. Colin's whimpers echoed in the large foyer with a large chandelier that looked like something out of a gothic novel. Without looking behind her, she stepped back toward the door. This wasn't a hotel. The police had made a mistake.

"What the hell are you doing in here?" A deep male voice asked in a low, angry tone.

Colin screamed.

The piercing sound was so close to her ear it sent shards of pain to her head. He shook so hard she almost dropped him.

Mya spun toward the deep voice and stared at the outline of a man. Most of him was in the shadows, and she couldn't see him clearly.

"I apologize. The Police officer gave me directions to come here when I told him I needed to get my son out of the storm. I thought this was a hotel." She hefted Colin in her arms and walked to the door.

Thunder boomed in the distance, followed by cracks of lightning. Colin screamed and tried to climb inside her body. It would be hard getting him back in the car.

"You're Ms. Curtain? The new housekeeper? No one told me you had a child or that a child would come with you," he said in a low voice.

"What?" She could hardly concentrate on what he was saying while calming her son. "No. I'm not Ms. Curtain. The police officer must've thought that's who I was and sent me here." She rubbed Colin's back as he continued to cry.

"What's the matter with him? Is he sickly?"

"No, he's not. It's the storm. He doesn't like thunder," she explained while listening. Soon as the storm died down, they would leave.

"Were you lost?"

"No, the road was closed, and the police were redirecting traffic." Her arms grew tired. She glanced at a brocade padded bench in the foyer, just inside the door.

"Have a seat, wait out the storm. I left the door open for Ms. Curtain. Chances are she won't arrive today," he said and stepped backward, disappearing from her sight.

"Thank you," she said as she took the seat.

Colin whimpered but kept a tight grip around her neck as he turned his face toward the voice.

Thunder rolled across the sky again. Colin screamed while shaking, and buried his face against her chest.

"It's okay, baby. It's okay," she whispered, wishing she was in her car or some place less creepy. What if the cop and this guy had some kind of racket going on where they lured women to this place and… she locked down that thought and palmed her keys with the small canister of mace.

Outside, the storm continued to rage.

Colin shook so badly she had a hard time holding him on her lap. Normally, she would put him in bed with her and turn on the television to drown the noise outside. This time they were right next to the door, and she refused to close it, which meant they heard everything.

The guy never reappeared.

Mya searched the dimly lit area where he had been standing while keeping an eye on her primary escape avenue, the front door. How old was this place? Was it one of the historical homes? Or the place the German criminal lived? Although she appreciated the shelter which allowed her son to calm down, she couldn't stop thinking of the town named for hiding criminals. The guy had remained hidden in the shadows could very well be someone hiding from the law.

When the rain let up and the skies lightened, 10 minutes had passed. Colin sobbed but eased up on the death grip as he took her hand in preparation to leave.

"Thank you for your hospitality, Sir. I'll close the door behind me," she yelled as she walked outside toward her car. She put Colin in his car seat, locked him in, and ran to the driver's side. The sooner they got out of here, the better.

She turned around and headed back in the direction she had come.

CHAPTER TWO

A SHER HEARD THE DOOR close, looked at the closed-circuit security cameras and replaced the gun in its holster as she drove off. What the hell had Jack been thinking to send that woman and small child to this place? He could've gotten them killed.

He ran a hand through his hair, took a deep breath, and headed back toward the hidden panel that led to the underground tunnels where his men waited. After pressing his palm on the scanner, then his eye, he typed in a code.

The door opened. He walked down the steps as the door closed silently behind him. Lights came on as he continued down the long stairs that would take him deep beneath the house into a tunnel that ended in a cavern in the mountain. Miners created the tunnels in the 1800s when the silver mines were productive. Once he and his cousins returned to Versteck, they spent a large amount of money to extend and add support to the tunnels so that they could come and go unseen.

They built a business around it.

He heard the men before he saw them on the landing, waiting for him.

"Menendez sent a woman with a kid?" Tombs asked in his slow, southern, raspy voice. Retired, in his mid-fifties, and somewhat stooped with short brown hair and blue eyes. He could throw a blade with pin-point accuracy ten out of ten times and vanish before his victim hit the ground.

"No. I don't think so. Jack sent her to get out of the rain," Asher said, allowing the tone of his voice to tell them what he thought of that idea.

"Moron," Connor said, shaking his head. Tall and slender with shaggy white hair, Connor was the best long-distance shooter on the team and was in high demand despite being retired from the life. "Good thing he's on our side, or we'd be in deep shit."

"True," Asher said, his thoughts returning to the problem at hand. *What happened to the housekeeper?* Had they discovered the trap Asher set and aborted? Menendez, the head of Gabriel's Shipping publicly and thug wannabe privately had finally tracked Asher to Versteck Valley. Menendez would be pissed and see the location as a challenge, which it was.

Within the past few years, Asher had moved his base of operations here. Two years ago, he took and completed a contract from the Feds to locate a shipment of arms. Word came down recently that Menendez learned of Asher's role in the government locating and seizing the illegal shipment of guns and ammo. Menendez had lost money, lost face and had to use considerable collateral to remain out of prison, although several of his closest associates were now guests in the penitentiary behind the botched deal. Unable to believe anyone could touch him, Menendez searched high and low until he got wind of Asher and his group of operatives.

A former associate had sold Asher out after coming down with a severe case of diarrhea of the mouth. In their line of business, there was only one cure for that problem. That person recently suffered irreplaceable losses that cost him his family and an arrest on drug trafficking charges. In prison, the man would cease to breathe. It didn't pay to be a rat, especially when you didn't know who owned a bigger mousetrap.

Menendez was out for blood.

Asher's blood.

His phone vibrated. He read the message from Jack, the local Sheriff. "Should I let her through?"

The woman with the crying child must have made it back to the blockade. "Yes."

"Sure?"

Asher silently cursed. "She's not the one." *Imbecile.*

"Sorry, thought she was the housekeeper." And that's why Sheriff Jack Jackson was on Asher's payroll, but not a part of his inner team. The man didn't think things through and wasn't thorough.

"NP." He sent the message and disconnected.

"What do you think Menendez is planning?" Tombs asked.

"His people are nearby, somewhere. The call yesterday was to make sure I was in town, accessible. The question is, where the hell are they? Why haven't they shown up?" Asher said. He called the Sheriff. "Is there a van or truck you don't recognize parked someplace in town or nearby?"

"Haven't seen any. I've been averting traffic from the area of town you specified," Jack said. "I can go look or have one of my guys do it."

"Yeah, do that. Let me know if you see anything."

"Can you tell me what this is about?" Jack asked. "I might be in a better position to help if I understood what was going on."

"Sure, I'll let you know once I've got a handle on everything, is that alright?" He would never share his secrets with Jack.

"Sure. I'll take a drive around town and let you know if I see anything." The sheriff sounded happy, as if they were friends. The man tried too hard.

"Movement above-ground," Mercer said, watching the monitors from the small control room. "Looks like five on the move toward the house, spreading out. I'm locking down the doors and windows, so they don't go inside and damage the place."

Eager to welcome their uninvited guests, Asher agreed and looked at the men. "We keep this outside. Drop 'em, bag 'em, and torch them. Any problems, head to the tunnels. We'll meet in Mecca for debriefing later."

Retreating to the safety of the tunnels was standard procedure and had saved their lives more than once. While most residents knew about the tunnels, it was local folklore after-all, few could navigate them successfully without knowing where they led. A person could get lost in the underground caverns, which was why Asher's tunnels were pass-coded and accessible only to his team.

"Tell Boots to fire up the incinerator," Asher said.

"Will do," Mercer said. His arthritic fingers weren't as fast as they had been when he first arrived four years ago, but he was steady and mentally keen as a whip.

Asher pulled the cameras up on his tablet and studied the positions of the five heading toward them. "Each one takes one," he said as the others crowded around to look at the screen. "I'll bring one back for questioning." He looked over the heads of the older men at Bryson, a native of Versteck with a recent medical discharge from the military. "Find a place for me to bring him so you can have a talk with him."

Bryson nodded, turned and ran further down the tunnel.

"They're at the fence," Mercer announced.

"Let's go," Asher said, pulling his hair back and pulling on a dark ski mask. He checked his weapons and ammo again before they traveled up another set of stairs that led to an abandoned house close to Asher's aunt's place.

Moving silently, it didn't take long to see their targets. The whiz of Tombs' blade was the only sound in the stillness. The person dropped to the ground. Connor shot the person climbing the wall and heading to the roof. He fell and hit the concrete patio hard. Two others ran toward their comrades and were shot or stabbed.

Asher caught sight of the fifth person attempting to enter the front door beneath the veranda. Something about the way the person moved stopped him from pulling the trigger to administer a disarming shot.

As if realizing they were being watched, the person stopped, turned and looked in his direction before speaking. "I have an appointment here for a job, but no one's opening the door. Can you help me?"

Asher remained in the shadows and cursed. No one on his team would hurt a woman. Not even him. This sucked. He backed up silently and motioned for the men to move with him. When they were a sufficient distance, he contacted Mercer to find out the status of the female and learned she continued trying to break into the house. She had a bag at her feet, and he was concerned about what was inside.

Unsure how to handle this recent development, Asher wasn't surprised when a familiar car pulled up, and a female stepped out holding a gun on the woman. Laura was deadly accurate and had no problem shooting her same gender, especially one who came to Versteck to cause problems.

"Boss, Laura's taking the woman with her. When she drives off, you can remove the bag at the door and disarm whatever's in it," Mercer said with some humor.

Asher and the others couldn't see what was happening, but he knew Laura. "What did she do?"

"Made the woman strip and leave everything and I mean everything on the porch. That's after she shot her on the earlobe. Got her silencer on." He laughed.

"I'm not going to ask how Laura knew we would need her special skills, but thanks. Need to tidy up out here and get over to the funeral home," Asher said, feeling relieved. Laura would ask the right questions, get the answers and handle the problem in a way none of them would.

"They just pulled off. You can go in and clean up. I'll let Bryson know about the change in plans," Mercer said. "He's going to be disappointed he won't get a chance to play."

Asher snorted as they moved back toward the house. It didn't take long to bag the bodies. Bryson arrived with a white cargo van with the name Higher Dimensions on the side. Asher didn't have time to complain about the awful choice of transportation as he sent the older men home through the tunnels and rode with Bryson.

"What do you think Laura's doing with the chick?" Bryson asked as they drove down the back road toward the funeral home.

"Questioning her," Asher said while looking out the window. It wasn't that late, around nine in the evening, but few cars were on the road, most shops were closed, leaving the two restaurants and three bars open for patrons. Versteck was a quiet, sleepy town, perfect for his business, and he loved it.

When they reached the funeral home, the room was ready. They placed the first bag on the loading table and pressed the button. The cremator door opened, and the bag moved forward into the flames. Six hours later, he returned to his aunt's house, tired and hungry. Menendez would no doubt retaliate, but not tonight. Tonight, there were four, possibly five, he corrected when he thought of the cryptic text from Laura—*Menendez hit, keep the fire burning*, fewer people to do Menendez's bidding.

Asher unlocked the front door and stopped in the middle of the foyer, hand on the hilt of his weapon, and inhaled. The slightest hint of lavender wafted through the air, a token left from the woman and child.

He turned and stared at the bench where she'd sat comforting the boy. Asher had picked up on the child's terror before he saw them. That hadn't been an act. That's what made him come out of hiding to face them.

The woman's gaze. All of her attention had been on the boy. She'd been frightened. He saw it in her eyes as he watched her on the cam. But she forced down that emotion to give the child what he needed. She was aware of her surroundings and never fully let her guard down. Her gaze flitted nervously around, and she never closed the front door. If she felt danger, she'd have rushed outside with her son. No doubt about it. It wasn't often he saw selfless courage or sacrifice like that. It had impressed him.

Asher's phone vibrated. Text from Jack. "Found a van, rental for a guy from out of town. He's just taking in the sights and moved along when I approached."

"Thank you. I was just curious." The last thing Asher wanted was Jack going after those guys alone. They'd kill him and escape. Although Jack was holding the Sheriff's position until the regular sheriff returned, he was too valuable and difficult to replace at the moment.

"Headed close by your place. Want a beer?"

Asher looked at the clock. It was late. He wasn't in the mood to play word games with the Sheriff. He wanted to leave this place, check some things on the computer and make new plans. As the owner of the largest security company in the area, Asher wanted to keep the local law on his side and sometimes needed to play polite, if not nice. Besides, he didn't want Jack to know he didn't live here.

Asher replied to Jack's question, naming the brand of beer he enjoyed and went to take a shower.

CHAPTER THREE

"**Y**OU KILLED HIM. HE died because of you."

"No, that's not true, it's not true," she wept while covering her ears. "Stop it," she said, running from the vile words.

"You killed my son. It's your fault he's dead," the mocking voice said, following her, chasing her.

"No," she yelled and sat up, wide eyed and shaking. It had been over two years since she'd had that nightmare. She sucked in air and rubbed her stiff arms while getting her bearings in the unfamiliar room. Reality returned slowly with each breath.

Versteck. New job. New school for Colin.

She took another deep breath and looked at the clock on the nightstand. She had overslept, which wasn't surprising given the day she had yesterday. Once they left that creepy house on the hill, she didn't bother stopping to ask the cop, which she later learned was the Sheriff, for directions. Instead, she drove straight past him as if she didn't see him standing next to his car on the phone. She wondered where they found him? The man was virtually useless.

They drove through town, saw several businesses, a two-story government building, shops, a park, theater. Elevated in the distance, maybe a mile or two away, stood a large red brick building with interesting woodwork near the windows and doors. It looked like it watched over the town. She tried to recall any information she had read about it, but couldn't remember as she turned onto the road leading to the subdivision of her rental house.

Streetlights made the roads glisten from the recent rain. Similar homes lined both sides of the street as she slowed to find the rental. The agent had kindly left on the porch light on the one and a half story home. She'd breathed a sigh of relief as they pulled into the driveway. Colin had been asleep and hadn't seen the open floor plan, with large living and dining areas and kitchen. Both of their bedrooms were on the first floor. She put him to bed before bringing in their luggage and pulling her car into the two-car garage.

The house looked better in person than the video or photos she had seen. The bedroom sets had arrived and were set up in their rooms, which was all that mattered for now. Later, she would purchase furniture for the rest of the house.

It still pissed her off when she recalled sitting in a stranger's home praying he was decent and wouldn't hurt her or Colin when this house was less than five miles away. That an officer of the law put her in that position still irked her.

"Come on, Colin, we need to check out your new school, get some shopping done and then I've got orientation," she said as she stretched and slid off the bed.

He didn't answer as he rolled out of her bed, an indulgence she allowed because of the weather, and padded to the hall bathroom. She hadn't unpacked and laid out a pair of jeans, socks, underwear, shirt, and a sweater for him to put on. They would grab something to eat on the way.

Pleased to have a bathroom in the master suite, it didn't take her long to dress. Excitement thrummed through her. The move was a step toward complete independence. Finishing college while raising Colin and living with her mom had been the right thing to do. But they needed a change. Colin was exceptionally smart. It had become increasingly difficult to find the right school for him where the teachers or students didn't respond to him as if he had a problem. She chose Colorado over Oklahoma because her son got into a gifted preschool. The tuition was high, but with her salary and the survivor's benefit check she received from the government for Colin, she could swing it.

Dressed and looking so handsome, Colin walked toward her and stopped near the door. "I'm ready."

"Good, let's eat first and then head to the school. We need to buy groceries later today," she said.

"The refrigerator's smaller than Nana's," he said.

"Yes, but there's only two of us, not three, so we won't buy as much."

He nodded as he picked up his overcoat. "Are you sure I can't take my books with me?"

"Not today. After you look around the classroom, let me know if you need to take anything like we did back in Tulsa. I'll talk to the teacher about it, alright?"

He nodded.

"Say the words, Colin. No teaching the teacher. I'll talk to her if you need more work or additional books. Not you, understand?" She waited until his large gray eyes met hers. He looked so much like his father. Her heart dropped. Not because she missed or loved Colin Sr. They hadn't had that kind of relationship. Her son would never see his father or speak with him again. His death in Iraq made sure of that, and that saddened her. Once the paternity test proved Colin Sr. was the father, he was onboard and as involved as he could be while thousands of miles away.

"I understand and won't say anything to her. Just to you."

She bit back a smile at the snark in his voice and let it slide. Being in a new place, neither of them had slept well last night. She planned to get him back on schedule soon.

Versteck Valley was an interesting town. Not quite a city, but not a rural community, either. Several well-known stores filled the shopping centers, as well as grocery chains. They pulled into a drive-through and ordered breakfast, an unusual treat that had Colin smiling and leaning out of his car seat.

Driving through town, she recognized several clothing shops, a theater, and a small museum. The school was on the outskirts of town in the same direction as the facility where she would soon start work.

Higher Dimensions Academy was a large one-story brick building that took up a huge portion of the block. From the outside, it looked clean and welcoming. Three playgrounds with fences separating them and different levels of equipment took up most of the outdoor space.

"Nice." She looked at Colin in the rear-view mirror, noticed his curiosity, and counted it as a good sign. "Finished eating your biscuit?"

"Yes. I put the paper in the bag to go in the trash," he said without looking at her.

"Thank you. Let's go inside." Her official appointment was in 18 minutes with the director, but she hoped they could look around until then.

He unbuckled his car seat and waited for her to open the door. She extended her hand, and he took it. Feeling pleased with the results of this new chapter in her life, she moved toward the building with a smile and purpose. The security guard greeted them and contacted the director regarding their presence.

Unsure if she should be concerned or relieved at the sight of security, Mya waited patiently in the lobby area for Ms. Wails. The woman didn't keep her waiting long. She entered the lobby with long-legged strides, a welcoming smile, and fulsome praise over Colin's test scores. Dressed in serviceable dark brown dress trousers, a short-sleeved cream-colored blouse, and sensible shoes, she bent forward and pushed aside the lock of brown hair that had fallen across her face.

"Hello Colin, welcome to Higher Dimensions. I'm Ms. Bonnie Wails, the Director. That's Mr. Bryson, head of security and this…" A lady with a deep tan and gorgeous blue eyes, slightly shorter than Ms. Wails, walked up beside her. "This is Ms. Jenkins, your teacher." Ms. Jenkins dressed similarly to Ms. Wails. Both women had slender builds.

As the parent, Mya wasn't accustomed to being ignored. All eyes were on Colin, the entire conversation was with him, and if the wide smile he wore was an indication, he loved it.

"Would you like to look around the school?" Ms. Wails asked, looking at Colin.

"Yes, we would," Mya said, inserting herself into the conversation.

Ms. Wails looked up at her, smiled, and straightened. "Sorry, how are you, Ms. Burch?"

Mya smiled. "I'm fine, and we're glad to be here. This is a beautiful school." She glanced at the guard, who pretended not to notice them.

Ms. Wails smiled and extended her hand toward the hall she'd just arrived from. "Please, come with us so we can give you a quick tour and then Colin can join his class. I think you'll like it here."

Colin looked at Ms. Wails and then at his mom. "Thank you."

The library was the first stop and was an immediate hit with her son. His eyes widened over the rows and rows of books.

"Of course, we have access to thousands more books online, but our students spend a lot of time here," Ms. Wails said, watching Colin.

"Whoa," he said, looking around slowly, wide-eyed.

Mya laughed along with the others as a knot loosened in her chest. He would fit in here. There'd be no name calling, no dumbing down to make teachers feel better. He could learn as much as fast as his mind could absorb. They continued through the facility to see the gym, cafeteria, band room, drama, dance. All the arts were there, along with science and biology labs and computers. They assigned every student a laptop to complete significant portions of their work.

Mya was amazed at the vast array of resources available at the preschool and fully understood the high cost of tuition. She followed the others to Colin's class. Inside were eight kids, three girls and five boys of various ethnicities. Carol King, Bev Harry, and Sheila Brown were Ms. Jenkins' assistants and worked with the kids.

"Can you pause from where you are for a moment?" Ms. Jenkins said. The kids looked at her and then at Colin.

"This is Colin Henry, Junior. He's new to Higher Dimensions and our class. He moved here from Tulsa and is new in the area. Everyone welcome Colin to Colorado and our class."

"Welcome." The students offered welcomes with a decided lack of enthusiasm, as if they couldn't be bothered.

Mya almost laughed because their attitudes mirrored Colin's. "Would you like him to stay here while we finish the paperwork?" Ms. Wails asked. Which really meant while you come and pay his bill.

"Yes, that's fine." Mya touched Colin's shoulder. "Why don't you check out the classroom and computers while I finish talking to Ms. Wails? I'll be back in a few minutes." She had explained to him he didn't have to stay at school today if he didn't want to since she didn't start work for a couple of days.

"Alright." He zeroed in on the bookshelves and headed in that direction. Smiling, she shook her head. *Only my son.* She looked at the others and changed that. Maybe not. With one last look at him as he studied the titles of each book, Mya followed Ms. Wails to the administrative section of the school.

"We're opening a private elementary school for our students. The campus is almost completed and should be open for the next school term," she said. "Something to keep in mind for Colin."

"Thank you, I will." If things worked out well for Colin here, she would definitely enroll him in that elementary school.

"Although we call it an elementary school, by the time our students leave this preschool, they're too advanced for public school and most private schools. We had so many parents asking us to consider continuing the education process into the next level we had to study the possibility. Current and past students always have priority placements."

Good to know. "Thank you. I'm sure that's something I'd like to do when the time comes. You received his tuition payment?" Mya asked. Since she saw the debit in her bank account, she knew they had, but wanted to hear it from the Director.

"Yes. Yes, he's paid up. There are a few incidentals, lockers, meal plan, and lab fees that need to be taken care of," she said. "What do you think of our facility?"

Mya hoped the woman would ask. "It's beautiful, state-of-the art and convenient." She smiled. "But what's with the security guard?"

Ms. Wails smiled. "Some students who attend the Academy are from families that require we monitor their children at all times. Rather than have the halls filled with guards, we hired armed security and beefed up school security. Don't misunderstand, their guards are still somewhere nearby, just not on the grounds. So if Colin sees someone carrying a weapon and escorting a student into a car, that's what's going on."

"I see." Mya didn't like the idea of Colin seeing anyone with a gun.

"Here's the list of additional expenses. All his school supplies, laptop, gym clothes, everything's included in tuition, and these fees are the last of it. All he needs to do is show up. We provide the rest."

Mya handed over her credit card to pay the $1,558 in fees. "Can he bring books?"

Ms. Wails frowned. "Why would he bring books to school?"

"Some of his favorites, that's all. If it's a problem, I'll tell him," she said, backtracking when she remembered the massive library.

Ms. Wails returned Mya's card. "I see. Why not do this? If we don't have his favorite book in the library, he can bring it from home. Will that work?"

"Yes, I'm sure it will." Relieved, Mya mentally patted herself on the back for remembering to bring it up.

Ms. Wails turned a large monitor to Mya. "He's talking to the other students," she said.

Mya's chest loosened with pleasure and relief as she watched Colin interact with the other kids, something he rarely did. They were discussing a book in his hand. Of course, they'd bond over books, she thought, watching as her heart lightened.

Colin laughed and opened the book to another page, pointed at it as he showed it to one boy who nodded in agreement. The kid showed Colin something on his laptop. Colin stared at it for a few moments, and they talked.

Seeing him interact, discuss and listen with interest was worth the move, worth the high tuition, worth more than she could ever say. This, she had gotten this right.

"Think he wants to stay today?" Ms. Wails asked with a slight smile.

"We'll see." Mya stood and shook the director's hand. "Thank you."

"Colin is an exceptional child who will be challenged daily. We allow them to learn at their own pace, but the students in that class are serious achievers. If you ever think he's under too much pressure, we can always move him to another class with equally gifted students who are more sociable."

Mya nodded. Colin kept to himself and didn't engage with other children. She hoped being in a new school or surroundings would change that. But maybe he wasn't built that way. This small setting with students doing their own thing might be the right formula for him. Time would tell. She glanced at the wall clock and headed to the door. "I need to see if he's staying today or starting in the morning," Mya said.

"I'll show you the way to that wing of the building," Ms. Wails said. They walked in silence and stopped in front of Colin's class.

Mya tapped on the door. Ms. Jenkins sent Colin to talk with her. "How are the books in there?" she whispered.

He nodded. "Pretty good. Michael read Moby Dick and Huckleberry Finn." It was obvious Michael impressed him.

"Sounds pretty good. Did you check out the computers? Are they any good?" she whispered.

"Yeah, those are great. I'll get my own when I start," he said. "When am I starting?"

"Do you want to stay today? You can. I'll pick you up after school," she said, pretty sure he would stay.

"Alright, I'll stay today, so I can get my laptop and get started."

"Can I kiss you goodbye until later? Just a quick one, because I'm going to miss you so much."

He frowned and then smiled. "Okay."

She brushed her lips against his forehead and hadn't stood straight before he ran back inside to asked Ms. Jenkins about his laptop.

Mya sat in her car in the parking lot of Versteck Arms and stared at the two large buildings. One stood behind the other, both held two floors, and were surrounded by a large beige brick wall with a heavy iron gate. The modern brick and glass buildings looked out-of-place inside the ancient wall. *Had they torn down whatever had been here before?* It looked that way.

She wasn't sure what to make of the wall or the security guards walking around the grounds. Why would a rehabilitation facility require security guards? Maybe she made a wrong turn. Turning in her seat, she read the name prominently displayed on the wall again; it matched the one on her offer of employment. This was the right place.

Mya checked her appearance in the mirror. With her natural hair freshly trimmed and minimal makeup, her big brown eyes and full lips stood out. She glanced at her watch again, shut off her car, stepped out and headed to the entrance. No one stopped her as she entered through the thick glass door and spoke to the receptionist.

"I have an appointment with Dr. C. Lloyd."

"One moment," the older woman said and placed a call.

Surprised no one asked her name, Mya moved toward the chairs and took a seat. They tastefully decorated the lobby in pastels and soothing colors. A large flat screen television hung in silence on the wall.

"Miss Burch?"

Mya nodded as she looked at the receptionist. The older woman's face lit with a smile. "Dr. Lloyd will see you now. Please follow me. Can I get you a soft drink? A bottle of water? Or some coffee?"

"No, but thank you." Mya stood, glanced down to make sure her skirt was straight and blouse buttoned. It had a tendency to stretch across her breasts and disengage without her knowledge. But it didn't require ironing and made for quick dressing this morning.

Although she saw signs of life behind two double doors, they turned down a hall before they reached them. This area was quiet. People moved with purpose and offered smiles. They stopped in front of a closed door.

The receptionist opened it and stepped aside.

Mya thanked her and entered the outer office. Another older woman with salt and pepper hair and piercing blue eyes sat behind a desk. She looked up and smiled. "One moment, I'll let the Doctor know you're here."

"Thank you," Mya said and moved to take a seat, thought better of it and looked at the pictures on the wall instead.

"Mya Burch?" A moderate voice said behind her.

"Yes." She turned and looked at the petite Asian woman standing near the desk. "I'm Dr. Chastity Lloyd. It's nice to put the face with the paperwork." She extended her hand and Mya took it.

"Nice to meet you, too."

"Please come on back." Dr. Lloyd turned and walked down a hall.

Smiling at the woman behind the desk, Mya followed the doctor into a large office. Plaques, framed pictures, framed degrees, and accolades lined the wall. Impressed, Mya glanced at them before settling in a chair in front of the glass and chrome desk.

This was it.

Her first professional job after acquiring her degrees. Heart racing, she crossed her feet at the ankles and then uncrossed them before crossing them again.

"When did you arrive?" the doctor asked.

"Yesterday. More like last night." Why was her throat so tight? *I can do this. Relax. Smile. Listen and only speak at the appropriate times.*

"Good. Good. Did you find the house okay? Any problems there?"

Dr. Lloyd had recommended a real estate agent to purchase a home initially. If Mya remained, she would buy a place. "The home is beautiful and perfect for my son and me."

Dr. Lloyd frowned. "That's right, you have a young son. How old is he?"

"He turned five six months ago," Mya said, hoping this woman didn't get amnesia and have a problem with the hours they agreed on before she accepted the job. She didn't work weekends and needed to be off work every day by five at the latest, earlier, if possible.

"Who keeps him while you're at work?"

"He attends Higher Dimensions."

The doctor's brow rose. "That's a hard school to get in. I know several people who would give anything to get their child accepted. How did you do it?" She leaned forward and watched Mya.

"One of the temporary teachers at his previous school suggested it. She did the preliminary work and gave me the information. When they contacted me, we set up a time for Colin to be tested --"

"Tested? How'd they do that with you living so far away?"

"We logged onto a testing lab. They watched as he answered the questions, tabulated his score, and said he was eligible for the school."

"You knew immediately?"

"Yes. It was all done online, took about two and a half hours, close to three." What does this have to do with my job here? She wondered.

"Congratulations to you and your son. That place is one of the best in the country for preschoolers. They'll be opening a private elementary school next year. It's going to be just as tough to get in there, I suppose." She gave Mya a questioning look as if she knew details.

Mya shrugged. "I don't know."

"Sorry. It's just... never mind. Is there a Mr. Burch somewhere?"

"No. I'm a single mom. Before you ask, Colin's father died in Iraq when my son was two. The only contact he ever had with his father was online, some videos he made before he died and on the phone."

"I'm sorry for your loss and grateful for his service," Dr. Lloyd said.

Mya nodded. She never knew how to handle condolences for Colin. They had dated briefly while he was on leave. He was handsome with dark hair, gray eyes, nice body, lighthearted, fun, a good distraction right after finals. When he returned to the field, they had said goodbye with no intention of seeing each other again. When she discovered the pregnancy, she told him about it. The only thing he asked for was a DNA test, which she had no problem providing. They hadn't been in love or an actual couple, just parents. Even so, his death had hit hard. The thought of Colin Jr with no dad hadn't been in the plans. They hadn't been informed of the funeral or anything else about him after that. Colin had been on his insurance and received military benefits and a monthly check which paid his tuition.

Dr. Lloyd asked a few more personal questions. Did she want more kids? Would her mother be moving to Versteck? Was she involved with anyone back home?

"No. Maybe. No." Her frustration with the questions must have shown.

"There's a reason I'm asking these questions, Mya. You're a young woman, and Versteck Valley is in a remote location, an hour and a half from Denver. We lose staff to the lure of the city often. I'd rather avoid training someone who might get bored and leave within six months. When I say there's not a lot to do here, not for singles anyway, I mean it. Couples, families love it and burrow in. I apologize if you feel I've crossed a line with my questions."

There was nothing in the doctor's voice that said she was sorry. It was clear she would do her job even if it made others uncomfortable. For some strange reason, that made Mya feel better, and she relaxed a bit.

"I understand." She didn't, but she'd moved across the country. Her son loved the school, and she would do a good job here if it killed her.

"Fine. Do you have questions about the job?" The one thing they discussed ad nauseum was the Counselor job description.

Mya leaned forward. "Not the job, but my clients. I'm not clear how that works."

Dr. Lloyd nodded as if she expected the question. "Ah yes. There are some things we don't share without the employment contract. Your clients are the residents of this facility."

Mya bit back her surprise. "Residents?"

"Yes. Our client's lease suites in our facility. Some require medical assistance, others, an occasional helping hand. Counseling is mandatory, as are other activities. It's a cross between a skilled nursing and assisted living facility."

Mya tried to process what she was hearing and blinked slowly. *Suites?* Was this a rehabilitation country club?

"Our clients expect and receive a higher level of care, food and lifestyle. When they come to talk to you, it'll be akin to talking to a Priest for some. Most will lie or tell you pipe dreams. The important thing is for them to have someone to talk to, so they don't remain in their heads all the time."

"You said that while we discussed the job. I didn't know this was a residential facility and the clients would rotate in," Mya said, unsure how she felt about that.

"Does it change your mind about the job?"

"No, not really. It's more personal than I originally imagined. Seeing the same people daily results in forming relationships which can become a handicap as a counselor," she said. *Plus, they get all in your business.*

"I knew I liked you. That's the gist of the drawback of this job. It's a struggle to keep your clients at arms-length when they're always around. Things can get personal, and it's hard to draw the line sometimes. It's also one reason you get six weeks of paid vacations, pay increases and a seven-hour workday. I know it's going to be hard to remain neutral, but you'll have to do it without getting burned out. Don't allow them to dump on you or make you responsible for their decisions. Listen, but don't become their advisor. No medical or personal advice."

Mya nodded and hoped she could do it. She was a sucker for a sob story.

"Are you still interested in the job?" Dr. Lloyd asked.

"Yes, of course." Mya jerked in surprise at the question as she looked at her.

"Alright, let's get your badge taken care of, and I'll take you back to the zoo." She stood, offered her hand to Mya again. "Sharon will take your picture, and we'll leave for the tour."

The woman seated out front took Mya's picture and, a few moments later, handed her the badge. She and Dr. Lloyd walked toward the back of the double doors.

"Swipe your badge to enter. Keep it with you at all times and never allow your clients to handle it. They'll steal it just for kicks."

Butterflies filled Mya's stomach as she swiped the badge. The door opened. Voices, talking and laughing, hit her as they entered the corridor.

"Maggie," Dr. Lloyd called out to a tall, statuesque black female. When she turned and smiled, her light brown eyes sparkled with delight as she looked at the doctor.

"Hi, Chastity, what brings you to the zoo today?" She glanced at Mya and smiled.

"Maggie, this is Mya Burch, our new counselor. Don't let them run her off like they ran the others off. I'm counting on you helping to keep them in line."

Maggie extended her hand to Mya. "It's nice to meet you." She winked at Mya while the doctor wasn't looking. "But watching out for people you hire isn't my job."

Dr. Lloyd turned, looked at Maggie, and laughed. "Stop playing, Mya may realize you're tough and heartless before she starts. Can you show her around your area while I make sure her office is ready?"

"Sure, no problem," Maggie said and waved for Mya to come with her. "I'm responsible for the nursing staff. Mostly female, a few men. Two doctors rotate in during the week. These are their offices, always locked." She pointed to the doors. "Here's the nurse's station. Behind there is their lunch room, lockers, private space." She pointed to another area. "Basically, we make sure our clients are comfortable with medications if they need them. They pay a lot to be left alone to live or die in relative comfort."

"Like hospice?" Mya asked, curious as she looked around. Everything was neat, the area clean, orderly. She liked it.

"In theory only. None of our clients are at death's door. They may have some kind of illness or need some help to get around. We don't get clients who're ambulatory here. Most either walk or use motorized chairs to get around."

"It's private, no Medicaid, or Medicare, so we don't follow their rules. In here, the doctor and client come to agreements on their care."

Different for sure. "Sounds like a private club," Mya said.

"Close." Maggie looked at her. "Where are you from?"

"Tulsa. You?"

"Miami," Maggie said, watching her.

"How long have you worked here?" Mya asked.

"Three years next month. The pay is great, the clients are mostly nice, and it's a pleasant place to work. From time to time, someone arrives who doesn't quite fit in. They never last long, though." She paused. "Kids?"

"One, he's five. You?" Mya asked.

"Two boys, three and six. Are you staying in town?"

Mya told her the name of the subdivision where she rented the house.

"Nice area. We're not that far from you. Maybe we can get the boys together one day for pizza," Maggie offered.

Colin hated pizza. "Sounds nice, let me know, and we'll plan something." She watched Dr. Lloyd walk toward them, waving, sending greetings and blowing kisses to residents as they called out to her along the way.

"Ready?" she asked Mya.

"Yes." Mya turned to Maggie. "Thanks for the tour. I'll see you in a couple days."

"Is that when you're starting?" Maggie asked.

"Yes." Mya turned and walked with the doctor down the corridor, past the open door where men sat at tables playing games or watching television. Several stopped and watched as the two of them walked by.

"Ignore them," Dr. Lloyd whispered.

"Those are the clients?"

"Yes."

Mya frowned. "Are all your clients' men? No women?"

They reached a door and opened it. An older woman sat at the desk and jumped when they entered. Her silver hair brushed against her shoulders as she stared up at the doctor in surprise.

"Dr. Lloyd, I didn't know you were coming today."

"Gina, this is Mya Burch, the new counselor." Dr. Lloyd turned to Mya. "Gina worked for the past counselor and can continue in her post if you'd like. However, she's been claiming time for when she hasn't been in the office."

"I...I... I had an emergency and had to go home," Gina said, red-faced.

"You're just arriving at work," the doctor countered.

"That's what I meant. I had an emergency and was late," Gina amended.

Mya didn't want that kind of headache. "Hello, Gina."

Gina offered a weak smile that said she knew she was in trouble. "Hello, Miss... Ms.?"

"Come with me, I'll show you your office," Dr. Lloyd said, ignoring Gina as she walked past her.

The doctor led Mya to a spacious and airy area that left her impressed. Two overstuffed chairs were off to the side of her glass and chrome desk. It looked just like the one in Dr. Lloyd's office. Maybe they got a discount or something to buy in bulk. Mya wouldn't have chosen it, but it would do.

A top of the line computer was near the desk with a large monitor sitting on top. A mini-fridge, microwave, and coffee bar were across the room. It was the perfect set-up to listen to men tell tall tales.

"Don't worry, I'll deal with Gina. You'll have a replacement by the time you start. If you need anything, let my Admin know, and she'll take care of it for you." She gave Mya a set of keys and an envelope.

"What's this?" Mya asked.

"Keys to the office and side door. Your parking space is right out back. I'll show it to you, so you don't walk all the way around the building." She opened a door. "This is your bathroom."

Mya stepped inside, noted the shower, vanity, and toilet.

Chastity spoke from the doorway. "We provide tissue, and it's cleaned daily. Bring towels and anything else you want to keep in there. That key locks it as well."

Impressed and bordering on being overwhelmed, Mya nodded and looked at the envelope.

"Signing bonus. I didn't mention it during the interview because I wanted you to come for the job, not just the money. Take this packet with you to review before you start. Call me if you have questions; otherwise, I'll see you Thursday at eight."

"I'll be working eight to four, right?" She hadn't known about the seven-hour workday, which gave her an hour for lunch and allowed her to leave in plenty of time to pick up Colin.

"As agreed. Let me show you your parking space."

They headed outside, used the key to re-enter and headed back to the front, where Dr. Lloyd said goodbye.

Mya walked daze-like to her car and sat in it for a few moments. This was too good to be true. There had to be something wrong with Versteck Arms. She looked at the $2,500 check, and her concerns floated away. Colin would be in school at least another three hours. There were several things she could get done between now and then. Groceries, linen, and other things for the house. Elated to have the rest of the day free, she headed out to shop. Who knows? Maybe she'll find something that helps her get past her writer's block. Anything could happen.

CHAPTER FOUR

THREE DAYS LATER, SETTLED into one of the houses he owned, Asher took a sip of water while listening to the news. "Bunch of sissies," he muttered when a reporter asked a prominent Senator about the investigation of missing Marines who showed up on a social media site blindfolded and tied up in a hostile country. The way the Senator ducked and dodged the question made Asher sick.

"Tell the fucking truth. Just say you don't know and if you did, you wouldn't tell because your silence has been bought and paid for, you sick son of a bitch," Asher yelled and clicked the remote. The screen went blank.

The whole stinking cover-up made him sick to his stomach. Five men from a special Marine task force left two months ago to do a job in the Middle East. His cousin Moses was one of those men. None returned. No one knew where they were or what happened to them.

Correction.

Someone knew. They just weren't talking, not yet anyway. Asher searched for clues, followed leads and came up blank. This situation couldn't end this way. He wouldn't let Moses' name or story slip forgotten into the shadows. No matter how many people became uncomfortable, he would find out what happened to his cousin. His best friend.

His phone beeped. *Sheriff Jackson*. Asher inhaled and released his breath slowly. The other night, he allowed the Sheriff one hour of his time before sending him away. Today would not be a repeat of that.

"Jack, what's going on?" he asked, striving to sound good-natured.

"Thank goodness you're not at home. I wasn't sure." The man sounded spooked, not the best trait in an officer of the law.

Asher didn't have a particular home, places he rested and worked, yes. But he didn't think of them as home. "Why? What's up?" he asked, although he suspected Menendez had done something to the house.

"An explosion at your place. It's burning out-of-control right now. It's a fucking nightmare. Fred and the volunteer fire department are working on putting it out, but I don't think they'll be able to save much. Roof's gone. Whole thing's a ball of fire, I swear."

The house belonged to his aunt, Moses' mother. He never liked the bitter woman or how she treated her sons. "Damn, that's... I don't know what to say. I'll try to get there before dark. Right now, I'm busy with meetings. Later, I need to find a place to stay. Maybe I'll head to Denver, get a room or something for a week or two." Jack would pass that information on to anyone who asked. It'd be better if Menendez thought he was dead, but Asher refused to give him that minor victory. Within the hour, everyone in Versteck would know Asher survived the fire.

"You're welcome to stay at my place," Jack offered. "We've got extra space, or you can get a place in town instead of going all the way to Denver."

"Thanks for letting me know about the fire. It's a shame it happened. I'll miss that place. I'll contact you when I get back to town." Asher disconnected and laughed. "Ballsy. Not unexpected. Thought you'd wait a little longer until you realized your men wouldn't return." He paused, playing it out in his mind. "Unless the guys in the van told you they were already dead. Okay, now I understand." He shook his head and went to the kitchen upstairs to fix a sandwich.

He looked out the window and saw the woman with the small boy take several bags from her car into the house. At first, it annoyed him to find out someone rented the house on the right that he owned. As soon as he realized he had a neighbor, he stopped the Realtor from renting his other properties on the left and the one directly across the street from this one until he moved to a new location. He despised being boxed in or spied on, which was the reason he purchased the adjoining houses.

The opening of her car door drew his attention again. *Why hadn't she parked in the garage?* Dressed in a dark blue, snug fitting jacket, matching skirt, and heels, she looked sharp, professional. She moved quickly with long-legged strides and a little jiggle in the back. The way she kept looking at her watch made him wonder where she planned to go. She slammed the door and took in the last bag.

He fixed a peanut butter and jelly sandwich with chips and a soft drink while figuring his next move against Menendez. As much as he enjoyed matching wits against the man, it was growing old. Plus, he'd been dreaming about Moses again and preferred to focus his energies on finding the man who saved his life. He hoped Moses was still alive somewhere trying to escape and needed help. Just as his cousin searched for him several years ago, saving his life, he could do no less. Time to wrap things up with Menendez and amp the search for Moses.

Decision made, he rinsed his plate and placed it into the dishwasher. A door slammed. The woman next door ran out in a pair of hip-hugging jeans, a yellow tank top, and a lightweight jacket, hopped in her car, and drove off.

Asher turned to head downstairs when he noticed a car peel away from the curb down the street and drive in the same direction as his neighbor's car. Out of curiosity, he went to the basement and checked the security cam that gave visuals of the entire street.

That car had pulled onto the street after his neighbor arrived home a short while ago. He frowned. Had the car followed her? Or was this Menendez? He didn't think so. It was too soon for his nemesis to learn of this location, plus there was the fire at the big house.

Asher sat and reviewed the security cams for the past few days. The first car arrived yesterday and parked further down the street, watching the house next door.

"Who's watching your house, fierce mama? What do they want with you?" he murmured as the car followed her when she left that morning. He wrote the license plate to run later, but was fairly certain it was a rental. He leaned back in his seat while staring at the screen and released a sigh. "This is why I don't like neighbors," he muttered. With everything he had going on, he didn't need outside surveillance next door.

Moving from this location wasn't in his immediate plans. This house had an underground bunker and accessed a tunnel that led to a cavern in the mountains if he needed to escape and hide quickly. If she had too much baggage, he'd break the lease and have her moved elsewhere.

First, he needed to inform Drake about the house fire and sent an alert. He received a text message with a number and called.

"The house burned down," Asher said by way of a greeting.

"Good. Always hated that place," Drake said, his voice low, cultured, and perfect for seducing secrets from the unwary and swaying a jury.

"The insurance company will get in touch with your administrator about it. I'm sure it was arson," Asher said, stretching his legs, getting comfortable.

"Menendez or someone else? Never know with you. You enjoy pissing people off."

Asher smiled. He hadn't talked to his cousin in a while. It was good hearing his voice. "Menendez. I'm pretty sure. He came for me, sent in five who never returned. Guess it pissed him off." Asher shrugged. "It's getting old."

"Glad to hear it. Why not let me shut him down so you can move on?" Drake said, no longer teasing.

"You've learned something?" Asher sat up. He and Drake had been searching for Moses for the past few weeks.

"Couple of threads for you to tug. Got two names. Senator Charles Bing, he's on the Arms Services Committee and a weak link. You can squeeze him for information. There's a lot he doesn't want to come out about his dirty habits. I'll send you what I have. But if I could find this information, it'll be a piece of cake for you and your merry-men."

"We all have our skills," Asher said as he typed in the Senator's name and started an intensive search while waiting for the next name.

"The other I heard in passing. Not sure if he's involved or what's going on. Gregory Parson, owner of Triple M Labs. Big time government contractor several years ago, had a lot of setbacks, screw-ups, almost bankrupt and is trying to get back in the game. Word behind closed doors is he ran illegal experiments that caused deaths. I'm assuming human deaths, otherwise why the hush-hush?"

"Experimented on soldiers? Moses?" Asher locked down the anger so he could focus on the information.

"Doubtful. Just another string to pull, see where it leads. I hope we find my brother soon because I'm tired of being polite, smiling at these hypocrites. I'd rather work in the shadows and bring them down one by one."

Asher smiled at Drake's irritation. "Like I said, we all have our skills. Nobody dishes out BS like you. It's a gift."

Drake growled. "Tell me we're getting closer."

"We're getting closer."

"Asshole."

"That's me." Asher sobered. Drake was two years younger than Moses and worshiped his brother. Moses' disappearance took a toll on them both. "I'm on it. Just continue with the plan. You're the face, the inside man gathering information, staying clean, on paper at least, and I'll work behind the scenes to get the job done. I'll never stop searching for answers about Moses, not as long as I breathe, believe that."

"I know. Which is why I'm going to have Menendez and his second, third and fourth in command removed from the equation to give you breathing room. When the Senator talks, you'll need to move fast without looking over your shoulder."

Asher thought about it.

Drake was right. Based on what he learned about the Senator he would start squeezing the man for information on Moses' whereabouts. He could send in a small team within 24 hours to start electronic surveillance. "I hate missing the grand finale with Menendez, but Moses is more important. We need to find him soon."

"Consider it done."

Asher knew Drake would handle the job personally and didn't remark on the glee in his cousin's voice. "Thanks for the information. Make sure your guys watch your six."

"I would say the same to you, but Beamer tells me the Arms is more profitable than we imagined when we started. The residents resemble a buffet of skilled criminals itching to do work from a safe distance," Drake teased.

Asher thought of the men in the building Chastity oversaw. Most of them had retired from a life of crime and sought a safe place to live without legal hassles. Versteck Arms provided that service for a hefty fee, a vow of silence, occasional work, and loyalty to the others living in the building.

The second building, Mecca, belonged to Asher alone and didn't take in residents.

"I haven't looked at the quarterly report, but I'm sure you're right. The place never has a vacancy and has a waiting list." His thoughts ventured to the Senator and the type of pressure they needed to put on the man to find Moses. He didn't realize Drake had disconnected until moments later.

While the computer hummed along, researching, and cross-referencing information on the Senator, Asher closed the digital files on Menendez and stored them in his virtual vault.

Next, he entered the secure database for Versteck Arms to research the current talent in residence. He wasn't sure how they would deal with the Senator or Parson, but he wanted a surveillance team in DC within 24 hours. In the end, it was easier to use Connor, Tombs, and Mercer, a three-man team he'd used before. They were ready to do some outside work and prepared for a briefing later that day.

CHAPTER FIVE

MYA GLANCED AT THE clock and released a long sigh before looking out the window at the mountains in the distance to think. Today marked the last day of her first full week on the job. She planned to spend some time at the farmer's market, visit a few shops in town and do some work around the house this weekend since her mom planned to visit next week.

Three days after Mya had accepted the job, her mom had gone on a shopping spree, gifting Mya with several new outfits to kick off her new career. She looked down at one of the new suits and wondered what her mom would think now if she knew they wasted these clothes. She could wear jeans and a tee shirt to do this job. Still, the gesture had been nice.

Besides, the men seemed to appreciate she dressed professionally. Their occasional compliments never crossed the line, and at their advanced ages, she doubted they could do more than flirt without drugs.

"How's it going?" Maggie stuck her head in the door and asked, as she had done several times in the past few days.

Mya forced a smile on her face and beat back the certainty that this job would not help fulfill her dream of owning or partnering in private practice. Could Maggie see her disappointment? Mya hoped not.

"Alright. Tombs canceled, he's going out of town to visit family. And I have one more session in an hour. What about you? Are they running you ragged?" Mya asked to give her time to refocus and lock away her private discontent.

Maggie grinned, stepped into the office, and closed the door. Grace, Mya's assistant, had already left for the day. "No. One benefit of this job is the work's ridiculously easy and routine. What about you? First week's almost done. Think you'll stay?"

"Oh, I'm not going anywhere, believe that. For what they pay me to listen to guys talk an hour, I'm good." And that sucked big balls. She squelched the mental visual of that, but she couldn't afford to leave and knew she'd be bored stiff while staying. The old saying if it looks too good to be true it probably is, summed up her situation beautifully. If only she could find her muse and start writing again, that would definitely help liven things up. Seems she had lost that as well.

"But... it's not what you expected. Not what you studied in school, right?" Maggie pressed.

Mya didn't want to complain, had nothing to complain about, but she was bored. Not that she'd ever say it out loud. The guys came in, talked, some stories they told were right out of a crime novel or a television series. She'd been told they would tell make-believe tales and she should appear interested, not ask questions, and forget what they said when they left. She had no problem with the last because she normally zoned out after they started describing a heist they had done or how they tricked the Feds and escaped with diamonds or some kidnapping scheme. One guy gave details on making an explosive to rid himself of some annoying competitor. She gave them high marks for vivid imaginations.

"No, it's not what I expected or experienced. I'm adapting to silent counseling."

Maggie laughed. "Good idea."

"I'm thinking of changing my title to Priest," she joked.

Maggie laughed harder. "That's more what you're doing without offering penance."

"True." Mya liked the laid-back staff. Everyone seemed to get along. "Is there a rule to only hire women and only accept men as residents?"

"I think Chastity prefers to hire women, specifically singles or single parents, and pay them well. She's really a nice person, so is her husband, Beam. He's in charge of security. Big guy with a soft spot for his wife and kids. Whoever owns the place decides on the clients."

Mya nodded. "I'm glad she hired me. Colin was struggling in school and was so unhappy. I didn't know what to do. It was driving me crazy."

"He's doing better since you moved here?" Maggie asked.

Mya smiled as her heart lightened. "It's like I've got my child back. He's smiling, playing with others, making friends, and doing well at school. He's excited about math, science and biology, things I admit I'm clueless about." She paused, pushed down the demons of her past and took a deep breath of her present. "I've made a lot of mistakes in my life, but I did this right. Moving here, putting him in that school was the best thing for him, which makes it the best thing for me."

"I heard that," Maggie said. When she told Maggie Colin attended Higher Dimensions, the woman had been ecstatic on her behalf. She asked a few questions regarding the entry requirements and congratulated her again. "The things we do to make sure our kids are happy and have what they need, right?"

"Yeah." Mya looked at Maggie, saw the look of sadness, and wondered what caused it. She hadn't and wouldn't pry. Her plate of personal dilemmas overflowed, but she wondered what put that wounded look on her friend's face.

Maggie stood. "Your last appointment will be here soon, and I need to wrap things up for the weekend crew. If I don't see you again, have a pleasant weekend."

"Thanks and you too," Mya said just before the door closed. The office phone beeped. "Mya Burch."

"Ms. Burch, there's a certified envelope here at the front desk for you. I'd bring it back, but there's no one here to cover the desk."

"That's okay, Donna. I'll be there in a minute." She checked her watch. There was enough time to make it up front and return for her appointment. Taking her badge and keys, she locked the office and headed to the front.

A few of the men she had met with earlier in the week waved and greeted her. Offers of marriage and everlasting love punctuated the air. Laughing, she waved and continued on her way.

Donna handed her the envelope. It was from an attorney in Seattle. Frowning, she returned to her office and read it. Shock raced through her. Colin's grandfather, Joshua Henry, was suing her for visitation rights of his grandson. She put the paper down, closed her eyes and read it again. The man had lost his mind. The only time he reached out to her had been to question the legitimacy of her son's inheritance.

Her son's father had made Colin the sole beneficiary in his will and on his insurance policy with his friend Griffin as the executor. She had never spoken to any of Colin's family or friends and had no desire to do so. Whatever Colin left for her son was between them. Otherwise, she received monthly benefit checks for Colin and handled the rest.

There was a discreet knock on her door.

Frazzled, she had forgotten her appointment and waved Wesley inside. He was a sweet, older man with a quiet disposition. She enjoyed listening to him talk about the way life had been 30, 40 years ago.

"What's wrong?" he asked, stepping inside and closing the door behind him.

"Something aggravating I've got to deal with later. Have a seat." She waved to the chair as she left from behind her desk and sat in the chair next to him. "How're you feeling? Taking your medication?"

He nodded. "Fine and yes. Now, what's the problem?"

She blinked a couple of times. "Wesley, when you come in here, we talk about you and whatever you want to discuss, not me."

He waved down her comment. "Today I want to talk about that piece of paper. Looks like a legal document. I was a lawyer once, you know. I can tell when someone's received bad news. Now, what's the problem?"

Mya didn't want to offend him. However, the last time he visited her, he claimed to have been an accountant who cooked the books for an unnamed criminal figure. It's possible that he could have been both an attorney and an accountant, but she doubted it.

"My son's grandfather is suing for visitation rights."

Wesley frowned. "Why would he do that?"

She didn't want to go into all of that. "I'll handle it, no worries."

"Where's the boy's father?"

Ugh, this was so not his business. "Wesley, you're asking personal questions."

"Yes, I know. But how else can I help fix this if I don't know the details? Where's the boy's father?" If his eyes hadn't softened and showed his genuine concern, she would've said, none of your business.

"He died in Iraq a few years ago. My son had just turned two and doesn't remember him. Plus, he's never met his grandfather or any of his dad's family. Colin didn't get along with his dad and didn't plan on taking our son to meet him."

"I see," Wesley said, staring at the papers on her desk. "Military takes care of their own. The boy should be fine financially," he murmured. "The old man can't get his hand on any money that way. So why would he want to see the child now? Has something happened?" He looked at her.

"Money? What are you talking about?" She hadn't thought there would be an alternative, possibly nefarious, reason behind the lawsuit.

"My dear, people always do things for a reason, usually money. Since he cannot access your son's finances, there must be another reason, hence my question of why now?"

"We just moved here," she said, trying to come up with a feasible answer.

"For work? This job?" He stared at her.

"Yes, but more for my son to attend a school for gifted kids," she said honestly.

"You're sure this has nothing to do with you working here?" he asked, staring hard at her.

"I can't imagine him caring where I work. We've never met or talked to each other. I didn't have a long relationship with his son, either. The only mention of me in the lawsuit is in relationship to my son," she said.

"You weren't married to the boy's father?"

"No."

"Hmm, grandparent's visitation is difficult to win, especially with no previous relationship with your son. Yet he's gone through the trouble of filing a motion. Interesting," he murmured.

"Really?" She hadn't known grandparents could sue for visitation rights.

"No. On what grounds? The child's life isn't in danger. You're not an unfit parent, and he's never contacted the boy before. Therefore, his non-involvement with the child won't affect your son's life. Your rights trump his. His attorney would've told him this, but as you know, you can sue for any reason, no matter how dumb," he said.

She didn't know, but it was nice to hear.

"Would you like me to make a few calls and have a reputable attorney contact you to handle that?"

It had been on the tip of her tongue to say yes, but she paused. Dr. Lloyd said she couldn't take anything these men said seriously. Although Wesley made sense and appeared lucid, she wouldn't put her son's situation solely in his hands. She couldn't do that.

"Sure, but I plan to talk to Chastity about it, get her take and advice as well," she said casually.

"Great idea. She knows everyone, and her contacts are a lot more recent than mine. We'll have this taken care of in no time. No one messes with one of ours. You better believe that."

Touched by his fierce defense, she smiled and covered his hand with hers. "Thanks, Wesley, that means a lot to me. Now, what else do you want to talk about?"

When Wesley's time was up, he left. Mya headed for her boss' office. Chastity had been standing in the outer office, took one look at Mya's face, and waved her inside immediately. "What's wrong?" she asked the moment the door closed behind them.

Mya showed her boss the papers.

"What the hell?" Chastity said while reading.

"Exactly," Mya told her what Wesley said.

Instead of discounting the man's advice, Chastity made two phone calls and faxed the papers to an attorney. While waiting to hear from the lawyer, Mya shared the rest of her experience with Wesley.

"He was so sweet, I really needed that," Mya said, feeling good that someone thought highly enough of her to want to help. Other than her mom and brother, Jefferson, she hadn't experienced that before.

Chastity sat back in her chair and nodded. "Wesley's a good guy, fanciful with his memories, but harmless. He posed a good question: why is someone you've never talked to or met suing for visitation rights in Colorado? Although grandparents have rights, he doesn't have a case."

"Honestly, I don't know. Colin and I didn't date long." She shared her brief history with her son's father, the pregnancy, and paternity test. "Once Colin realized he was going to be a father, he was all in. He asked me to name our son after him if it was a boy. I agreed, and we discussed co-parenting. We got along well, but I didn't love him, and had no plans of marrying him or anything. We were parents. He helped support Colin from the day he was born with no hassle. Sometimes he saw Colin online and talked to him. Of course, he was a baby and doesn't remember any of that. He made some videos for Colin in case things went wrong. I got those after he died."

"Did Colin ever mention his family? His parents?"

"His parents divorced. Mother remarried, but they didn't have a close relationship. I remember him saying something like I was fortunate to have such a good relationship with my mom because he couldn't be in the same room with his or something like that. Think he has siblings but don't remember exactly. He wanted nothing to do with his father. Couldn't stand him and made sure Griffin, a good friend of his, wouldn't allow his father or family anywhere near whatever he left for Colin."

"You don't know what he left for him?" Chastity asked, surprised.

"No. I've never asked. I got a letter informing me of Colin's trust account, Griffin's number, but never contacted him. There was no reason. That's a gift from father to son. It's got nothing to do with me."

"You're a better woman than me," Chastity said. "I'd want to know everything, keep tabs on how it was being invested and reinvested, all of that."

Mya waved down her comments. When my son is a teenager, he'll be informed and likely do that and more. For now, I just want him to be a little boy with no worries."

"Totally understandable," Chastity said as her phone rang. She held up her finger and spoke into the receiver. "She's sitting right here. I'll put you on speaker."

"Hello, Mya, this is Laura Williams. How are you?"

"Better after talking to Chastity. What do you think of the lawsuit?" her gaze met Chastity's.

"It's a petition for Grandparent Visitation rights. In the state of Colorado, there are three reasons this type of suit can be filed. One is the death of the parent, which applies in this case. However, the parent has been dead for almost three years. The grandparent has never sought contact with the child before and was aware of the child's existence. If they push, we can go forward, but they have no grounds to win."

"You think he'll push?" Mya asked, shocked.

"For him to start this is a surprise, so I wouldn't be surprised if he pushed. We'll request he pays my fee, of course." Laura chuckled. "If you'd like, I'll draft a response and go over it with you before filing it."

"Yes. Thank you. Thank you. I've never met the man and can't imagine why he's doing this. My son's father didn't have anything to do with his father and didn't want our son to have anything to do with the man, either. So, I do not want my son to have visitation rights with a stranger."

"Got it. I'll contact you sometime next week to go over this. Chastity, don't forget you promised to work with me on the Charity Ball. It's not that far away, and you've missed every meeting so far. No more excuses. If I have to be there, you have to be there. Next Thursday at noon."

Laughing, Chastity saluted. "Yes, ma'am."

"Damn straight. Goodbye, Mya." Laura said on a chuckle and disconnected.

Mya felt a sense of relief and relaxed in the chair, rubbing her forehead with her fingertips. "I appreciate your help in finding the right person to take care of this."

"No problem. There's a lot of professionals around willing to help when needed. Not only is Laura one of the best around, she's reasonable, won't break your bank," Chastity said.

"Even better," Mya said, her thoughts on the stranger and the lawsuit.

"If you have some free time, we could use some help with the Charity Ball," Chastity said.

"Huh?" The woman's sly smile made Mya think of a million and one reasons she couldn't volunteer to help. "What kind of charity?"

Chastity smiled, and it lit her dark eyes. Jet black hair stopped at her shoulders and framed her oval-shaped face. Dressed in an apricot colored A-line dress, she looked every bit the executive in charge.

Mya didn't understand the joke and waited until the laughter died down. "Must be some ball."

Chastity grinned. "I keep forgetting you're new here and don't know anything about the town."

"I've been here less than two weeks."

"Apologies. Forgive me for laughing."

Mya nodded as she watched Chastity dab the corner of her eyes with a tissue.

"What do you know about the history of Versteck Valley?" Chastity asked.

"A German guy bought a lot of the land, named the town hideaway, Versteck in German and helped bad guys disappear," Mya said in a rush while trying to remember the rest of what she had read but couldn't.

"Wow, okay, so you got a highly edited version." Chastity smiled, so Mya didn't think she offended the woman.

"Pretty much," she said.

"You're right, Robert Von Block was a German who bought most of the land in the silver mining town once it went bust. He didn't arrive intending to make money like most of the miners, but the stories of the wild west captivated him. In Germany, there was a guy they called Schinderhannes." She waved her hand. "A German version of Robin Hood."

"Never heard of him," Mya said, interested.

"He was a criminal beheaded by the French in the early 1800s."

Startled by the matter-of-fact comment, Mya nodded slowly.

"Anyway, Von Block had this thing about Cowboys and outlaws. Made several visits to Wyoming to visit Butch Cassidy's hideout, traveled the Outlaw Trail to see other places where there are monuments to Cowboys and Outlaws," Chastity continued. Her voice softened, as if she shared the man's wonder of the distant past. "The Outlaw Trail was a series of hideouts from Montana through Wyoming, Colorado, Utah, New Mexico, Arizona, Texas, and even into Mexico."

"There's a lot of that here? In Colorado I mean?" Mya asked.

"The most famous was Brown's Hole or Park. Have you heard of it?"

She shook her head. "No."

"It's a canyon in Colorado near the Wyoming and Utah borders. Lots of... erm, people used that place to hide. The most famous is Robbers Roost in southeastern Utah, where Butch Cassidy and his gang hid. If you watch old westerns and see them change horses and keep going, they don't stop until they reach a mountainous area that's really hard to navigate. Back then, once they went in, they couldn't be found."

"Really?" Mya hadn't known any of that. She'd look for an old western and watch it.

Chastity nodded. "The government owns them now and one other as well." She snapped her fingers as her brow furrowed. "The Hole-in-the-Wall. How could I forget that one? A gang even named itself after that place. Have you heard of Kid Curry, Black Jack Ketchum or Butch Cassidy's Wild Bunch gang?" She looked so excited it hurt to disappoint her.

"Not all of them," Mya said. "Just Cassidy. I didn't know he was a part of a gang. I hope there's not going to be a test on the Wild West," she joked.

Chastity laughed. "No. Not by me. But lots of people in the area are huge history buffs and take pride in the events of the past, both positive and negative. Anyway, the Hole-in-the-Wall is in Wyoming and was another favorite hideaway the government now owns."

"Sounds interesting. I'll look it up." Mya tapped the names into her phone.

"I had to give you a little more history so that you'd understand the purpose of the Charity Ball. It was something Von Block started." She hesitated and looked at Mya. "The Ball is a fundraiser to help families in need."

Mya had the feeling there was more, a lot more to it than that. "So why did you laugh?" There was nothing remotely funny about helping families in need.

Chastity's face pinked as she sat forward in her chair. For a few moments, neither spoke. "With Laura asking, no demanding I attend meetings... meetings I'd been deliberately dodging with a certain level of panache, the whole thing seemed funny. Now that I've reminded myself of the purpose of the Ball, I'm ashamed." She didn't meet Mya's gaze as she drew circled on the desk with her fingertip. "Every year we raise a lot of money to help families in need. It's a worthy cause."

Since the woman didn't meet her gaze, Mya wasn't sure Chastity was being completely honest but short of calling her out, there was nothing she could do. Well, there was one thing. "Thanks for explaining it to me. It sounds good, but I'm still settling in and don't think I'll be much help. Maybe next year." Smile in place, Mya stood, grabbed her bag, the letter from the desk and headed toward the door.

"No problem. It's an annual event, and you can help later. Laura will contact you about that legal issue, and if you need me for anything else, my door's open to you. I know you haven't been here long, but the feedback I've gotten from the residents about you is positive. They've adopted you and think you're doing a great job."

Wesley had said she was one of them and it made her feel good. She smiled. "They're really nice guys and make my job so easy."

"Glad to hear it. Have a great weekend, see you Monday," Chastity said, her smile not as bright as before.

CHAPTER SIX

THE PAST TWO DAYS had been a whirlwind of activity. Asher had placed Connor, Mercer, and Tombs on a private flight to Maryland first thing, along with the equipment they would need to complete the job. They would pick up a modified truck from one of Asher's associates and head into Silver Springs to a house he set up for them. From there they would gather more intel on Senator Bing.

Drake had been right. If you knew where to look, there was a lot of information on the Senator. That could create a problem if someone, a larger organization, got to him first, which was why Asher pressed to get his men on the ground as fast as possible. They should be able to pull it off, in and out, get the information and leave.

Once they arrived, things would move fast. The Senator spoke at a fundraiser in Alexandria, Virginia tonight, which would give Mercer a window to access the Senator's hidey hole and set up his surveillance equipment.

Asher sent Drake a message. Moments later, the phone rang. "Everything's good?" his cousin asked in a clipped tone.

"Couldn't be better." Asher rubbed the bridge between his nose. He needed to get some sleep but hadn't been able to grab more than a few hours at a time since Moses' disappearance.

"I'm almost done here as well." Drake cursed. "Talk to you later, gotta deal with this."

Asher looked at the monitor. He hadn't listened to the news today and wasn't sure if Menendez was dead or alive. Based on Drake's curt remark and temperament, someone in that organization was dead. *Good.*

He rubbed the back of his neck to ease the tightness, closed his eyes and took a deep breath. When he opened them, his gaze landed on the monitor. A file named background check was on his desktop. With everything going on, he hadn't read it.

He checked the time, realized he had some downtime, and opened the file. "Mya Lynay Burch. Mother alive. Father unknown. One younger brother named Jefferson. Married at 17 and divorced from Ahmed Johnson within 18 months. Went to community college, pregnant from a guy on leave. Son is a junior, mixed kid." The report wasn't that long.

Based on this, she was as dull as white bread. He would be content if he hadn't witnessed her being followed for a week. There was no explanation for her surveillance in this report. He suspected things were about to get worse and looked at her photo on his screen.

"Mya Lynay Burch. Took your last name back. Moved away from home. Put your son into an exclusive school. The job at the Arms is more of a sounding board position than therapist. Why is that car following you? What are you hiding?"

He glanced at the time and stood to pocket a few tools. After checking the security camera for cars on the street, he left through his back door, climbed the fence, and walked next door. Before inserting his key, he scanned for a security system.

When the device beeped, signaling an active system, Mya rose a notch in esteem in his opinion. It didn't take long for his device to deactivate it and he walked inside. Anyone watching would think he lived there.

Stainless steel appliances, granite countertops, and dark cherry maple cabinets adorned the expansive eat-in kitchen. He hadn't been particular about what went into the houses he purchased and allowed the sales agent to add on quite a few upgrades. He took a quick glance around the kitchen, walked through the dining area into the living room. None of the rooms had much furniture in them yet. The place looked empty.

He headed to the master bedroom on the first floor, along with one other bedroom. The half floor above held two more bedrooms with private baths.

The smaller bedroom door remained opened. This was where she put her money. The kid's room had one of those coordinated bedroom sets that you see in furniture stores. He couldn't recall a delivery truck, but obviously, they had come at some point. The master suite was across the hall. A pearl-gray bedroom set which included a padded queen-sized head and footboards dominated the room. There was art all over the walls that you could buy anywhere. A matching dresser, chest, and large comfortable chair completed the set. A lone glass and black metal computer desk with a chair sat in the corner.

He smiled and fingered the tools in his pocket as he moved purposefully and turned on the computer. It was pass coded. He inserted a USB decoder, typed in a few commands, and allowed it to work. It would beep once it identified her password. Meanwhile, he looked around the first floor. In both bedrooms, the beds were neatly made. Everything in its place. No clutter. He took a quick glance in the bathroom. Same thing, neat.

At least they're taking good care of my investment. He walked upstairs. It was empty. He wondered if they even came up here. He looked out a window toward the house he was using. It was dark. Blinds and curtains closed.

Good.

A ping from downstairs drew his attention. Prepared to discover the real identity of the woman and why she was being followed, he returned to her room to check out her computer. A picture of her and the boy filled the screen. Rather than look at her emails or personal information, Asher clicked the history button to get a feel of what interested Mya Burch.

"Well, well, well," he said, sitting up and clicking on a few places she had been. She had an account on a few erotic literature sites and used a pen name. "What's a nice lady like you doing visiting these kinds of sites?" he murmured.

He found a file in her documents folder under the name, "Lynay Luvs." Chuckling, he clicked on it and whistled at some titles: Strip Joint Love. Lost in Face. Taken by 3 and several more with various themes.

There were files that went back five years, no make that seven. Some titles made him laugh. "Titty Cat? Chocolate Cream Lover?" Fascinated by her imagination, he read a few. Looks were definitely deceiving. Appearance wise, Mya looked like a straight-laced, PTA, soccer mom relegated to a lifetime of missionary positions. She stood several inches beneath his six-two frame. Curvy with hips, nice body. She wore her hair short, curly, maybe natural, he wasn't sure. While he had no particular preference for curvy women, her online pictures captivated him, maybe because of the playful glint in her eyes or her suggestive nature that had him picturing steamy nights.

She was beautiful. Nothing in her attire screamed Titty Cat, but she had indeed written a short story called that.

Conscious of the time, he clicked on three erotic websites and saw the name: Lynay Luvs. "You've been busy, haven't you?" he said, typing the names of the sites into his phone to check when he had more time.

He continued checking her browser history and frowned at the link for grandparents' rights. She had checked Oklahoma and Colorado laws. He hadn't realized they had any rights, but apparently, they did. Was that for her son? The boy's father was dead, which left Mya's mother. Was her mom fighting for custody? It didn't ring true but could've been. If the mom wanted proof, she wasn't caring for the boy properly. That might be the reason for the surveillance.

When he finished with the browser history, he shut down the computer and erased his presence. "Still don't know why those cars are tailing you, but you've definitely become a lot more interesting in my book," he said as he left through the kitchen door, locked it and turned the alarm back on.

He got home and checked out the first website with the Titty Cat story. She had high rankings and a lot of comments. He hesitated at the raunchy remarks. It sounded like porn. *Written porn?*

He rubbed his right cheek, felt the long-jagged scar from temple to chin and sat back in his chair staring at her huge number of followers. "Shit." What if one of her fans tracked her down and was stalking her? Could it be that simple? Did some horny-assed dude want to make one of her stories a reality?

The timing sucked.

Asher couldn't afford to have strangers lurking around, not with Menendez in the background or the hunt for Moses ratcheting up. He'd be using the tunnels and couldn't be seen. He thought about having the Realtor move them to one of his other places in town. They weren't as nice as the one next door and the neighborhood wasn't as safe, but she and her lurkers would be gone.

His phone rang. He looked at the number. His heart jumped.

"Talk to me." The call was from Eli, the man he hired to track information on Moses. He had been out of the country. This was their first conversation in a week. Asher needed to hear something. Time was running out.

"They identified a soldier on Moses' team. Not dead, but badly injured in a small village near the Iranian border. I don't know if the entire team is intact, but a rescue op is underway and should go down within the next 24 hours."

Asher closed his eyes and took a deep breath. "Best damn news I've heard all day. We won't know about Moses specifically until after that?"

"Yeah. It's an unauthorized op. I'm not sure where they'll take them afterward. Soon as I learn more, I'll let you know."

"Thanks, I'll send your package." Asher referred to Eli's fee.

"Appreciated." He disconnected.

Asher closed his eyes and hoped Moses was alive. Anything else they could work with. He stroked the scar on his cheek and recalled the blade that had ruined his face and life several years ago. If he could survive that, his cousin could survive anything they threw at him.

Eli sent an update three hours later, confirming that they safely extracted all five men from the hostile zone and were undergoing debriefing. He promised to contact Asher the moment he knew more about Moses' condition.

Drake had contacted him within the past hour and all but cried with relief at the news that his brother was alive. Asher understood and lost track of time discussing likely locations Moses could've been sent, when they might hear from him, and his current physical and mental condition. The conversation had been full of hope and an eagerness to do whatever they could to help Moses.

Drake surprised Asher by not mentioning Menendez during their conversation. News of the man's death in an explosion at his factory earlier this morning, along with all of his top men, was on every channel. Television anchors had been discussing Menendez' enterprise and the unfortunate death non-stop. They called it an accident. Asher wondered how long that would hold up.

He stepped into the kitchen and caught sight of a tall man dressed in black pants and a dark tee-shirt on Mya's porch fiddling with the door. The next moment, he entered the house.

Surprised, Asher looked at the clock. It was a few minutes past two. Mya was still at work, the boy in school. Who had just broken into her home? It wasn't something that happened in a place like Versteck; the residents knew better. There were too many people with skeletons in their closets and guns in their pockets to go poking around uninvited in their private, personal space.

"Damn it," Asher growled. Another reason he didn't like neighbors. He hated getting involved in things that weren't his business. He turned to walk downstairs and stopped.

What if that asshole accessed her computer and discovered she wrote porn? Would that impact the grandparents' claim? No. Maybe. Hell, he had no idea and didn't want to know. But that someone other than him snuck into her home, and read her stories bothered him.

He picked up his phone and called Jack.

"Hey Asher, how's it going? Are you back in town?" Jack asked.

Asher had forgotten the man thought he was in Denver. "Yes, had a meeting. Listen, I just drove past a house and saw a break-in."

"What? Where?" the Sheriff asked all business.

Asher gave him the address next door.

"Thanks, on my way." Jack disconnected.

Asher remained at the window to see if the intruder left before Jack arrived. Versteck wasn't as large as Denver, so it didn't take long for the Sheriff and another car to arrive. The Deputy went around back, while Jack went to the front door and rang the doorbell. Of course, no one came to the door.

Moments later, a late model Ford pulled up, and Francis Kelly, the Realtor, waved toward Jack, holding a key.

"Smart," Asher said, watching as Francis drove off.

Jack was returning to the front door when it opened. Asher tried to get a good look at the man but couldn't. Jack made the guy step outside, kneel, and handcuffed him. The Deputy entered the house and walked out a few moments later. Francis returned, and the three of them talked to the side.

Jack escorted the man to the back of his car. A few moments later, Asher's neighbor pulled into the driveway. Chastity and Maggie were in the car with her. Jack had his hands full trying to calm the women and finally got them inside.

Asher would've given anything to be a fly on the wall listening to Jack trying to handle those three females. Beamer's arrival in a black SUV, carrying his equipment bag, didn't surprise him. Tall, the man stood several inches over six feet with a wide muscular chest loaded with tattoos and scars. He had fractured his nose on two occasions, and one of his eyelids remained partially closed. Beamer was a menacing sight who took his job as head of security at the Arms seriously. No doubt Chastity insisted he come and scan the house for bugs or anything else.

What would Mya think of that? Did she realize Versteck was a different town? How would she react when she realized the lines between the law and lawbreakers blurred in this part of the world?

When Jack and Beamer walked out of the house, Chastity, the top of her head reaching the middle of Beamer's chest, was with them. They talked to Jack for several moments before returning to the SUV and driving away. Asher wanted to know what they found, but refused to risk exposure. With Menendez' recent death, Asher planned to remain off the radar to avoid suspicion and notice.

The Sheriff and deputy departed minutes later, leaving Maggie and Mya at the house. Uneasy without knowing why, Asher remained near the window, watching the other house. "What will you do now?" he murmured. "I've got a $100 that says you'll bounce for the night."

It didn't take long for Mya and Maggie to leave with a small suitcase and drive off.

Smiling, Asher returned to his office below and checked the street cam. The man had parked a block away and walked straight to the house as if he belonged in the neighborhood. There had been no car tailing Mya back to her house. Had he been the man tailing her the past week? Or were there two or more of them?

Asher's gut said there were at least two, which meant this wasn't over. Someone wanted something from Mya and wouldn't stop until they had it.

CHAPTER SEVEN

MYA SAT IN THE conference room next to her attorney, Laura. Before they entered the room, Laura made it clear to Mya that things operated a little differently here in Versteck. In this situation, the Sheriff would leave pressing charges for breaking and entering up to her and her attorney. He would only get involved if they could not reach an agreement. When she asked questions, Laura patted her arm solicitously and ushered her inside.

The slender woman sat erect. The loose band barely contained her reddish-brown natural curls. Occasionally, her wide nose flared, and freckles darkened across her face as she listened intently to Mr. Sung, the attorney of the guy who broke into her home.

Last night, she stayed at the only hotel in town until someone installed a new system at the house. Francis was there now, supervising the installation of the upgraded system.

"Are we to understand your client broke into my client's home, set up surveillance equipment with the intent purpose of invading her privacy and it was the wrong house? Is that what you expect us to believe?"

"Yes," the hapless man said as sweat beaded on his flat forehead. He took out a white handkerchief and wiped his brow. "This has all been a huge mistake. I hope we can work this out without taking it further."

"Show me the paperwork for the correct house," Laura said, her tone doubtful.

The other attorney's eyes narrowed. "I cannot do that. It's confidential."

"You'll have to provide it in court." Laura stood and motioned for Mya to do the same. "He'll lose his license to practice investigations in the State of Colorado. Since he did not have legal permission to install the surveillance equipment, we'll ask for the maximum remedy." She pointed at Mr. Sung. "Never call me again when you have nothing to offer."

Impressed by the woman's ferocity on her behalf, Mya stood slightly behind Laura and watched the other attorney's face redden.

"We always had something to offer. My client is prepared to pay whatever you deem appropriate to drop the charges," he said, his voice attempted to sound amicable but came out in a low, frustrated growl.

Mya wasn't sure the man could buy her off. He had committed a crime. She remained silent in the background.

Laura placed both hands on the conference table and leaned toward Mr. Sung. "Your client violated the sanctity of my client's home. He broke in and installed devices to record her every move. How do you put a price tag on her peace of mind?"

His gaze flicked to Mya and back to her attorney. "We start by negotiating."

"I want to know who's following me and why?" Mya blurted. She hadn't been in Versteck long enough to have enemies. Had Colin's grandfather sent the investigator? She didn't think he had that kind of money, but someone did, and she wanted to know who.

The man looked at her, surprised. "My client's not following you. He arrived in town yesterday morning. I can prove that."

Mya had noticed the same car following her to work and back home. She had talked to Ms. Wails at the school and the security guard. They assured her they would watch her son closely and keep him safe.

"I'm not interested in the money. If the only way to find out who sent this guy to set stuff up in my house is by going to court, that's what I want to do," Mya said.

Laura nodded and looked at the frowning attorney. "You heard her." She turned to walk out of the room. Just as they reached the door, the attorney spoke.

"Alright," he said.

"Alright, what?" Laura winked at Mya before facing Mr. Sung fully.

Stunned by his capitulation, it took Mya a few seconds longer to realize they were about to start the real negotiations.

"I can answer your questions." He did not look happy as he stared at Laura and then Mya.

Laura held up her hand. "Before you speak, let me tell you everything we want."

He looked resigned and nodded.

By the time Laura finished, the attorney agreed to pay all legal fees, pay Beamer's fees for the job he had done yesterday, all of Mya's expenses for the extra security measures that were being installed in the house, a $100,000 cash payment to Mya and give them the information she wanted.

Mya couldn't utter a word as the two attorneys argued back and forth. Not once had she considered she would receive any kind of financial compensation or that Beamer had to be paid for scanning the house. The dollar amounts were insane, but the attorney never argued over those. He wasted energy trying to control the amount of information his client would share with her.

Either she got it all, or they took it to court.

In the end, Laura prevailed and made sure the other attorney understood they would only forgo pressing charges against his client after Mya was satisfied that she knew everything about the break-in.

The attorney wrote several checks. A check on Mya's behalf for $100,000, two more for Laura and Beamer's fees. And two additional ones to cover all the expenses for a new security system and a gift to the Charity Ball. Laura's assistant stepped into the room, took the checks, including Mya's, and left.

"Your client is a private detective. Why did he break into my client's home and set up surveillance?" Laura asked, while staring across the table at the attorney.

"It was a job to determine if she's a fit parent for the boy. The grandfather hired him."

Mya's heart clenched. Fear fluttered in her chest as the realization that someone wanted her son hit home. She had thought the old man was behind it. Having it verified made it more real, more devious. Despite Laura's assurances that he would not win, this whole thing scared her.

"Will others be coming?" Laura asked, pulling Mya out of the gray area where her thoughts didn't line up.

"Possibly. He doesn't know."

"Why the sudden interest in the boy?" Laura asked.

The attorney shook his head. "He does not know. It was a job. Nothing more or less."

The truth was anti-climatic.

Mya didn't know what to say or think. She'd never met this man, and yet he wanted her son. It made no sense. Not once had he ever reached out to meet or know Colin.

Numb, she stood and headed toward the door. Her head hurt. Laura said the man had no case and yet he persisted. Behind her, she heard the two talking but ignored them. She wanted to go home, take a bath, and sleep for several hours.

"Tell Laura I'm headed home and will talk with her later," Mya told the assistant.

"Okay, will do. Get some rest. Laura will handle it. The money should show up in your account before the end of the day."

Trusting that to be true, Mya fished her sunglasses out of her purse, slid them on, and left the office building. It didn't take long to reach the house. Francis was locking the door as she pulled into the driveway beside the other car and waved.

"Just in time," Francis said as she waited for Mya to meet her on the porch. "Let me show you what was done." They entered the house. Francis pointed out the new equipment, the controls, and explained how everything worked. It was a lot better than before.

"This is serious stuff," Mya said, relieved while looking at the steel doors, locks, and cameras. "Where'd you get all of this so fast?"

"The owner heard what happened and took care of it. He wanted to be sure the house was safe for you and Colin," Francis said, looking around.

"Thanks. Seeing this makes me feel a lot better about moving back in. My mom is coming in a few days for a visit, and I wanted everything to be right." Mya was happy the expense of the doors and security equipment had been paid and wouldn't show up as a rent increase.

Thinking hurt.

Right now, she needed to close her eyes and center her thoughts before picking Colin up from school and hitting the furniture store. With her mom coming, she had to finish furnishing the bed and living rooms. Now that she had extra money, a lot of money, she wouldn't have to put it on credit.

Francis walked to the door as she spoke. "Totally understand. If you need anything at all, let me know."

Mya nodded and walked to the door. Once Francis slid behind the wheel, Mya locked up and went to her room to undress and get comfortable. She had removed all her clothes and pulled on a soft oversized shirt that reached mid-thigh when she remembered her toiletries and overnight bag were in the car. Intent on moving the car into the garage, she walked outside barefoot with keys in hand.

A tall, muscular man stood on the sidewalk between her house and the house next door. She froze when she saw him. Thoughts of her recent break-in flew across her mind as fear threatened to choke her.

Run back inside.

Although her brain gave the order, her legs refused to obey. Her throat tightened, robbing her of the ability to speak. Like prey in front of a predator, she remained frozen, staring into his light-colored eye for several seconds.

Move or say something, she thought desperately. This could be someone the old man sent to spy on her. *Save yourself.*

"Hello."

The deep voice broke her paralysis. Her chest heaved as she sucked in air. Had she forgotten to breathe? *Yes.* Her lungs burned as her hand trembled.

"Hello." The word came out ragged and low. Neither said anything else for a few moments. Now that she could think, like a dolt, she stood in place trying to decide if she should continue to the car as if her heart wasn't trying to break out of her chest, or run like hell and lock the steel door behind her.

"Are you alright? I saw the police here yesterday. Actually, I called in the burglary. I was driving by and saw him on the porch."

He moved slightly, and she saw the side of his face clearer. His dark tee shirt had some writing on it. She couldn't read all of it, but she noticed his muscular arm and chest and his flat belly. Without conscious thought, she sucked in everything and stood straighter.

"The Sheriff said someone called it in. Thank you. I appreciate you doing that." Swallowing down her fear, she moved toward the car, holding her keys tight in her hand.

He stepped toward her.

She stopped, read his tee-shirt and laughed. "I can't go to hell. Satan has a restraining order on me. That's... I've never seen that one."

He smiled, and it transformed his face. Made it appear softer, more human, more masculine and stirred things low and tight in her belly. She stopped laughing and took in his high cheekbones and crooked nose, which looked as if it had been broken and healed with a slight bump. The jeans he wore fit snug across his waist, down his long legs with a definite protrusion near his crotch. Untied sneakers graced his feet as he moved again and stopped.

"At the time I thought it appropriate," he said in that deep voice that pulled at her core, waking a need inside that hadn't stirred in months.

Unable to speak, she continued staring at him as ideas for new stories flooded through her mind like a rushing river. For what seemed like forever, she had experienced writer's block. A lack of inspiration had dried her ocean of ideas and left her bereft. She hadn't felt like this in a long time.

"You okay?" he asked.

Mya blinked as heat traveled to her face. Mentally, she had been writing a sex scene with him as the star.

"Yes. Yes, stressful day." She didn't look at him again and opened the car door.

"I'm Asher."

He had moved closer to the car without her hearing him. If she didn't look in his direction, she could put the insane idea of holding his thick cock in her hand out of her mind. It was one thing writing about faceless men, another writing about someone who made her nipples hard and moisture lick the apex of her thighs. Dressed only in an enormous shirt, it wouldn't take much for him to see her arousal.

"Mya." She removed her luggage and held one bag high enough to block her nipples. When she stepped back, his gaze had been locked on her ass. Had her shirt risen in the back? Probably. Rather than feeling embarrassed, she found joy in the admiration reflected on his face.

This is when I normally get into trouble. She had a healthy sex drive and enjoyed sex, even though she hadn't indulged with a real person in years.

She and Ahmed, her ex-husband, had sex almost every day during her senior year of high school, and she'd loved it. When she got pregnant before graduation, his parents insisted they marry, and her mom agreed.

Married sex lacked the thrill of discovery but wasn't bad, just not as often. She didn't mind working or being married, but when the sex slowed to a trickle and Ahmed had sex with other girls, being married sucked. His father cheated on his wife, and no one said anything. Mya knew she wouldn't remain married to Ahmed under those conditions and moved back with her mom.

Embarrassed, Ahmed made all kinds of promises to get her back and moved in with her at her mom's. The sex was better than before. She believed he was faithful until the baby was stillborn. Then he became ugly, mean, and abusive. He claimed her desire for sex killed their son, even though the doctor told him that wasn't true. To this day, she believed he grabbed the death of their child as an excuse to get out of their marriage.

They had been too young, and even though they tried to remain married, it was too much work. In the end, he spread rumors she was the reason the baby died, said she didn't want the child, claimed she was a sex freak, a nymphomaniac, always ready to go at it. Guys she had never spoken to approached her for sex. His demonizing the loss of their son and their intimate moments almost destroyed her. She dropped out of college. Things got so bad she, her mom and brother moved to Tulsa to get away from that small town and started over.

It took years of therapy to accept and love herself. While pregnant with Colin, she had been extra careful and prayed daily he'd be born healthy. There were times she believed Colin was God's way of telling her she was a good person and losing the first baby wasn't her fault.

"Are you from here?" she asked as she locked the car door before stepping toward the porch. *How come I'm not scared?* He could grab or snatch her right now... and what?

"Wasn't born here, but I live here now." He leaned against her car's fender and crossed his arms over his muscular chest. For the first time, she saw the right side of his face. Pink scars ran from his chin to the temple. Her imagination went into overdrive as he became a tortured hero in her story. Her fingertips itched to touch his face so she could accurately describe them.

"That's an interesting reaction," he said with some humor.

His voice startled her, and she jerked to meet his gaze. "What?"

"You were staring at my face."

Heat rushed to her cheeks. She was glad of her darker complexion. "Sorry. I've... they look like they have textures to them. I wondered what they felt like." She closed her eyes and shook her head. "God, that was a weird thing to say. I'm sorry."

He chuckled. The sound skittered across her skin raising goosebumps. "Definitely a different reaction."

She looked at him again, realized he wasn't offended and smiled. "Should I keep apologizing for saying the wrong things?"

"No. Just be honest, say what you feel and mean, makes life simpler. Besides, guessing is a bitch."

Taken aback by his candid remarks, she nodded slowly as she wondered if she would see him again. With her work schedule and Colin's extra school activities, she doubted it. No, she would be forever grateful to him for jump-starting her creative juices and libido but would not do anything that would endanger Colin. For all she knew, this hunk could be a plant by the old man to tempt her into doing something he could use against her.

That thought was the equivalent of pouring ice water on her rising lust. She cleared her throat and walked back to the porch. "In that case, thanks so much for reporting the break-in, I really appreciate it."

"Have dinner with me."

His voice did things low and deep to her libido. She could imagine them in bed together, but not now.

"I can't."

"Lunch?"

She frowned at his persistence. Even though he hadn't moved from his spot against her car she sensed coiled energy in him. Colin's father had been that way too. It was still damned attractive.

"The timing is wrong," she said with genuine regret. "I can't get involved with anyone right now. There are a lot of things happening that I've got to stay on top of."

His brow rose, but he didn't ask questions or push. A point in his favor.

"Can I give you my number or have yours? We can talk until you're ready," he offered.

Mya stared at his imperfect face. Pale, angular and strong. He needed to spend time in a tanning bed or on the beach for some much-needed color. The tattoos on his arm, neck, and fingers screamed he wasn't the kind of man you met in Sunday School or at PTA meetings. Definitely not husband or daddy material. Everything about him indicated he wasn't a nice, wholesome guy. In the past, she had done wholesome and was over it.

"Sure. My phone's inside, give me your number, and I'll call you in a bit. That way you'll have my number." One part of her yelled. "*No, he's dangerous. You can't trust him or yourself around him. He could be a part of a trap to build a case against you.*" The other part of her yelled. "*Shut the hell up. We're here to start over, make a new and better life. Plus, we're attracted to him.*"

"Got something to write it down? Or you wanna get your phone right quick?"

Her gaze met his.

"Makes more sense to get my phone. Hold on, be right back." She dashed inside and ran to her room. Once there she remembered she hadn't locked the front door behind her and prayed her instincts to trust him were right. It didn't take long to grab her phone, glance in the mirror to groan in despair at her appearance and return to the porch.

He hadn't moved. When he saw her he called out his number. Moments later, his phone rang. His gaze held hers as he answered.

"Hello, Mya. I want to get to know you better, will you let me do that?" he asked.

The husky timbre of his voice slid over and through her before settling between her legs. Hunger, a sexual need so intense it rocked her. It had been years since she'd indulged in sex and was starved. Most days she turned to her sweet vibrator that never disappointed. After talking to Asher, she doubted her toy would work its magic today. She wanted something with a pulse, and he stood in front of her.

"Yes, I'd like that, Asher," she said dropping her voice an octave. Pleasure washed over her at his expression. He wanted her and didn't bother hiding it. "I've got to get a few things done before I pick my son up from school. Can I call you later tonight?"

"I'd be disappointed if you didn't," he said without humor.

She liked that. "Talk to you later," she said and returned inside.

"Indeed you will," he answered and disconnected the call.

Excited and horny, Mya took a deep breath as she strode to her computer. For the first time in months, she wanted to write.

CHAPTER EIGHT

ASHER WATCHED MYA'S HIPS swing as she spun around and entered the front door. Her smooth, dark complexion glowed beneath the midday sun. He had been right about her hair. She wore it in tight curls with longer curls on the side like a bang. When she smiled, even white teeth, full lips on a wide mouth parted, sending his imagination into overdrive. She was gorgeous. It surprised him that she was attracted to him.

He could still see her large dark brown eyes staring at him as she told him she wanted to get to know him. The challenge in her gaze and the curl of her lips made his dick hard as nails. Desire, hot and heady swept through him. She wasn't a tease, he had met enough in the past to spot them a mile away.

Mya was interested.

Initially, he had planned to go back to his place after instructing his security guys on what to install. Most of his properties had steel entry doors and energy efficient windows. Adding a few cameras to Mya's rental benefited him in the end.

None of that explained the reason he had come outside after Francis left. Or why he hung around, watching and yes, hoping Mya would see him.

The moment she stepped out and saw him, her fear had been almost tangible. She looked innocent and nothing like the vixen her stories conjured in his mind. As her eyes rounded and lips quivered, he thought she would bolt back into the house. But she hadn't, which earned her points in his book.

When she stared at him, the greeting locked in his throat. Nothing prepared him for seeing her in that long, thin tee-shirt. Her high, full breasts, and pert nipples made his mouth water in remembrance of her story, Titty Cat. The woman in that short story had allowed her lover to slide his gorged cock between her huge breasts enfolding his dick like a hot-dog bun as she licked the tip when he pushed through. His pants grew uncomfortable.

Seeing her unleashed breasts made his dick throb and his brain go to mush. At that moment, he wanted to reenact that story and do so much more. Finally, his cock released his brain, and he could think and speak. No matter what he said from that point on, his mind locked onto his end game. He wanted to fuck her. No, he would fuck her. They simply hadn't picked the time and place.

Her response to his scars surprised him. None of her stories, at least none that he had seen so far, romanticized imperfect people. All the men were handsome with great bodies and fantastic never-get-tired lovers. Since he planned to have a physical relationship with her, she needed to see his scar early on and get used to it. He wasn't sure what response he expected, but the fascinated longing in her gaze threw him for a loop. He hadn't known what to make of it. If he didn't know she dabbled in make-believe and erotica, he might've thought she was daft when she mentioned his scars having textures.

Showing the right side of his face seemed to ease her fears, which made no sense. He wasn't handsome, had never been. Most women he dealt with understood it was about sex and only sex and never pushed for more.

Mya had both surprised and confused him. He hadn't expected her to be so damned sexy or a straight shooter. She didn't hide her attraction to him. That threw him and made him take things further than he originally planned. Now he had her number on his phone. Granted he could've gotten it from her file, but there was satisfaction in knowing she wanted him to have it.

He slid behind the wheel of his truck and started the engine. Would Mya go for an uncomplicated fling? She was more educated than the women he typically screwed around with. Plus, she had a kid. Would she want the boy to know about them sleeping together? Probably not.

He pulled onto the street and headed to the Arms to gather more information about Mya. Something was going on with her, and he needed to know what. Asher admitted outside of work, he wasn't the most patient of men and could be an ass when things didn't go his way. But he wanted to slide between Mya's breasts first and then her thighs as soon as possible. That meant he had to remove whatever problem had come up and stood in the way of them going forward.

Chastity and Beamer would know.

Before he reached the corner, the Sheriff called.

"Hey, Jack. How's it going?"

"Good. Just wanted to update and tell you about the burglary yesterday. You remember calling me about someone breaking into a house?"

"Yeah, I do."

"I caught the guy. Private investigator out of Washington named Delaney. He'd installed cameras in the house. Beamer checked it out and gave them to me. Laura's the victim's attorney." He went on to explain what they learned about the job.

Asher whistled. "Pity him." Laura was a good attorney who wouldn't quit or cheat. If she hadn't run into problems eight years ago, she might still be practicing law in California or maybe not. At some point, they all planned to return home.

Jack chuckled. "They reached an agreement. I'll be letting him go in a bit." He told Asher the name of the attorney and the guy in holding. "I told Laura you called it in."

Loose lips and all that, Asher thought sourly.

"No problem," Asher said, this time, he added silently. Laura was a part of the community and could be trusted. Jack's propensity to share information was a problem in need of correction. Right now, he wanted to have a private conversation with Delaney. "Well done, Jack. When are you releasing him?"

"In a few minutes, why?"

"I want to talk to him after his release. Can you give me a few minutes? I'll call when I'm there. Then release him." He added a bit of bass to his voice, so the words came across as an order, not a suggestion.

"Will do. Let me know when you're here." Jack disconnected without asking questions.

Asher headed downtown toward the Sheriff's office and pulled into a spot across the street from the jail. He stepped out and sat on a bench before making the call. He took out his tablet, entered the code and opened the software which allowed him to watch the streets through hidden exterior cameras in this area.

True to his word, less than ten minutes later, Delaney stepped outside and looked up and down the street. He stuffed his hands into his pocket and walked to the right and around the corner.

Delaney walked to the end of the block, looked both ways again and crossed the street. He wasn't very tall, possibly around five six or seven. Dressed in dark jeans and a black short-sleeved shirt he looked pale and slender. Strands of his dark brown hair stood straight up as he continued walking until he reached the Von Buck house at the end of town.

"Interesting," Asher murmured.

Delaney pressed the button at the gate several times. Nothing happened. He pulled up his collar and pressed the button again. The gate remained closed. Asher wondered if someone in the big house would offer Delaney sanctuary and was happy to see the man denied. Delaney looked in the direction he had walked and strode in the opposite direction toward the shops.

Asher watched for a few minutes more and slid into his truck. It was time to meet Delaney.

Within five minutes, Asher strolled into the corner deli where Alonso and his wife, Maria, served their lunch clientele. Maria looked surprised to see him. Alonso took the unusual visit in stride and, moments later, handed him a tray with a peanut butter and grape jelly sandwich cut in half, a bag of chips and a cold bottle of water.

"Thank you." Asher left a $10 bill next to the register and walked outside to join Delaney, who nursed a bottle of water.

Asher didn't ask if it was alright to sit down at the table as he pulled out the chair.

Delaney didn't appear surprised, either. Instead, he watched Asher take a bite out of his sandwich.

"I've settled the debt and am on my way out of town. Just waiting for my ride," Delaney said, when Asher finished the first half of his sandwich.

"You didn't seek permission first," Asher said, in a low tone. He wasn't sure what to do about Delaney yet. So much depended on the man's attitude in the next few minutes.

Delaney took a deep breath and shook his head. "No. That was stupid of me. To be fair, the name of the town changed. On the map, it's Wellesby Valley, not Versteck."

"Town name hasn't changed. The Post Office did that for mail," Asher said, in a voice devoid of emotion.

"I see. Still, I should've checked before I accepted the job. Should've realized there was a problem when others refused. The attorney dropped the charges and cleaned out my savings. If I'm allowed to leave this time, you have my word I won't be back," Delaney said.

"Tell me about the person who hired you," Asher said, and bit down on a chip.

Delaney explained the man wanted dirt on his grandson's mother so he could get visitation rights or something along that line. So far, she turned up clean and would easily win an award for Mother of the Year. When he told his client there was nothing, the man didn't think anyone could be that good and insisted he traveled here to bug her home.

Asher listened. "Why? Why is he doing this? He's spending a lot of money for a case he can't win without planting information. And don't tell me he didn't want you to do that."

Delaney scowled. "The bastard wanted me to plant enough drugs in her house that she'd never get out of jail. Has no idea how the law or an excellent attorney works. I told him no to the drugs and yes to the surveillance."

"Who is this man?" Asher asked, in a low voice.

"Joshua Henry, father of the boy's dead father, Colin Senior. He wants to spend time with the boy. But..."

Asher looked at him. "What?"

"Something's not right with the whole thing. I got the feeling he had a reason, other than family loyalty or whatever it's called, for doing this. He seems desperate. Like he's under pressure or something. I quit the job the moment the Sheriff knocked on the door. I don't like the way any of it went down," Delaney said.

"So it's not the love of his son or grandson driving him?" Asher asked, as he finished his food.

"Maybe he's one of those cold bastards who doesn't show affection and hides it deep. But I don't recall him ever mentioning his dead son or speaking of his grandson with anything close to compassion or kindness. It seems like it's more of a mission to win," Delaney said, and leaned back in his seat, watching Asher.

That seemed strange to Asher, but as an only child who didn't have a good relationship with his father or grandfather, he did not know how things worked. He would talk to Laura next and get more answers.

"Why did you go to the Von Buck Manor?"

Delaney's eyes widened fractionally before he released a long sigh. "My partner, Harris told me to go there if there were any problems." He glanced at Asher and leaned forward. "He said someone in the house would help me get out of town."

Asher stared blankly at the man.

"Have you heard anything like that before?" he asked.

"Not in those words," Asher said.

Delaney continued staring at him and nodded. "Bunch of rumors."

"Is that the reason you came here? To see if the rumors were true?" Asher said, confident he was at the crux of the matter. Fewer people came these days trying to gain information regarding Versteck and Von Buck's modern Robber's Roost. Jack was supposed to weed these guys out.

"Once I got here and discovered I was in Versteck, I thought I'd see if the rumors were true," Delaney said.

"What rumors would that be?" Asher said, watching Delaney's cheeks redden.

"You know what rumors. That's why you're here." He paused and glared at Asher. "Isn't it?"

"You committed a horrible crime in Versteck. If you know anything about Von Buck and the purpose of this town, understand we value our privacy above everything. We hold our secrets close. Spying and stealing secrets is right up there with murder."

Delaney blanched. His mouth opened and closed a few times. "But I've made that right already. The checks had to clear before my release. I even made a donation to the Charity Ball."

Asher nodded. "Good deal. That's a fine accomplishment. However, you asked why I was here. I wanted to assure you it's not because of the rumors surrounding Von Buck Manor, but because of the seriousness of your violation."

Delaney stared at him for a few seconds. "Answer me this. Am I leaving this town alive?"

"That's up to you," Asher said.

"Please explain," Delaney said.

"Tell me what rumors you've heard," Asher answered.

"Von Buck wanted to replicate Butch Cassidy's hideout and built his own Robbers Roost inside the manor. There's supposed to be places a person can hide for months and never be found by the law."

When he said nothing else, Asher prodded. "What else did you hear?"

Delaney took a deep breath, looked around before facing Asher. "Heard Von Buck's ghost still roams the place, and if he likes you, the gates open. If he doesn't, they don't.

Silly, I know, but there are so many old places in Colorado that advertise ghost sightings, I wasn't sure."

"They've never advertised any Von Buck sightings," Asher said with certainty. Although he grew up hearing about Von Buck and the Manor, no one talked about ghosts. This was something new. He would pass on the information to the groundskeepers at the Manor.

"No one's advertised anything about Versteck. I was making a point of other places, like The Stanley in Estes Park. You know the one Stephen King based his book…" He snapped his fingers. "The Shining. Made a movie about it too. It was based on that haunted hotel. Lots more of them, too. I was just making a comparison, that's all," Delaney said.

Asher didn't like the direction of the conversation. "So you came to see if the Manor was haunted, is that it?"

Delaney sighed. "Sounds stupid now. But like most kids who cheer on the not-so-good guys, I wanted to see Von Buck's Robber's Roost. Butch Cassidy's hideout is a place anyone can visit and get a look at how he and his gang evaded the law for years. So's the Hole-in-the-Wall but not Von Buck's Manor."

"Different decades," Asher said to nip this conversation and Delaney's fascination with the Manor in the bud. The last thing Delaney wanted to do was try to break into Von Buck's house. That could very well be the last thing the man did.

"Yeah, I know. Just curious." He looked at Asher. "Have you been inside?"

"Are you waiting for someone?" Asher countered.

"Lawyer's sending a cab to pick me up and take me to the airport," Delaney said, looking up the street and back at Asher. "So, are we good? Do I need to keep looking over my back because of this?"

Asher understood and, as tempted as he was to say yes, he had no reason to justify drawing more attention to the town. If Delaney kept the information quiet, neither the good citizens of Versteck Valley nor the legal authorities would take any legal action.

"Not that I know of," Asher said, as a cab turned the corner and stopped in front of them.

Delaney stood, nodded goodbye, and headed to the back door of the cab.

Asher placed his trash in the can and returned the tray inside. With a fingertip on his forehead, he nodded, left the deli, and headed to town to talk to Laura.

CHAPTER NINE

G REGORY PARSON SAT IN his office after-hours waiting for his late appointment. He popped two antacids into his mouth, stood and stared out the window. It couldn't end this way, he thought. His father and grandfather started Triple P Labs decades ago. It hadn't been called Triple P, he changed the name once he took control of the company 15 years ago. He had been so eager, so full of new ideas, and ready to take on the world. Despite his father and grandfather's advice against moving too fast, he chartered a fresh course and went after military contracts.

At first, things were great. With new technology and the right Chemists, the company had been on track to blow away the competition. He hadn't counted on the ferocity of industrial espionage. The competition wooed away one by one his top chemists. Company secrets stolen or lost, or chemical compositions couldn't be successfully replicated.

Thankfully, his grandfather passed before the company started losing money. His father had sold his shares at the peak of their success, and no longer had anything to do with the company. Lucky bastard.

With his younger sister and half-brother waiting at the door to snatch control of the firm from him, Gregory needed to prove to the military the compound his company created worked. And the man who would help him do that would arrive momentarily.

His stomach clenched, and he took another antacid.

There was a light tap on the door.

Gregory glanced at the wall clock. "Right on time," he murmured. "Come in." He had done everything he could to reverse his fortunes. Henry was his last hope.

Joshua Henry strode into the room, dressed in a gray pin-striped suit, white shirt, and a red and gray tie. The color made Henry's gray eyes all the more startling in his hawkish looking face. He took a few steps inside the office, closed the door behind him and extended a long, slender hand.

"Nice to see you again, Parsons."

Gregory accepted the older man's hand and pumped it once before releasing it. There was something oily about Joshua Henry. No matter what he wore or how he carried himself, he gave off dishonest vibes.

"Likewise," Gregory said, and waved to one of the upholstered chairs near a round table. "Please have a seat. Can I get you something to drink?"

"I thought we were having dinner," Henry said, as he unbuttoned his coat before sitting down.

"I can order something. What would you like?" Gregory had hoped to get this conversation over with quickly and head home. His wife was entertaining his sister and her husband, and he wanted to monitor their talk.

"Nothing. I'll grab something later on. Gin and tonic is fine," Henry said, as he crossed his leg and looked around the office.

Relieved but schooling his features, Gregory fixed them both drinks and handed his guest the glass. Henry lifted it in a salute and took a large gulp.

Hope he doesn't get drunk while he's here. Gregory took another sip of his drink, cleared his throat, and asked. "When will you get the boy? I need to run a few tests on him and --"

Henry held up his hand. "I don't know. So far, the bitch is clean. I've changed lawyers three times. They all agree I don't stand a shot at winning in the courts. Useless laws. Why have them on the books if you can't enforce them?"

"I told you to introduce yourself to her, make friends and ask nicely to spend time with your grandson. If you'd done that, we wouldn't be having this conversation," Gregory snapped.

Henry waved him off. "We do this my way or not at all. I'm not interested or comfortable in being nice to that bitch. She seduced my boy and convinced him to leave all his money to her."

Gregory could see his plans for a renewed contract evaporating. Caught up in his own version of history, this fool failed to see the bigger picture. "Your son left his money to his child, not the woman."

Henry waved down his comments. "Give to one, you give to the other. My son may have been taken in by her, but I won't. The boy is his. He had the smarts to make sure of that --"

"Which is why he is your son's heir and not you. Have you spent all the money I gave you?" Anger rose in Gregory's chest as he watched the wastrel brush imaginary lint from his jacket.

"I've had several expenses," Henry said.

"I'm paying the Investigators, not you." There was no reason to mention no one would work for Joshua Henry and thought Gregory was crazy for dealing with him, too.

"True. But I'm working on another avenue to reach our shared goal. I'm planning a trip to meet the boy. I'll try to slip him out of town and get him to you within a week. Will that be sufficient for your schedule?"

"Yes, but are you sure it's a good idea to go there? What if she doesn't want you around the boy? Or calls the cops? If you're talking about kidnapping, I want nothing to do with that." Having two kids of his own, Gregory wasn't that desperate. He'd turn the company over to Stephan, his half-brother, first.

"All you need is a little blood, right?" The older man looked at him beneath lowered lids. Whatever he planned probably wasn't good.

Gregory thought of all the tests that needed to be done. He already had the boy's medical and school records, along with recent photos. He could fudge a few things if he had vials of blood.

"We could make that work. I'll find a lab in the area where you can take him." It wasn't an ideal solution, but he could make it work. In the end, the boy would return home to his mother no worse for wear.

"Agreed." Henry stood and re-buttoned his coat. "I'll need money for expenses."

Gregory bit back a groan. He knew this was coming and rather than argue; he went to his desk, pulled out the envelope with some of the cash his new backers had given him this morning and handed it to Henry.

"This is the last until I get blood from the boy. Make it last." He held Henry's gaze a moment longer until the man nodded his agreement and left the room in silence.

CHAPTER TEN

YA LEANED BACK AGAINST the headboard with a satisfied smile. She couldn't recall the last time the words flowed so fast and seamlessly from one paragraph to the next. Either she was becoming a better writer or Asher was the perfect muse. The man set her mouth to watering as she wrote the sex scenes. God, if he was half as good in reality as in her imagination, they, if she was lucky, could set the world on fire.

A side glance at the wall clock made her yell. "No." She closed the file and set the laptop aside. If she didn't push it, she would be late picking up Colin. He never noticed when she was a few moments late, but it always made her feel as though she had failed. Toss in the fact she left work before noon to meet with her attorney, and she had no real excuse for being late. It didn't take long to dress and race out the door after engaging the new security equipment.

The line of cars for pickups was much shorter than normal, indicating her tardiness. When she pulled to the front, the security guard, Bryson, walked to the car and asked her to come inside.

Immediately concerned about Colin, she pulled into a visitor's slot without asking questions. Bryson rarely said anything other than hello or goodbye, for him to want to speak with her. Something was wrong.

Dressed in gray sweats, matching sweat top, and sneakers, Mya moved quickly to the entrance where Bryson waited.

"Is Colin alright?" she held his gaze for a moment before bracing her hands on her knees. She took several deep breaths to calm her racing heart.

"Yes, he's in his class. They're running a little behind. Ms. Wails wanted to talk to you about the situation you mentioned to her last week. She wants to be kept current, won't take long. By the time you're done, Colin and the class will be ready to leave." He didn't smile. She couldn't recall ever seeing the stout man smile, but his eyes were kind.

"Whew, you scared me. I didn't know what to think." She straightened and placed her hand on her chest. Her heartbeat hadn't slowed much.

"Sorry about that. Should've explained things better when I asked you to come inside. The other parents are in the class waiting. I didn't want you to go there first," he said, before returning to his post.

Mya moved at a slower pace to the administrator's office. It didn't make sense for her to be so out of breath, she should start working out again, maybe walking or something.

"Ms. Wails wants to see me," Mya told the receptionist.

"One moment, I'll tell her you're here."

Mya stuffed her hands into the pockets of her top and counted to ten to pull herself together. Before she finished, Ms. Wails walked out to greet her.

"Hello, Mya. Thanks for taking a few moments to talk to me. Please come in." She waved Mya into her office.

Conscious of being bra-less, Mya crossed her arms to keep her breasts from moving too much and drawing attention. If she hadn't been so worried about Colin, she would've worn her large jacket instead of leaving it in the car. Seated she waited for Ms. Wails to explain what was going on.

"I just wanted to touch bases with you regarding the security challenges you may be facing with Colin. I heard someone broke into your home yesterday and left surveillance equipment. Seems Mr. Henry is becoming a nuisance over this grandparent thing. Have you heard anything else from his attorney?"

Mya relaxed fractionally. This she could talk about. "Not since Laura sent a response. She's sure it'll be thrown out of court, he'll lose his petition. We're just waiting for the judge."

"So, you don't have to go to court?" she asked.

"No. If it goes further, Laura will go and handle it," Mya said.

"Good. We haven't had any problems here and will let you know if that changes. Bryson has added another guard to help keep watch. In the short time Colin's been here, he's become family, and we look out for our own. No one will get to him while he's here, I promise you that."

"Thank you, I appreciate it." Mya wondered how Ms. Wails could make such a promise with two security guards, students, and academic staff. Were they all packing weapons? She bit back a smile at the thought of Ms. Jenkins, Colin's teacher, wielding a pistol. The small woman looked like she'd faint at the sight of trouble, let alone gunfire. Still, she appreciated Ms. Wails attempt at making her feel better.

"Colin's class is just finishing their last project. Sorry, you missed it, but Ms. Jenkins didn't want anyone entering the room once they started, so I took the opportunity to discuss this matter. I hope that's alright."

"Sure, but if I knew Colin had a project, or there was a program going on, I would've been here. I don't like missing his class events. If something like this happens again, please let me know ahead of time so I can be there to support him," Mya said trying to hide the rising disappointment from her voice.

"Of course. This was more a class assignment that wasn't finished, and the kids asked for more time. Ms. Jenkins asked the parents to come inside and wait quietly with the promise of allowing each student to explain their projects. Each time the door opened, and a parent walked in, it set the students back. That's why she stopped others from entering the class. She wanted them to finish without the distractions," Ms. Wails explained as they walked toward the main lobby.

Colin stood next to Ms. Jenkins, his friend Michael, and another little girl. Her son smiled at her. "Mommy, look!" He held a large white cardboard box for her to take. "Look inside. See what I put inside it."

Tickled by his bursting excitement, she took the box and did as he asked. Colors of every shade swirled along long, wide rods. "This is beautiful." She looked down at him and kissed his forehead. "You'll have to explain to me how it's spinning by itself." Taking his hand, she smiled her thanks to Ms. Jenkins and headed toward the car listening to Colin's explanation of how the class had to solve the problem and the solutions they came up with.

"I told Michael his idea wouldn't work, and we wasted a lot of time trying to get it right. Paris finally had the best idea and it worked," he said while strapping himself into the car seat.

"That sounds like a lot of fun," Mya said as she placed the box next to Colin, closed his door, walked to the driver's side, and slid behind the wheel.

"It was interesting," he said as he picked up the box again. "The colors are pretty like Paris."

Mya turned and looked at him. His hair had grown longer since they arrived, she'd get it cut this weekend. "Paris is pretty."

Startled gray eyes looked at her. "You know her?"

"She's the new student in your class, right? Short, hazel eyes, long braids?"

He nodded. "She speaks three languages." The way he said it meant it was a big deal and a challenge.

Mya pulled out of the parking lot and headed toward the furniture store. Last weekend she picked out the living, dining, and bedroom furniture for upstairs and placed it on hold until she got paid next week. Thanks to the check she received today, she would pay it off and have it delivered well in advance before her mom arrived.

"You're learning Spanish," Mya said.

"I already know how to read Spanish. I just say some of the words wrong." He paused. "I'm learning French. Soon I'll know three languages, too."

Mya smiled as she turned onto the highway. "Does Paris speak French?"

"No. She speaks German. Her family is half-black, half-German. She's never been there though," he said.

"She told you that? About being half-black?"

"No. She said she was mixed like me. I'm not mixed. She said her mama is German and her daddy is black." He shook the box. "Mixed means more than one race. You're black, my daddy was white. But I'm not mixed, and I told her that."

Unsure what to say, Mya waited.

"I'm Black," he said sounding like Jefferson, her brother, who always talked to Colin about his heritage.

Alrighty then.

"Once you learn French, we'll take a vacation to France, would you like that?" she looked at him in the rear-view mirror. He continued looking inside the box.

"That would be nice. I could speak the language with everyone else. What about Spanish? Are we going to Spain? Or South America?"

"Maybe Pueblo or Denver. A lot of people speak Spanish there, everywhere actually," she said.

"That's true." He put the box aside. "I read something on your computer I shouldn't have, Mommy."

Thinking he read some of her erotic stories, her heart dropped. Heat birthed from rising embarrassment filled her face. She didn't know if she should explain or fuss at him for bypassing her password.

"What?" When words fail, say less. This tactic gave her additional time to think and gave him a chance to explain exactly what he saw.

He held his head down. "I'm sorry. I wanted to look up something that we saw in class. Your computer was on, and I used it while you were laying down at the hotel last night."

She glanced at him in the rear-view mirror again. "What did you read, Colin?" She hadn't pulled up any of the websites where she posted her stories in weeks, so he hadn't seen those.

"What are Grandparent's Rights?"

The air left her chest in a swoosh. Last night after the break-in she had done a little more research on the matter. Her concern over Colin's grandfather's actions pushed her to the edge. The man paid someone to spy on her.

"It's when grandparents go to court and ask a judge to force parents to allow them to see their grandchildren." She stared straight ahead so he couldn't see how much she did not want to have this conversation.

"Why would they do that?"

"Not all people are loving or kind or want what's best for their grandkids like Nana. It's up to moms and dads to protect their children from anyone who might hurt them in any way. Your daddy died as a hero fighting in the war. We never heard from his mom or dad or brothers or sisters. We don't know anything about them. Your daddy didn't talk about them either. So how do we know what kind of people they are?"

"Does that make them bad?"

"What?" She glanced in the rear-view mirror.

"That they've never called or talked to us. Does that mean they're bad people?" He met her gaze in the mirror. She stared at those serious eyes, so much like his father and released a sigh.

Knowing how close he listened and would mull over every word, she chose them carefully. "No, baby. It doesn't make them bad people. But they are missing out on something really important though, and that makes them... unfortunate."

He frowned. "What? Why are they unfortunate?"

"They don't know you. They've missed an amazing opportunity to know what a remarkable person you are. That's their loss." She watched him smiled and thought of the seriousness of the lawsuit. "Colin?"

He looked at her as she pulled into the parking lot of the large furniture store, parked and turned off the car.

"For some reason your daddy's father, a man who has never spoken to you or met you, wants you to visit him. I want you to know I've said no. No for now. Once you're older and can defend yourself against anyone who tries to hurt you, I'll let you go for a visit if they still want it. But not until then. I won't change my mind about that."

Colin's eyes widened. "He might hurt me?"

"I don't know, because I don't know him. Do you understand that? I won't allow you to go anywhere with anyone I don't know," she stressed. It was important for him to understand just in case the old man decided to show up in town with a sob-story. Colin asked very few questions about his father or anyone else, but that didn't mean he wouldn't become interested if the man said the right things or asked the right questions. Above all else, Colin was curious.

"Yes, Mommy. He's a stranger, and I'm not supposed to go with strangers no matter who they are." He paused. "What if he wasn't a stranger? Would I visit him then?"

"When you're older and can defend yourself, yes you can visit him. But not until then. Promise me, Colin. You will never go with your father's father or mother or any of his relatives or friends or strangers. Promise you won't go off with anyone that I have not specifically said you could go with." She turned in the seat and looked at him.

"I promise. Just you and Nana when she comes. Until then, just you. If anyone else tries to get me to go I'll scream and fight like you told me," he said looking too serious for a five-year-old.

Her heart melted as he leaned forward and brushed her hair back. "It's okay, Mommy. Don't be scared."

"I love you so much," she whispered blinking back tears. This child was her world, and until he could be his own champion, she would stand for him, slaying his dragons.

He smiled and unbuckled his seat belt. "Love you too, Mommy. We're going to look at furniture again?"

She wiped the tears from the corner of her eyes, grabbed her cell from her purse to check her bank account. The money had been transferred. "No. This time we're going to buy furniture."

CHAPTER ELEVEN

A SHER SAT IN THE same conference room Mya and Laura had been in earlier that day. Laura was finishing an appointment and would be with him in a few moments. With her full schedule, she offered to meet with him later or in the morning, but since he was already there, he would wait.

What would they do about Delaney's client? Based on everything he knew and heard, the old man didn't have a case, yet he paid to have Mya watched. That cost money and didn't sound like someone with intentions to stop.

Why now? What made the man come after Mya and the boy now? Colin's dad died three years ago. If the grandfather was concerned about having a relationship with the child, why hadn't he been involved in his life before? Delaney said his client appeared desperate. Like he's under pressure or something. That could mean several things.

Asher would run an extensive background check on the man and have someone shadow him. If the grandfather decided to sneak into town, Asher wanted to know about it before he approached Mya.

The door to the conference room opened. Laura strolled in. She had tamed her thick, woolly, natural hair into a long, single braid. Her freckles stood out more than normal, and her smile didn't reach her eyes. She was pissed about something. That wasn't good.

"Everything alright?" he asked, watching her closely.

"Let's talk in my office." She turned and walked down the hall, stopping in front of a closed door. "Hold my calls," she told her assistant as she and Asher entered her office.

Older than him by a few years, Laura had a slow burn, but when her temper lit, she blew hot and long. It wasn't pretty. He watched her carefully as he moved to stand in front of her desk.

"What the hell happened with Menendez?" she snapped. "His entire first string was eliminated. There was no need for a clean sweep right now." She pointed at him. "Don't tell me you didn't do it. You've been messing with him for years, just back and forth stuff. Why kill him now? We don't need this shit."

He relaxed a bit.

Laura understood their business but didn't like anything that could blow back on them or the town. Over the years they worked hard building this place. It took millions of dollars and a lot of hard work. None of them wanted to see Versteck Valley fall apart or come under government scrutiny.

"He was angry when his team of five didn't return," he said reminding her that she'd been responsible for eliminating the fifth person.

"I was there, remember?" she said. "We all know he burned down the house, a real landmark." She gave him a wry look and chuckled. "One that no one other than your aunt is going to miss. Still, that asshole came here to do damage. I knew you'd retaliate but to take out his core team? They'll be looking for you." She sounded worried.

"I wasn't the only enemy he had. Nor have I ever done anything that bold. Why do you think they'll suspect me or mine for such a major hit? Hell, Menendez screwed over so many people, had his fingers in so many pies, my name shouldn't be anywhere near the top of the list for that one."

She held his gaze for a few more seconds and then nodded. "Damn, I'm glad he's dead. The man was a boil on society, infecting everything he touched. I just don't want his hounds coming after you or anyone here," she said as she leaned against the corner of her desk with her arms folded across her chest. "Have you heard more on Moses?"

Crisis averted, Asher nodded. "I did. The news is keeping quiet about it, but they sent in a rescue team to get him and the others out. I'm waiting to hear how he's holding up."

She closed her eyes and took a deep breath. "I'm praying he's alright. None of us will be good if he's not. Moses... well, like his namesake, he's a good guy."

Moses and Drake grew up in Versteck Valley with their parents. Laura, her sister Crystal, and cousin, Jessica, were descendants of Von Buck and had deep roots in the town. All of them went to school together and over the years became close friends.

Asher spent his summers in town with Moses and Drake. It didn't take long for them to accept him in their close-knit group. Back then they talked about Von Buck's Manor and how cool it would be to turn the town into a real paradise for those who fell on the wrong side of the law. In those days it was just talking, something teenagers did when they were bored.

After high school graduation, they all went their separate ways, either to college, the military or someplace further away to make their mark on the world. After the death of his grandfather and later his father in a boating accident, Asher used his inheritance to buy huge tracks of land south of Versteck Valley and anything that came on the market in town. Within three years he was a major landowner, second only to Von Buck's heirs. He kept several acres vacant to create a sizable buffer between Versteck and the next closest town. It was important to remain somewhat isolated and limit access to the tunnels to a few individuals.

Years ago, Laura had personal problems in California, which she never discussed and returned to Versteck. As a descendant of Von Buck, she couldn't ever sell the land but would always have access to acreage to build a home or any enterprise of her choosing. Laura built four large townhouses, renting the other three and a two-story office building. She used the second floor for her practice and rented the first. When Asher and his cousins returned and built the Arms, they were beginning to see their teenaged dreams fulfilled.

"Yeah, that he is. He's alive. That's the most important thing. Everything else can be fixed," he said rubbing his chin. When her gaze followed his hand movements, he stopped and dropped his hand to the side. "I had a conversation with Delaney."

"I saw. He paid a high price for a bungled job. Somebody's got deep pockets somewhere. I could've gotten Mya more, but she's happy, which is all that matters."

Asher nodded and gave her a brief recap of the conversation.

"Haunted? Did he really say that?" she asked surprised.

"Yes, he did but don't get any ideas about using the place to scare people away, it'll backfire, and that's not the kind of attention we want around here," he said watching the expressions cross her face.

"But it would be so much fun." She laughed and clapped her hands. "No, we can't do that, but you have to admit it would be so cool to spend the night in the Manor, maybe have a seance, call out old man Von Buck, ask him how things are going on the other side."

He shook his head. Laura would do it. "We already spent the night at the Manor, several times, there were no ghosts. No Von Buck. No seances. I thought you grew out of that years ago."

Smiling, she stood and walked to one of the chairs in front of her desk and sat. "Those were exciting times. I don't miss them per se, just the adventure of sneaking in and not getting caught. Now, the risk is so much higher."

"A lot of people depend on you to keep your head on straight," he said taking the seat next to hers. "You're one of the legitimate faces in this town that keeps the Po-po off our asses."

"Yeah." She looked at him. "You too. The Arms isn't just a home for those guys, it's a haven and a job pool. They know the jobs are decent and low risk because you vet the offers first. That's a valuable service and a way to live with your dignity intact. It was a great business move and feeds into your legitimate security company."

The finder's fees were extremely profitable along with the quarterly payments to live in the arms. His inheritance had topped 5 million. Over the years his investments here in town and other places around the country paid off, easily tripling that amount. "Our version of a Robber's Roost, right?"

She smiled. "I remember the night the three of you talked about it. We were all half drunk and the ideas were flowing wild and bizarre. You guys wanted a state-of-the-art facility, best security on the market, large comfortable units, best medical care, a gourmet kitchen for the best foods. Everything had to be the best for your Robbers Cave."

"Hey," he objected on a laugh, remembering that night. They had returned to the big house for Christmas to make his recently widowed Aunt Mae happy. They'd been in the basement drinking and talking. "Not a cave. We spent close to a million on those buildings."

"Because of the escape tunnels," she teased. "You or Drake, I can't remember which, started writing stuff down and made a drunken vow to build it. At first, I wasn't sure you could do it until you came back with the drawings and told me you had several residency applications already. And that was before you broke ground."

"I've met a lot of interesting people in my career working in the Diplomatic Corps, so has Moses and Drake. Once we got the money, we went for it. Best decision we've ever made. All above board, on paper anyway." He winked.

"Lots of good talent, that's for sure. A couple of them have saved me tons of money and time."

"True." He paused. "About Delaney's client. Do you think he'll show up here?"

"Unfortunately, yes. I've alerted Jack. He's going to have a deputy tailing her for a few weeks to let me know when Joshua Henry arrives."

Asher shared Delaney's thoughts about the man appearing desperate. "What do you think he really wants? And why now?"

Laura appeared thoughtful. "I've asked myself that question a few times and haven't come up with anything. Would you look at the background information I have on him and give me your opinion?"

He nodded. "How deep did you go?"

"Not as deep as you could, so feel free to dig deeper. I like Mya and her son, so does Wesley, Charity, and several of the others. They, we, all want them to stay." She watched him for a few moments, pulled out her phone and tapped on the keys. "I sent it to your secure files."

Wesley was a former attorney who had specialized in tax law and had lived in Versteck all his life. In his late 40's he ran a pyramid scheme operation that netted him and his top players' serious cash before it fell apart and cost him his license without spending time in jail. Fortunately, he invested well enough to retire early. These days he worked underground, advising several clients on how to navigate the complicated tax codes. The man was a genius with the Midas touch and a member of their coalition. His word carried serious weight.

"You think Henry is a threat to our way of life?" Asher asked as he clasped his hands across his lap.

"Don't' know about that. What I'm thinking is he's threatening one of ours, and that's not a good thing to do any day of the week."

"She hasn't been here a month, how is she one of ours?" Asher's interest in Mya was physical, and he didn't want her to leave, not yet anyway. But he was curious why Laura and Wesley considered her one of theirs.

"She's nesting. Wants to raise her son in peace. Her first marriage wasn't good, the guy was a jerk. She's here to start over." It was the way Laura said "start over" that caught Asher's attention. So many of the residents moved here for that same reason with no questions asked. As long as they didn't violate Versteck's code of ethics, nobody bothered anyone.

Laura continued. "When she told Bonnie about the possible threat to her son, you know the school went into "fuck off" mode. Bryson added security and is carrying live ammo just in case."

"He told me," Asher said recalling the conversation with Bryson last week. The man had been livid over the threat. Bryson had been raised by his mom and identified with the struggles of single parenting. There were only two single-parent students at the school, and Bryson gave them extra attention. If Henry attempted to see the boy at the school that might be the last thing he ever did.

"According to Bonnie, Colin's on track to be the star student this year, nothing from the outside should interfere with that." Laura and Bonnie had been dating for the past six months after Bonnie's former girlfriend complained Bonnie spent too much time at the school and moved away.

Rather than poke holes in Laura's comments, Asher nodded. As Higher Dimensions administrator, Bonnie Wails knew best about the students. "What's the legal position on this?"

"The grandfather has no case. Mya stipulated in the response she does not want any contact with the man at this point and has refused visitation rights. The law's pretty clear on that. I'm just waiting to receive a dismissal from the court. Still, it goes back to your question of why now? He's never contacted the boy, not even for the funeral. After making a brief inquiry over the legality of Colin being his son's heir, Mya never heard anything from him again."

"What about the Trustee?" Asher asked.

"What about him?"

"Has she heard from him or her? Are they involved with Henry in this mess?" Asher asked. "You said someone has deep pockets, maybe the money is coming from the boy's trust fund."

She pursed her lips. "Good point. I hadn't thought of that, but it's a possibility. I'll talk to Mya later today and get that information. It won't hurt to find out what's the Trustee's position. Thanks."

"No problem." He hesitated. Should he mention meeting Mya? Would she tell anyone about their conversation? Or that they were talking on the phone? It had been so long since it mattered, he wasn't sure. "I'm staying in my place next to her. I saw Delaney break-in and called it in. With the situation with Moses and Menendez, the last thing I need is to be next door to a house under surveillance."

Laura's gaze sharpened as she stared at his face. "I wondered where you were laying your head. Didn't think you were in town. Jack said you were in Denver."

Asher frowned. "What are you going to do about him? He talks too much."

"Nothing right now. I like that he's talking especially since he's loyal. Just don't tell him anything you don't want to be repeated. He'll fold like a cheap deck of cards," she advised. "Other than that, he loves Versteck."

"Do not tell him about our Robbers Roost," Asher said.

Her gaze chilled. "I've never told anyone about it, not even Bonnie."

"He talks too much," Asher said again.

"He's asked questions about the Arms," she said.

Asher looked at her with a raised brow.

"You guys have that buried under so many corporations, he was curious who owned it. I told him I did." She grinned. "I think he believed me for a few months."

"He accepts pay-offs." He looked at her. "From me. I don't trust him, but he's useful. I'll be glad when Pierre returns and takes his job back. I'd feel better with one of our original gang in charge of the police."

She nodded. "I agree. His commission will be over within the next year. I miss him and Shelly. It'll be good to have more of us back here."

He reached over and covered her hand.

"Have you talked to Mya?" She captured his gaze.

"Yes. Today, just after the new security system was installed." He and Laura didn't always agree on everything, but they didn't lie to each other.

"What did you think of her?"

He frowned. "Think of her? We didn't talk that long."

She continued staring at him.

He didn't blink. They didn't lie to each other, but they did keep personal secrets that did not impact the town.

"You're not going to say more, are you?"

"Like what?" he asked, going for a neutral tone.

Laura sighed as she stood. "Don't hurt her, Asher."

He tried to look offended. "Why would you say that? Have you ever known me to hurt a woman?"

She pointed at him. "Not physically. But there are other, more painful ways to hurt a person. Don't play games with her, that's all."

He held up his hand as if swearing an oath. "I've never cared enough to hurt a woman in any way and the only games I play are sexual. I won't agree not to play those."

She threw up her hands and laughed. "You're a mess. Just know if you hurt her, she might leave town, which will piss off the Arms residents and you don't want that."

Her words sobered him.

Those men were loyal and would go looking for blood if they felt one of theirs had been harmed in any way. Did he really want to deal with that?

CHAPTER TWELVE

L ATER THAT NIGHT, COLIN fell asleep shortly after dinner and his bath. He had played with the box while explaining how the colors moved. Mya half-listened while watching the clock and wondering if Asher would call her or if she would call him. It seemed that she should call him since she had a child to put to bed and he didn't.

Wait. How did she know he didn't have a child to put to bed? Or if he was married? Or shacking with someone? Lots of men didn't wear rings for a lot of valid reasons. That would be the first thing she asked. Getting involved, even private phone conversations, with someone's husband was a big no and lose my number for her.

She took a deep breath and stepped out of the shower. No need to borrow trouble. He didn't give off the kind of vibes men already in relationships did. Those guys knew they had to come with more than an "A" game to win the prize and often smacked of desperation based on lies.

Asher came across as interested but not going to jump through hoops for anything. If he lied to get into her panties, she would be surprised. Even with his scarred face, he seemed confident, and that was sexy as hell. Just as she finished rubbing Shea butter onto her arms and legs her phone rang.

Her heart leaped in her chest as she picked it up and read his name. "Hello, Asher. How are you?"

"Better now. Is this a good time or should I call back later?"

She glanced at the clock. It was nine. "This is fine. Colin's asleep."

"What about you? Are you getting ready for bed?" His voice dipped.

Goosebumps rose on her arms.

"Not yet. Are you married? In a relationship with someone? Have kids? Or any baby mama drama?"

He chuckled. "Guess we should get that out of the way first. No to all the above. For the record, if I were in a relationship with someone, I wouldn't have asked you for a date or your number. When people do that, the other relationship is not serious."

She frowned. Her ex-husband dated, certainly asked for phone numbers, and took other females on dates during their marriage. She had considered theirs a serious relationship. Perhaps she was the only one who did, and that's what Asher meant.

"I see," she said while thinking it through.

"Both parties have to agree on what the relationship means and entails," he said.

"True." The rules of marriage were basic and well known. Forsaking all others meant monogamy.

"I don't have any children, so no baby mama drama. What about you? Is someone going to come looking for me with a gun when I take you out to dinner?"

"What?" She heard the word gun and nothing else.

"Are you in a relationship with someone who would take offense over us going out?"

"No. No, of course not. Sorry, I got... Thanks for answering my questions. I wanted to be clear I don't poach or take a sideline position for anyone, not even as friends."

"Really?"

"If I can't be friends with your wife too and she isn't alright with me being your friend, I'll back off. It's less hassle all around that way. Some women are alright with their men maintaining friendships they had before they became a couple, others aren't. The last thing I want to do is cause problems for my friends. If it's a genuine friendship, it'll be okay," she said.

"That's an interesting way to look at it. I won't give up friends I've had for years to make someone else happy," he said, sounding implacable.

"Different people handle things differently." *Did she really want to have sex with this guy? He sounded inflexible.*

"True. How do you handle intimate relationships?"

She blinked. Did he ask what she thought he asked? *What did he mean intimate? Just for sex?*

"Depends," she said to give herself time to think up an answer. She lacked the skills to navigate that kind of relationship. Sure, she wrote about one or two-night stands all the time. But that was fiction. More like a dream, not something she wanted in real life. *Or did she?* Could she go out with a guy just for sex?

"On?"

"On what I want at the time." One of her characters had said something along that line. It worked in the story. *Yeah, anything works in stories when you're writing them.* The thought that she was out of her league ran through her mind. Did men indirectly ask for sex during the first conversation? In her stories, yes. But that was to move the story along.

Between school, raising Colin and helping her mom, she hadn't dated or been with anyone since Colin's dad. Even that short-lived relationship hadn't been simply for sex. He hadn't mentioned sex on their first date, although later he told her it had been on his mind. They had sex on their third date. By then she understood he would be leaving and couldn't make promises of a future. With school and her terrible experience with Ahmed, Colin had been exactly what she wanted. He had eased her back into the dating pool, something she had avoided since moving to Tulsa. Plus, the sex had been great.

But now? She wasn't sure she could go that route with her son in the house.

"Do you know what you want at this time?" he asked.

"Hadn't thought about it until you asked," she said truthfully and laid across the bed to think. "I can't do casual. I've done it in the past, and it worked. But with my son, that's not what I want this time." She hadn't realized that until this moment. "Sorry about that."

"Why're you apologizing? It's how you feel and what you want, isn't it?"

She said sorry, but it wasn't a real sorry. She didn't want to admit it, though. "Yes, it is." Deflated, she rolled over and covered her eyes with the back of her other arm. The timing sucked. The last thing she needed was Colin's grandfather claiming she had loose morals with various sexual partners. One shouldn't be a problem, but if he brought up the lies Ahmed had spread about her, one man could convince the judge. She wouldn't chance it, no matter how fine Asher was.

"Did you know Robert Von Buck, the man who founded Versteck Valley, never married? He had four children from three different women. Cynthia, a black woman he met here in the Valley. She had a son and daughter from him. Although he didn't marry her, he took good care of her and their children. He had two other daughters, both from German women, before he arrived in this country. Collectively, they own a lot of the land in this area."

Surprised by the change in conversation, Mya stammered. "No, no, I didn't know that. He had two children from a black woman?"

Actually, she was a mix of Black and Crete Indian and I heard she was stunning. But yes. The eldest daughter, whose name I can't recall, came from Germany to visit her birthplace and try to sell her share of the land. But the land's held in trust for his heirs and can't be sold, only used by them for their personal use."

Intrigued, Colin wasn't the only curious person in the house. She chuckled. "I bet she was pissed."

"That's putting it mildly. She blamed Cynthia, claimed the woman worked some kind of magic on Von Buck to make him stay in America and rob her of what she believed was rightfully hers. She took them to court and lost. In anger, she tried to burn down the Manor."

"What? That big house near the mountain?" Mya stared up at the ceiling in shock.

"Yes. If you look it up on the internet, the story should be there."

"What happened?" She didn't know this kind of thing happened in such a nice, quiet town.

"Like I said, she tried to set fire to it, but they built the walls of thick concrete blocks, which didn't burn. Some of the living room furniture caught fire, but the police got there before she could do more damage."

"Wow. What happened to her? Did she go to jail or the crazy house? Or did they just deport her?" Mya asked.

"No one knows. She disappeared."

"Stop playing." She shook her head at his nonsense.

"Von Buck had a lot of hiding places in that house. People say she hid from the police and got lost. No one ever heard from her again. She didn't go back to Germany. Her fiancé came looking for her, but no one ever found her."

"You're making this up."

"Seriously. That's part of the history of this town. Since we're going to have a relationship, you should know I have no plans to move or live anywhere else. Versteck Valley is home for me."

CHAPTER THIRTEEN

A FTER MEETING WITH LAURA earlier that day, Asher made a couple of calls and sent someone to tail Joshua Henry, who at this moment was in a hotel off the coast of Maine. For now, the man wasn't in Colorado. They'd know in advance when he moved in this direction.

Wesley sent word through Laura that he wanted to have dinner with Asher at the Arms tonight and wouldn't be swayed to meet another time. Their relationship was a loose partnership based on mutual respect for one another's talents. There was no question who ran the Arms enterprise. Asher was top dog with strong enforcers if needed. However, Wesley's influence on the residents couldn't be downplayed. They respected him. If there were such a thing as a union boss among the criminal class, that would be Wesley.

Asher could've blown it off, but Wesley rarely asked for anything. Initially, he thought Wesley wanted to talk about Menendez or Moses since they had discussed both in the past.

However, most of their conversation centered on keeping Versteck Valley's residents safe. Not an unusual topic, but certainly unexpected when Mya's name came up. Wesley knew Asher owned the house Mya rented and asked several questions about the break-in and the conversation with Delaney.

Asher hadn't expected Wesley's demand that Asher got involved and fix the matter. Asher explained his full plate with Moses, the Senator, and vetting jobs for the talented men who lived at the Arms. Neither the updated security system, nor the large dollar settlement, nor Delaney's promise not to return to Versteck mattered. Wesley listened deferentially to all Asher's objections, but his response was the same.

"Fix it."

Laura had called this one correctly. The men in the Arms liked Mya and wanted her and her son protected at all costs. He could still hear Wesley yelling. "We take care of our own."

Since arriving home, he delved into his projects and checked on the Senator's surveillance team. The men worked seamlessly together and had amassed a lot of valuable information. Once Asher knew more about Moses' situation, he would decide on this operation. It wouldn't hurt to have a strong lever, if necessary, to pry Moses loose.

Eli had not contacted him with more news about where they had taken Moses and his team. The last cryptic message had simply said he's out and alive. Great news on the surface, but he needed to know his cousin's physical and mental condition. Moses had been making noises about getting out of the military. Maybe he would do that sooner rather than later.

After showering, Asher checked the clock. It was close to nine. Mya had been on his mind most of the night and not just because of Wesley's conversation, either. He couldn't shake that damn story, *Titty Cat*. Looking at her earlier, he couldn't reconcile her as the writer of something so hot and freaky. There were layers to Mya Burch he wanted to peel off and taste.

Laura's warning made him pause. If he dealt with her the way he normally did, she might become offended and leave. If she left town... especially with Henry after her, Wesley and the others would go gangster to protect her. Which would draw attention, if not the law, to Versteck. That's if they didn't turn on him first.

Not being with her was out of the question. Perhaps after they reenacted that scene in Titty Cat, he could back off, but they would have sex first. If necessary, he would change his approach and not be so abrupt about what he wanted. Some women preferred a soft lead up, dinner or a date before getting around to sex. Since she didn't want the date, he suggested talking on the phone and hoped to get the same results.

What if all she wanted was sex?

He grunted at how simple that would make everything.

To discover what she wanted, he would be smooth, ask a few questions and play it by ear. His bottom line was to have sex with her. The more he read her stories, the harder his dick became, and the more he wanted her beneath him. Or on top or bent over or any way he could have her. Just thinking about doing some of things she described made him uncomfortably hard.

He grabbed his phone and called her. When she said his name, all his plans vanished. He hadn't meant to ask her about intimate relationships, hadn't meant to get her thinking about what she wanted, not this soon. They hadn't talked for five minutes. What happened to his damn control?

When she apologized, he realized she was saying goodbye. She thought he would bolt at the idea of a genuine relationship. Normally, he wouldn't consider it, but there was nothing normal about Mya, and he didn't mean that in a bad way. She truly was the lady in public with naughty thoughts in private, and he definitely planned to take those thoughts for a test drive with her.

For some insane reason, he told her the story about Laura's great-grandmother's relationship with Von Buck. It came out of nowhere. Maybe on a subconscious level, he wanted to connect to the storyteller in her. It worked. She stopped thinking about not having a relationship with him and became engaged in the story, giving him time to come back to his objective, getting together with her.

He hadn't planned on a relationship, but he would do it if that was the only way to be with her. Fortunately, she didn't ask questions or say anything right away. He might have messed things up by reverting to brutal honesty and doubted she wanted to hear him admit he wanted to have sex with her right now.

Asher had never had a girlfriend. Growing up, he moved between his dad and mom's house at first, then his dad and grandfather's home. He'd lived on military bases in several foreign countries, learned several dialects and languages and made a lot of contacts.

None were girlfriends.

Sexual partners, one-night stands, even a Mistress, but no one close enough to warrant a label. Today, the day after Mya experienced a break-in, had been the first conversation they ever had. And then he says this:

"... we're going to have a relationship..." *Stupid. Stop thinking with your dick and fix this before she thinks you're weird.*

"Who asked you to move?" she said.

Snatched out of the fog of reprimands, he said. "Huh?"

"You said I should know you aren't moving. Who asked you to move?"

What the hell? "Just wanted to put it out there," he said, unsure if he should backtrack, apologize, or go along with whatever she had to say.

"We don't have a relationship. I don't know you, but thanks for letting me know you won't be moving."

Uncertain if she was making a joke at his expense, he frowned and listened harder.

She laughed. It was a tinkling, light sound that made him smile.

"Are you laughing at me?" he said, grateful she hadn't hung up or called him names. Not yet anyway, preferably when they were both naked and sweating. *Stop thinking with your dick.*

"Yes, I am. Was that a true story?"

"Yes, it is. Von Buck was quite the lady's man."

"Must be in the air or the water," she said.

Quick wit. Sense of humor. Polite. He understood how those traits would be a bonus with her job and why Wesley and the others liked her. "Could be."

"If the timing were different, I'd take you up on your subtle offer and see what's what. But I can't. There's too much at stake right now," she said.

"What's going on?"

"Just some stuff with my son's family. The other side, not mine," she blurted.

"I can help."

"That's so sweet, thank you. My attorney's handling it and she's very good."

"So, it's almost over?"

She didn't say anything for a few moments. "Yes, I hope and believe so."

"Is your attorney local?"

"Huh?"

"Attorney? Local?"

"Yes. Yes, she is."

"Laura's the best. She won't stop until she wins on your behalf."

"You know her?"

"Yes. I live here. She's the best attorney for miles around," he said seriously. Laura was tough to beat.

"She is."

"I'd still like to take you to lunch or dinner," he said into the silence.

"Timing," she said.

"Can you explain that, please? I promise I'll never share what you tell me." He hated pretending he didn't know what was going on, but as she said, timing. If they hit it off, he would admit everything later on, but now was not the right time. She would pack and leave town tomorrow if she knew he had been in her home and on her computer.

"It's a long story. I'll give you the short version."

"Thank you." He valued her trust.

She explained her son's father's death, the lack of communication between families, her son not attending his father's funeral. "We've heard nothing from any of them. If he walked down the sidewalk, I wouldn't know who he was."

That bothered Asher. "They need to get a picture of him for you," he said. Laura had photos of the man in the file she sent him. He would suggest she show Mya one of them so she wouldn't be blind. It would be a good idea for her son to know what his grandfather looked like as well.

"That's a good idea. I hadn't thought of that. I'll mention it to my attorney," Mya said and continued discussing the lawsuit.

"Until this is over, I don't want to give that man any reason to say I'm not a fit mother."

Asher wondered how or why she jumped to that conclusion. It was normal for women to date occasionally. Unless she was bringing dangerous men around her child or placing the boy in danger, the courts wouldn't rule against her for dating. There had to be more going on there. Now wasn't the time to push, but they would eventually discuss it.

"I understand. But there's another way to look at it," he said.

"What?"

"You're a young, professional, single mother with a son. Wouldn't it be a positive mark in your column if there was a good man in your son's life as well as yours? It's more normal for a beautiful woman to be dating than not. I'm just saying I'd be willing to step in and help in any way I could."

She laughed.

So did he. It was BS of the highest caliber, even though it held kernels of truth. "Seriously, though, you might consider it. I'm not talking about dating a million guys, just one. Me. That won't be held against you, I'm sure of it."

"Hmm, if I had to pick one man to date..."

"Can I come over? We can talk about it on the porch or deck. It's nice outside tonight." He didn't know if he could pull off being soft and nice, but he'd try.

"Now?"

"Yes. It's nice outside."

"Do you live nearby?"

"Yes. It won't take long to get there. No pressure, just face to face talking for a little while."

"Okay. How long before you get here?"

"Ten minutes. Will that work?"

"Alright. I'll meet you on the porch. I don't have anything to sit on out there. We'll have to sit on your car."

He hadn't planned to drive. "I'll bring a couple of chairs."

"Oh, alright. I'll see you soon."

They disconnected.

Asher ran his hand through his damp hair as he searched for his keys. The collapsible chairs were in the garage. He'd grab them on the way out. He glanced in the mirror, specifically at the scar on his cheek, and ran his hand through his hair again to keep it out of his face.

Next, he pulled on a pair of jeans, tee shirt and slid his feet into a pair of sneakers. Before leaving, he checked the street cameras to make sure they weren't under surveillance, checked for messages from his out-of-town team, Eli, or any recent developments on Joshua Henry.

Nothing.

He pocketed his keys, grabbed the chairs, and left to walk next door.

Mya changed into a pair of jeans, a fitted tank top, and a pair of slippers. She didn't bother with makeup, but she used the curling iron to bump her hair in the front. Ten minutes wasn't a lot of time. Where was he coming from, she wondered as she stepped onto the porch and looked up at the cloudless sky.

It was a beautiful night full of possibilities. Living near the mountains, it always seemed as if she was closer to the stars. A few nights after moving in, she and Colin laid on the back deck naming the stars and talking about constellations and galaxies. She smiled at the memory. Her son's vivid imagination went into hyper-drive as he talked about what life on other planets would be.

"Hey."

She hadn't heard him arrive and jerked back. Her heart raced until she recognized his tall, muscular outline. Pleased to see him, she smiled as he reached the porch with two long bags slung over his shoulder.

"Hey. You were right, it is beautiful out here tonight," she said, watching him remove the bags and take out the chairs. "I've got to get a couple of these. They're convenient."

"Yes. Perfect for watching any kind of outdoor activities," he said.

Immediately, she thought of a story she'd written about a nude party outdoors where couples mingled and chose partners based on drawing raffle tickets. Her face warmed as she moved to sit in a chair.

"One sec," he said and wrapped one arm around her waist, drawing her close but not flush against him. She closed her eyes and relaxed into his warmth. He dropped his chin on the top of her head, took a deep breath, held it, and released it slowly. "You have no idea how good you smell and feel. I've wanted to do this all day."

She shivered at the husky timbre and words.

"Thanks for letting me come over."

What should she say to that? You're welcome? That sounded almost condescending. Compliment him too? Or tell him she had thought of him as well? What if he asked about her thoughts? She could not tell him he was the hero in her erotic fantasies or stories.

"I'm glad you came over. It's nice having company," she said honestly.

He placed a kiss on the top of her head and released her.

Unsteady, she sat down, took a deep breath, and looked at him. "Tell me the truth. You're more interested in having sex than being in a relationship. I just felt how happy you were to see me and since we haven't talked much, I know my sparkling personality is not the reason you've risen to the occasion."

He stared at her for a few seconds, his face half-shadowed by the moonlight.

"That was a question," she said into the charged silence and grinned.

"Give me a moment. I'm trying to think of a way to answer you with diplomatic honesty."

She laughed and shook her head. "In that case, I can't wait to hear your answer."

"Can't lie about wanting sex. You felt the proof of that," he said. "But I also understand what you mean about timing. You're beautiful, sexy, smart and if you'd give me more of you than sex, I'd prefer that."

Was he telling her the truth? She had just given him a graceful out, and he hadn't taken it. Would she be his fuck buddy? Unfortunately, no. As a single parent, she would only allow men around her son with the potential to be more. She didn't want Colin growing attached to men she had no future with.

"I have a son. He's five. That's another reason I haven't dated."

"He's jealous?" Asher asked.

"I don't think so. He's never seen me with anyone. I won't do that unless I'm in a serious relationship."

Asher nodded.

She looked at him. "I told you why I'm hesitant about relationships, and it's true I'm concerned about the lawsuit, but there's something else. My son and I are a package deal. His father's dead. It's possible he'll look at any man in my life as a father figure. My father is gone, and my brother Jefferson is in Tulsa. It's not unrealistic to expect my son to gravitate to a man I care about. Some men might see that as a step too far or too much responsibility. It's important that you know this upfront. We're a package deal." She held his gaze for several moments.

"Not only do I need your permission to spend time with you, but I also need his as well?" he asked.

And that was the real reason she hadn't dated anyone in a long time. It was just the two of them, and Colin came first. If he picked up weird vibes or felt threatened by Asher or any man, she wouldn't date them. She was young enough to wait until Colin was older to enter a serious relationship. It would suck big time. She'd have a lot of horny nights, probably wear out five vibrators, write a ton more stories... but she would do it in a heartbeat.

"Yes," she said.

"If he doesn't like me?"

"If he was your son, and he didn't like me, what would you do?" she asked.

"Good point," he said moments later. "Will my scars and tattoos bother him?" he asked.

"Maybe, I don't know. But I would mention those to him before the two of you met." She paused. "Just like you made it clear you wouldn't be moving, and I thought the comment was premature since we don't know each other, so is this, but it's a core issue like dating married men. It's best to get it out now so that I don't waste your time."

"Appreciated. Any other core issues you want to share?" he said, watching her.

"No cheating. No belittling or name calling. I hate when people do that."

"Alright. Agreed."

"And you? What core issues do you have?" She looked at him. Moonlight caressed the unmarred side of his face, making him classically handsome. What did it say about her that she preferred the imperfection of the other side better?

"I like yours. In time, I'll need you to trust me, and I'll need to trust you too. I own a security company. My life can be complicated at times, and I can't share everything with you right away. As we build a relationship, trust becomes essential. It won't work if you don't believe you can get to that point with me."

She thought about her writing under another name, her shameful past with Ahmed and the years of therapy, her sexual kinks, and other things she would only share with him if she trusted him. It'd be awesome to finally have someone know, accept, and grow to love the real her. That was the gold ring.

"Most definitely. In time, I think that's critical. A core issue. Thanks for bringing it up," she said, smiled as he covered her hand with his.

"Tell me about your job," he said.

Thinking of the men at Versteck Arms, she grinned. "I work as a counselor-slash-therapist with a great group of older men. They make my job easy."

"Good. What do you do for fun?"

The change in the topic made her pause. "Fun? Hmm, what's that?"

He grinned, and she realized she enjoyed seeing him smiled. It softened his face, made him appear more boyish, less tough.

"Mountain climbing?"

"Uh, no," she said with a snort.

"Skiing? Winter sports?"

"No."

"Roller skating? Indoor sports like hockey?"

"No, and No. Although I attended a hockey game once," she said.

"Did you enjoy it?"

"No." She grinned at his baffled expression.

"Water sports like swimming? Or skiing?"

"I enjoy swimming," she said. "In Tulsa, Colin and I took lessons and spent a lot of hours at the pool."

"Awesome." He squeezed her hand. "What about ball games?"

"I can watch some basketball, maybe the Super Bowl, but that's about it. Colin has less interest in sports than I do," she said, in case he planned on talking to her son about games.

"Has he ever tried out for anything?" he asked.

"No. He's five," she said, as if that explained it. She never thought of sports for him, since he never appeared interested.

"What about plays, movies, or museums? Do you enjoy those?"

"Yes, although I haven't been to any in a long time. I've promised my son a week-long trip to D. C. to visit the Smithsonian museums. Maybe next year." Now that she thought about it, she had made Colin a lot of promises to see various things and needed to make good on some of them soon.

"I enjoy those too."

She grinned. "Who knew we had so much in common?"

"What do you like to read?" he asked.

Mya froze for a few seconds. "Romantic fiction," she said. "You?"

"Mostly non-fiction, things that deal with my profession, investment information, economic data, that kind of thing. I read some fiction, not a lot, though," he said.

She met his gaze as he leaned forward. His firm lips brushed against hers, softly. Her core clenched with need.

"I like you," he whispered near her ear.

No one had ever said anything that simple. Ahmed had claimed to love her. Colin's father had said he wanted her. Hearing Asher's declaration pierced her heart.

"I like you too," she said.

He leaned back, stared down into her face, and kissed her. Softly, tentative, as if asking permission. She leaned closer and swiped her tongue against his lips, and he took over. They broke apart on a gasp but didn't move far as they each took several deep breaths.

"Damn, woman. You're potent and should have a warning label," he said as he leaned back and cupped her face in his palm.

Heat spilled onto her cheeks as her core throbbed, demanding to be filled and satisfied. She hadn't been this turned on since Colin's father. If she didn't stop now, she would toss caution to the wind and take him inside to bed. *Timing*. She couldn't risk it. Maybe once they knew each other better, she could have him come inside after Colin went to sleep.

An unchained memory from the past rose like a specter dampening her desire.

"You're no better than a slut who wants to have sex all the time," Ahmed said, his face filled with disgust.

"We're married, we're supposed to have sex," she said, attempting to defend herself against the shame coating her throat and rising nausea.

"Not all the time. Not when you're pregnant. You're sick like a nymphomaniac," he accused, pointing at her. "That's what killed my son. You killed him, always wanting to fuck."

Hurt by his accusation, by her desires to be with him, she stood pulling the sheet around her nude body. "The doctor said that had nothing to do with it," she said, tears rolling down her cheek. He'd been mean and cruel, using her desire against her.

"What do they know? He would be alive if you'd kept your legs closed. Something is wrong with you. Get out, I don't want a whore for a wife," he said as he pulled on his clothes.

For years, his words had found fertile ground despite the brave front she displayed when she left him and finally filed for a divorce. She'd been a virgin when they met. He turned their time together into something dirty and unclean. Broken and confused over her sexuality, her therapist encouraged her to write about her feelings. That turned into so much more.

Asher went to kiss her again.

She stopped him as their lips touched. "One thing I'm not is a tease."

"Tease me," he whispered.

She closed her eyes as moisture dampened her thighs. "No, I won't, and you won't tease me. We're both attracted to each other. There's serious chemistry here, and we will take it to another level soon. But not tonight."

He dropped his forehead onto hers and nodded. "Not tonight."

She smiled at the weariness in his voice.

"This was nice, better than I imagined," he said as he moved back to look at her.

Her body screamed in protest; she wanted him inside her in the worst way. The way he felt, smelled, and tasted had her body sizzling with unfulfilled need.

He brushed his lips against hers and scooted back. "What are you doing tomorrow?"

"Huh?" She blinked a few times to understand what he was said.

"What're your plans tomorrow?"

There was always something going on, but she hadn't made any concrete plans that she could think of. Hell, she couldn't think clearly about anything at the moment. "Not sure yet."

"I'd like to see you if you have time. No pressure, just something to think about." He stood and looked down at her. "You're right. The chemistry between us is definitely off the charts. Looking forward to taking things to another level."

She stood and stepped back.

"Keep the chairs here for next time," he said with a smile.

She watched as he collapsed the seats and returned them to their bags. "Will do." Confused by all the emotions and memories running amok in her mind, she didn't say much as he walked to the edge of the porch.

"Goodnight, talk to you soon," he said, looking at her over his shoulder.

"Goodnight, Asher." She turned and walked inside, fighting feelings of inadequacy and shame that rose whenever she thought of the latter part of her failed marriage and losing her first son.

She engaged security, checked on Colin, who lay sprawled across his bed asleep, and went into her room. Meditation was the weapon of choice to eradicate the demons of her past. She hoped it wouldn't take too long but would do what was necessary to shut down the memories before she went to sleep.

CHAPTER FOURTEEN

I N THE MIDDLE OF the following week, Mya arrived at work a little early. As she pulled into her parking spot, her mom called.

"Morning, Mom. How're you doing?" Mya asked while turning off the car.

"Not as good as the doctor likes, the old goat. He's grounded me for a month, maybe more, depending on how well I respond to treatment. He's got me working with a physical therapist to get better movement in my leg. I just found out yesterday and meant to call last night, but things got busy at church. I won't make it out there until next month or the next. I'm sorry. How're things going?"

Disappointed, but not overly so, Mya said. "Good. Love the job. The people are nice, work's fun. Bought new furniture. I'll send some pictures when I get home." She hadn't told her mom about the break-in or Colin's grandfather. If she did, nothing would stop her mom from getting on a plane and coming to Denver. A lifetime of putting your children first was hard to break, so Mya would do this for her. She would handle Colin's grandfather on her own and pray for the best.

"How's Colin? Does he still like his school? Is he making friends?"

The conversation continued with Mya answering questions and bringing her mom current on most things. When they finished, she hung up with the realization she was really on her own, like a bird kicked from the nest. Sink or swim time.

Versteck Valley proved to be a great place to live and raise Colin. They had a nice home, money in the bank for emergencies, a good job, and friends. Asher was the topping that made everything else better. Having a sexy guy interested did wonders for her ego. Feeling empowered and ready to take on the world, she left her car and went in.

She stopped as she entered her office. Maggie, Chastity, and Laura stood waiting for her just inside the door.

Her steps and smile faltered as she noticed their serious expressions. Fear lanced through her chest. "What happened? Is it Colin? Did the school call?" She dropped her purse, half the contents spilled to the floor as she searched for her phone. She grabbed it and didn't see a missed call.

"No, it's not Colin," Maggie said. "We need to talk." She stepped back as Mya stood holding her purse.

"Alright," Mya said, frowning as she looked at her friends. *Had she done something wrong? What had she done? Something offensive?* She couldn't think of anything. Laura had heard from the court, and the case had been dismissed. They both agreed Colin's grandfather may not have given up and might show up in town. Between the two of them, Asher as well, they came up with a strategy on how to deal with the man if he approached either her or Colin. Sheriff Jack assured her all of his officers would look for Colin's grandfather as well.

Both she and Colin had seen a recent picture of the man and would sound the alarm if they saw him in person. Other than that, she and Laura no longer had business. Chastity and Maggie worked with her, but she couldn't imagine why they appeared upset.

The moment the door closed, Mya whirled around and looked at them. "What's this about? What's going on?"

"Asher."

That knocked the wind out of her sails. How did they know about him? About them? She hadn't told anyone about their spending late evenings together, without sex, and was sure he hadn't either. "What?"

Laura inhaled and rubbed her forehead for a few moments. "When it comes to relationships, Versteck is a small town, and word gets around. Asher's a good friend of ours, and we're concerned about him, that's all. If you're not into him, please don't lead him on."

Lead him on? Confused, Mya stared at them. "What?"

"I don't think he's ever been interested in anyone in town before," Chastity said, looking at Maggie for confirmation.

"Not that I'm aware of either. For a long time, I thought he was gay," Maggie said.

"What?" Mya said again, unable to follow or believe the conversation. *Gay?* Were they talking about the same man?

Laura gave Maggie a look that said her comments were ridiculous. "We're not trying to get into your business. He's a grown man, but he's also our friend, and we don't want him hurt. That's all."

"What are you talking about? How? Why would I hurt Asher?" She had no idea where all this was coming from. As far as she knew, her relationship with him was going well. He admitted he lived next door and asked her not to tell anyone. Once she put Colin to bed, he came over, and they talked or watched television and had been doing that since that first night.

He made her laugh. He listened to her. They disagreed on several things; he had some radical views on revenge and vendettas but could discuss them rationally. Often, she understood his point of view, although it didn't change hers.

Last night, he commented on how good the house smelled. When she offered him the rest of the lasagna and salad from dinner, he acted as if she were Chef Louise or something. His genuine appreciation touched her to the point she planned to invite him to a late dinner Friday night if things went well tonight. First, she had to get through this weird conversation.

"He likes you," Chastity said.

Mya frowned. "Did he tell you that?"

"No," she hedged. "But the fact he's talking to you means he likes you."

Mya snorted and crossed her arms over her chest. "Are you saying he likes me because we talk?"

"Yes," all three of them said.

Mya frowned. "You realize what that sounds like, right?"

"Please sit down so we can talk. Your first appointment isn't for two hours," Chastity said as she pulled out a chair and sat. The others followed. Mya sat in the only vacant chair in the room, the one behind her desk.

"Who's going to explain what this intervention is really about?" Mya said, looking at them.

"Do you plan on staying in Versteck?" Maggie asked, watching her closely.

"Yes. I have a good job, my son is doing better here than ever before, and I think or thought I had good friends. Was I wrong?"

"No, you aren't wrong," Maggie said. "We've got your back, believe that. It's just Asher... he's always been a loner. Now that he's interested in someone, someone we love and respect, we just don't want this to blow up and him to get set back. Do you understand what I'm saying?"

Mya leaned back in her chair and met Chastity's gaze. "I think so. Are you guys serious? You think I... me... can hurt Asher and not the other way around?"

When they didn't answer and looked slightly surprised, she realized they never thought he could hurt her. That was a shock. "Do you think I'm some Femme fatale? A heartless vixen?" She shook her head. "I can't believe you're afraid I'll hurt him. He's the most confident, self-possessed man I've ever met. That any woman, or man for that matter, could use or abuse him... I can't fathom it."

"He's been hurt physically," Laura said.

"Yes, he told me someone cut his face," Mya said. Asher hadn't wanted to discuss it, so she hadn't pushed. If these ladies wanted to share details, she would definitely listen.

Laura sighed. "I warned Asher against hurting you."

"Thank you," Mya said, feeling slightly better.

"What you don't understand is we're seeing our friend act out of character. We don't know how you respond when you're falling for someone. You've been smiling and happy, but that's no different from your normal behavior," Chastity said.

"How is he acting out of character?" Mya asked, curious.

"The two of you are still talking," Laura said bluntly.

Mya frowned.

"Asher does not talk to women, does not date, does not do the hanging around the house thing. At least he's never done it before, which is why we're saying he's acting out of character and we really hope you're into him," Chastity said, leaning forward with an earnest expression.

"How can a man who looks as good as him not date or talk to a lot of women? I know they're attracted to him," Mya said, fighting disbelief and relief at the same time.

"He has relations with women, but he doesn't date, not what you two are doing," Laura said and cleared her throat. "You could put us out of our misery and tell us you like him."

"I like him." Mya stared at the desk as she spoke in a dry tone. Moments later, she looked up and read the sorrow on their faces. "Girl, I really like him. It's taking everything within me to keep from jumping him every time I see him."

Chastity's face lit like a neon sign. "Thank God. Now I can tease you, both of you, like they teased Beamer and me."

Laura placed her hand on her chest. "He's a brother to me. It would've hurt me to cut you for messing him over, but I would've done it. I'm so glad everything's working out for you two. Has he met Colin?"

Mya stared at her attorney. Did she say she would've cut her over Asher? Yeah, she did. What the hell was that about? "No. We haven't had sex yet," Mya said.

Maggie nodded in complete understanding as she relaxed in her chair. "No need for intros if the two of you don't make it in the bedroom or any room you want." She winked at Mya.

"Exactly. But... I don't think we'll have a problem in that area. He's smoking hot."

Laura covered her ears. "Did you hear me say I consider him my brother, not as your sex god, someone for you to bang at whim?"

"About that cutting," Mya said, staring at Laura. "Neither Asher nor I know how our relationship will end. Either of us could get hurt, but that's between the two of us. Not you or anyone else. I don't appreciate that threat."

Laura met her gaze and then smiled. "I was kidding. We're good. No worries." She stood. "My work here is done." She pointed at Mya. "You're good for him. He's good for you. I really hope everything works out. Both of you deserve to be happy. Don't let anyone come between the two of you." She glanced at Maggie. "After he proves himself in the sack, that is."

The ladies laughed.

"I still need help with the Charity Ball," Laura said.

Chastity groaned and covered the side of her face with her palm. "I'm already helping. I can't do more."

"I know, and I appreciate all you've done." Laura looked at Mya and then at Maggie. "Ladies, I could really use a little more help. Please consider volunteering."

Mya looked at Maggie, who appeared horrified by the idea. "Alright, let me know when you have the next meeting, and I'll be there. I'll have to bring Colin with me."

"That's fine. Bonnie comes to the meetings. I'll make sure she brings something for him to do," Laura said.

"Or I could bring things for my son to do," Mya said wryly.

"Sorry, you're right," Laura said, acknowledging she had crossed a line. She clapped her hands and grinned widely. Her freckles stood out as she waved her hand at them. "I met

Imani Barnes at the top 100 Influential Women's conference last week, and I asked her to handle the presentation at the Ball."

"Who?" Maggie asked, looking at Laura.

"Imani Barnes, gorgeous, smart, married Theo Barnes, the billionaire. Good looking, tall, big, sexy, pale hunk," Chastity said and licked her lips.

The women stared at her.

"What? I'm happily married, but I'm not blind and can appreciate a fine-looking specimen like the best of them," Chastity said and crossed her legs.

"Well, alright now," Maggie said, offering her fist to Chastity, who bumped it.

Laura chuckled before she continued. "She got back with me yesterday. Her husband's company handles some investments for Von Buck's trust that still bring in revenues. Wesley did business with the original owner, the grandfather. Can't recall his name. Anyway, Wesley made it seem like there was some history between Von Buck and the old man and until the grandfather died, he came every year to the Charity Ball giving a large donation."

"Did she agree to come this year?" Chastity asked.

"Not yet. She wanted me to know about the history link. At the turn of the century, a lot of European immigrants came to the country seeking their fortunes. Some were successful, others not so much. Somehow, these two, one from Norway, the other from Germany, met and were business associates," Laura said. "I got the feeling Theo, the new owner, and Imani's husband, will send a contribution whether or not they attend. She came across down to earth and nice. I'd like you guys to meet her."

Chastity nodded. "Sounds like a story there. If we don't meet her at the Ball, we can meet another time. Maybe something less formal, like lunch or dinner. She doesn't have to come speak, invite her to come and chill. There's no place like Versteck Valley."

Laura grinned. "That's true and a good idea, one I'll keep in mind if she doesn't make the ball." She waved and left the room.

Chastity and Maggie faced Mya with eager gazes. "Talk," Maggie said.

Giddy with excitement, Mya hadn't had girlfriends to share secrets with since middle school. For the first time in years, she had a set of people who weren't family, who genuinely liked her and were in her corner. It felt great.

"I really, really like him, but I don't want to rush in and make things worse." She shared her concerns about Colin's grandfather using her dating against her.

"Yeah, no, that kind of thinking is off and not something to worry about," Chastity said, shaking her head.

"We're not talking about opening a sex den. You're dating one, very responsible member of the community. Have you mentioned this to Laura?" Maggie asked.

"Yes, she said the same thing you just did." Mya bit her fingernail and tried to explain her irrational fear. "People judge women harder when it comes to sexual relationships. There's a set of acceptable rules for men and a different one for women. I'm scared of taking a chance that a judge would count having a man in my life, who isn't my husband, against me."

"You were raised in the Bible belt," Chastity said.

"I sound like my mama; I know but can't help it. I keep thinking how they'd brand me in the courts, and I'll lose my son," Mya said. *You lost one child by putting your desires; first, you'll lose this one too.*

"What do you plan to do about Asher, then? He's not going to let you string him along forever. At some point, you'll need to let him know how you're feeling. I think you're wrong, but feelings are just that, feelings," Maggie said.

"I'm building up to having that conversation with him," Mya admitted.

"After the sex, though," Maggie said.

"Most definitely," Mya agreed.

CHAPTER FIFTEEN

A SHER STARED AT THE blinking light on his computer and pressed the button. "Mountains and Valleys, no storm."

He released a long breath and sat back in the chair while reading the words over again. It came as no surprise when his phone beeped. "Yeah?"

"Mountains and valleys, no storm?" Drake said, sounding relieved.

"No storm," Asher said.

Drake snorted. "I had my bags packed and ready to go hunting. If that message had been six hours later, the shit would've gotten real. Still, it's good to know he's alright and remembered the code."

"Same here. He cut it close, but I'm glad he called off the search party. Would've been all the way live," Asher said, looking at the items, including weapons, he had pulled out in preparation to go search for Moses.

"Do we know where they took him?" Drake asked.

"No. But he said no storm, so it doesn't matter. Moses will contact us when he can, but he's alright and doesn't want us to interfere. So, we wait," Asher said.

"Your team still watching the Senator?" Drake asked.

"Yep. Got a lot of information we'll sit on for now. Moses may or may not need it later. I'll contact them in a bit to pack it up and return to base," Asher said, thinking through the steps to shut down the operation.

"It's been a hell of a week not knowing anything. Waiting to talk to him or see him won't be as bad. He'll head for Versteck once he's cleared. I'll come down when he arrives," Drake said.

"Sounds like a plan. Have you heard anything about Menendez's investigation?"

"A little. The funeral was yesterday, lots of who's who bigwigs attended. A few kids with different, unknown mama's, showed up. Lots of drama there. News media did some research and are asking questions about the legality of some of Menendez's businesses. Some say he was involved in organized crime and upset some high-ranking Cartel member. The police don't have much to go on but are working on it. Other than that, I've got nothing."

Asher whistled. "You could've stopped after the baby mama drama. The man was Catholic, and that would cause serious problems. But the Cartel? That's a stroke of genius."

"Indeed, it is, and mostly true," Drake said. "See you when Moses gets there."

The line went dead.

Asher sent a message to Tombs to shut down the operation on the Senator. The men should be back in the Arms tonight or tomorrow. After ensuring that the three men were dismantling the equipment and scheduled a private plane for their return, he leaned back to clear his mind.

Last night after leaving Mya, he read two more stories she had written. "All Things Chocolate," was as hedonistic as it sounded. Using milk chocolate syrup during foreplay left him stiff as a board. He wanted to taste her in the worst way and have her dribble chocolate over him. The thought of her licking him clean had him rearranging his package. The next one, "Toy Story," was nothing like the kiddie movie and everything about sex with toys. Definitely educational. He couldn't help wondering if she had a toy box filled with the ones in the story. If she didn't, he would buy her one and fill it.

Those two stories made him so hard and needy he had shut down the website and went to take another shower. Tonight, he needed to do more than kiss her. Maybe she would let him taste or play with her beautiful breasts and nipples. *Something. Anything*. Walking around with a hard-on was counter-productive, not to mention unhealthy.

If he didn't change the direction of his thoughts, he wouldn't get anything done. He contacted Wesley and Laura.

Wesley had been happy that Moses was well and didn't need help. Laura was happy, but hesitant.

"When's he coming home?" Laura asked.

"Don't know. He'll let us know more when he can. Some things we'll never know," he reminded her. There was certain information he learned while in his short tenure in the Diplomatic Corps he could never share. Never.

"I'll feel better once I see him for myself, that's all. I still remember how you and Moses played down your injuries when you were in trouble. Still pisses me off when I think about it."

"Sorry. Didn't want you to worry," he said the same thing he always said when she brought up this sore point.

She snorted.

He smiled and shook his head. Laura was tough.

"Anyway, I said something to Mya today. She was a trooper about it. There shouldn't be any backlash. Just wanted to give you a heads up." She told him about the conversation she, Maggie, and Chastity had with Mya.

His smile dropped as he listened in stunned silence. "You told her what?"

Tonight was the night.

Mya planned to tell him about her marriage, losing her firstborn, the problems she had with Ahmed, and then they could have sex. Closing her eyes, she swayed with need. She didn't want to wait. So far, she liked everything she knew about him. It wasn't much, but it was enough for sex. They could learn more about each other as things progressed. His light tap on the back door startled her.

She opened it and allowed him to pull her close for a kiss. The man had the absolute best lips in the world. His mouth slanted across hers and she lost herself in him.

"Hey," he said on a gasp as they broke apart. He closed the door and locked it without releasing her from his other arm.

"Hey yourself," she said, glad to see him. "You had a busy day."

"You had an intervention." Taking her hand, he walked toward the living room and sat on the sofa. "I'm a private person. They never should've done that."

"True. Laura threatened to cut me," she said, watching the shocked expression cross his face.

"Well... I don't know if I should apologize or tell you to be careful with me," he said.

She pushed his shoulder with a snort. "Is it true? You've never had a girlfriend? How old are you? Twenty? Thirty? Forty? How could you not have had a girlfriend before?"

"Thirty-five and it's never been necessary."

Based on the way he handled himself, she had guessed his age range, but the rest surprised her. "Meaning?"

"The women I've dealt with in the past met my needs without the benefit of a label or close relationship."

"Friends with benefits?" she asked.

"Friends?" He raised one brow.

"Just benefits?" *Fuck buddies?* There were a few women like that in the stories she wrote, but they were never the heroine. Typically, they were evil women trying to steal the heroine's man, emphasis on trying.

He shrugged non-committally.

She wanted to push, especially since she planned to come clean. But he pulled her close and kissed her long and hard, stealing her breath.

"I missed you today," she panted, stroking the scarred side of his face. She did that every time they came together. The raised, rough edges that marred his otherwise perfect face fascinated her. She loved the feel of them beneath her fingertips.

"Did you?" He touched her lips softly and lingered. "Good. That's the way it's supposed to be, right?"

No, you're supposed to miss me too, she thought as she pulled back emotionally. She'd made a fool of herself once and refused to do it again. Rather than answer, she leaned against his chest.

"My parents fought all the time. I thought they'd kill each other. Divorce was in everyone's best interest. I was just a kid when they made the final split. Believe me when I say I was relieved all the yelling stopped. Problem was, they didn't know what to do with me, which meant more fighting. In the end, my father, a Foreign Diplomat to Israel, won me." He snorted. "I never understood why he bothered fighting for custody. He spoke several languages, had an ear for it and his assignments had him moving around a lot. I barely spent time with him. I got into trouble in Middle School and went to live with my grandparents back in the States. A year later Nana died, and it was just the old man and me." He looked at her. "Some scars aren't visible."

Her heart clenched as she gazed at his face.

"He was a cold, calculating, mean bastard. It took four years for my height and weight to match my age. Until then, he beat and knocked sense into me for every imaginable infraction."

Mya gasped and took his hand.

"Taught me how to duck a blow and where to hit so that it doesn't show in public," he said in a mocking tone.

"Asher, I'm sorry you went through that," she said. Her heart bled for the child he had been.

"It shaped me into a hard man who didn't trust anyone except my cousins Moses and Drake. The old man let me spend summers with my aunt's family. She's like my grandfather, but without the capability to inflict physical pain. Emotional and mental ass-whippings were more her thing. At least until we became old enough to realize that's what she was doing and stood against her."

He chuckled.

"What?"

"That summer, I'd just turned 17 and was shorter than Moses by a couple inches. We measured." He winked. "But taller than Drake. Anyway, one night we talked, shared the abuse we'd received from our elders. The conversation went into the morning and meant everything. Literally, we changed the directions of our lives and refused to allow anyone to fuck us over again. We promised to have each other's back, no matter what."

"How'd your aunt respond?" Mya watched his face light up and smiled companionably.

"Livid. Nothing she said or did had an impact. Her tantrums, seen for what they were, became funny."

"You laughed at her?" Mya imagined three teen-aged boys defying their mother and aunt and shook her head. She couldn't have done it.

"Well, she was breaking her expensive China while yelling how ungrateful we were because we went to Denver to watch movies with Laura and the others. She wanted us to stay in that big ugly house with her, waiting on her every need. 'Bring me a bottle of water. Bring me my phone. Do this. Do that," he mimicked. "She wasn't sick. Sometimes her phone would be on a table across the room, and she'd call Drake or Moses from upstairs to get it for her." He snorted.

"Wow," she said, almost speechless.

Asher brushed his lips across her forehead. "She was a selfish... person, just like her father, my grandfather. He resented the way I turned out, said I was soft, weak, worthless, like my mom." He shook his head to dispel thoughts of the old man. "There was a time I really wanted him to approve of me, to see me as a man he could be proud of." He pointed to the scar. "This proved he only cared about himself."

She placed a kiss on the back of his hand.

Her lips seared his flesh and opened doors that'd been bolted and locked for years. It seemed as if he couldn't stop talking, couldn't shut down the vile memories that ate him like cancer for years until he got a handle on what was important.

"Like my old man, I have an ear for dialects and languages. I pick them up fast. After college, I joined the Diplomatic Corps." He shrugged. "Made sense back then."

"Because of my father's influence, and my experiences in a certain country when I was younger, they expedited my training and sent me into the field. I can't say anything about the places I served or what I was doing. That's classified."

"Of course."

"During my two-and-a-half-year deployment in a foreign country, I established strong connections and was given information that could have posed a problem. After verifying what I could, I made the mistake of sharing it with a couple of higher-ups. The next day I woke up in a hovel with a man bent on convincing me it was in my best interest to tell him who gave me the information."

"I... This stuff happens in real life?"

His jaw went slack as his eyes widened. *Was she serious*? Did she think he would lie about such a devastating event in his life? For days he had prayed for death, would've bargained with the devil to stop the pain and torture. Giving them what they wanted would've ended in the death of two people instead of just one, so he never told. In his nightmares, he could still smell the stench of that small room, hear his screams as they bounced off the walls and see the bloodlust in the eyes of the man as he wielded the knife.

She dropped her gaze, looking away as she spoke. "I mean, it's horrible, but it's the stuff you see in the movies."

Once he swallowed his disbelief and remembered she lived a sheltered life, he steadied and placed his finger beneath her chin. He wanted her to see the truth in his eyes. If he faced his demons to have a future with her, she damn well would go through them with him.

"Mya, we're going to take things to another level in our relationship and it's important that you understand a few things about me. There are reasons I've never had a girlfriend before. I'm sharing a very private, personal part of my life with you. It's not theater or something I do."

She took a deep breath while holding his gaze. "You're right, and I apologize. I'm trying not to cry and talked foolishly. I'll do my best to just listen and not do either," she promised.

He searched her face for a few seconds and continued. "Every day for four days he sliced one side of my face and areas on my chest, arms, and thighs. He intended to horrify people when they saw the smooth side of my face and then his handiwork on the other. Before the dawn of the fifth day, my cousin Moses arrived and took me out of there." He couldn't express how he'd felt that morning. It was like summer in the midst of winter, an unexpected but welcomed surprise. During captivity, they'd barely fed him. He had been weak. His face burned constantly from pain and reopened wounds. Fortunately, his face hadn't gotten infected. Moses had lifted him out of that small room and ran. They passed several dead bodies on the way. He'd passed out. When he woke and was lucid enough to talk, he was at his grandfather's house.

"My grandfather was horrified by the ruination of the Pendergrass' face. He insisted Moses take me someplace to heal after the surgery. Which he did. I never spoke to or saw the old man again."

He picked up her hand. "The old man wrote letters, left messages, sent a card apologizing, but I never responded. I hated him. Hated what they had did to me. All I could think about was killing those bastards and never being a victim again."

They had found the two men in the Corps who sold him out dead in a London alley while Asher recovered. He always suspected Drake had done it since Moses remained with him at the big house.

A month later, Asher told his father about the kidnapping and knifing. The following week, they killed the man who'd cut and tortured him in an ambush. Since his father relayed the information to him, Asher assumed his involvement. It helped their relationship some, but not much. Once he healed, he quit the Corps.

"When my grandfather died, I refused to go to his funeral. In his will, he left me everything. Pissed off his kids, my father, and aunt. I sold all his properties, re-invested, and moved here, expanded my security business. I'm no angel. Have my own code of honor.

My loyalty to my cousins and a few others is absolute. If they ever call and need me, I'm there to do whatever's necessary. You should know that."

"Totally understandable. He saved your life, and for that, he has my eternal gratitude," she said sincerely.

Pleased he had shared a few things with her, and she hadn't run away, he kissed her again. She melted against him. His palm rested on her breast as he flicked her nipple. Like his cock, it stiffened. Titty Cat, here we come, he thought as he squeezed her breast. Tonight, or tomorrow night, he would slip his dick between these luscious breasts as she sucked his tip.

She moaned into his mouth and pulled him closer.

They broke apart and stared into each other's eyes. "I'm not a good man, but I am the man who wants you more than anything right now," he said honestly. All he needed was to see her passion-filled eyes. Standing, he extended his hand.

Her gaze flicked to his crotch as she took it. In silence, they walked to her room. He stepped inside, turned and watched as she peeked into her son's room.

More turned on than he could ever remember. He unsnapped his jeans as she closed and locked the door while watching him with feminine appreciation. He wasn't as wide or muscular as Moses or Drake. They could compete professionally if they beefed up, but he was bigger than most of the men in town.

"I didn't realize you had so many tattoos," she said, admiring the ink on his chest, upper arm, and back.

"They cover the knife wounds. It's harder to see them," he said, pulling down his pants so she could see he wore nothing beneath.

She grinned. "Confident, were you?"

"What?" He tried to sound innocent and failed.

"Bare-assed?"

"It's what I wear after a shower," he said, watching her undress. Once her breasts were visible, his mouth watered. He reached for her, pulled her close, and they kissed flesh to flesh for the first time.

"Your skin is soft and beautiful." He leaned back and looked at her. "Different shades, all gorgeous."

She hugged him again for a few seconds, then took his hand and stepped to the bed. "I've never had a man in the house with Colin. He's a heavy sleeper, but we still need to be quiet." Sounding apologetic, she looked over her shoulder at him.

Obviously, despite his raging hard on, she had no idea how happy he was just to be with her. "No problem." He would've agreed to tape both of their mouths to slide between her thighs.

She smiled at him. "Good, because I really want this."

There it was. That mischievous glint that said there was another side of her he hadn't met. He had wondered how her stories could be filled with sexual fun and heat while she appeared so composed and polite. Maybe he could coax Lynay out to play tonight. As goals went, that was a good one.

She lay on the bed and extended her arms to him. Normally, sex on a bed was the last stop before falling asleep. There were so many more fascinating places, like the wall, chair, bent over something or the shower to have sex, but this was their first time, and he followed her lead. Taking her hands, he allowed her to pull him onto the bed and kiss him. It was nice, but she was too controlled, too aware of what they were doing, and it didn't feel right.

When they broke apart, she smiled at him.

He bent forward and took her nipple into his mouth and grazed the sensitive nub with his teeth.

She gasped.

His other hand trailed down her chest, over her belly, and stopped between her thighs. His long fingers stroked her moist lips. She widened her legs. He slid one finger inside, stroking and toying with her entrance, drawing more natural lubrication.

She purred.

Like a siren's lure, the sound went straight to his groin. He moved to the other breast, suckled, and teased it unmercifully. She was dripping wet. He slid in another finger. She moaned at the entry as she writhed beneath him. Her walls throbbed against his fingers, making him crave her taste.

"You're so damn tight and hot. Let me help you put out this fire," he said near her ear, watching his fingers, slick with her juices, slide in and out of her.

She surprised him when her body stiffened, her vaginal walls clenched and then throbbed as she orgasmed.

Breathing raggedly, she shuddered again and looked up at him. "This time I'll wait for you."

He grinned. "Take them any time you want. I'll try to keep up, but take whatever you want or need, alright?"

Her face changed. For a few moments, she looked entirely too serious about what they were doing. "Alright."

He kissed her again and made his way down her body. The need to taste her overwhelmed him. When he reached her thighs, he licked everywhere. She tasted divine and loved what he did. There was something liberating about oral sex with someone who really got into it. A lot of women allowed it to please their men and not because they enjoyed it. Mya genuinely loved what he was doing, which made him want to do it more. Could she orgasm this way?

He planned to see and slid a finger into her while sucking her clit and laving it with his tongue. She moved faster and made more purring sounds. He didn't think she realized how loud she was. He'd tell her... after. His tongue dipped inside her body briefly before he licked upward and sucked her clit into his mouth. He used the edge of his teeth on her clit while stroking inside her heat with two fingers. She tensed and orgasmed again, this time saying gibberish.

Shudders continued wracking her body, and he waited until her breathing calmed to crawl up and kiss her. She froze and then accepted his tongue. Was this the first time she'd tasted herself after oral sex?

They broke apart when she held his dick and squeezed. "If you don't have a condom, I have some in the drawer."

He had forgotten. "Thank you. Which drawer?"

She pointed to the nightstand.

He leaned over, pulled out a string of them, and pulled off the first one.

She watched as he rolled it on. He held his cock in hand and looked at her.

"Thanks for the appetizers, but this is what I need," she said, surprising him with her boldness.

He liked it. "Whatever you want," he said, covering her again before sliding into her tight, hot sheath.

Her breath caught.

He stilled and waited for her to tell him to move.

"Big. Tight. Hurt," she moaned as she moved her hips and opened her legs wider, taking more of him.

Mute, he stared at the top of her head, afraid to move and hurt her. Damn if she didn't feel good. He pulled on all his considerable experience not to blow his load. This was no time to lose control. He thought about the weather, the tunnels beneath the Arms that needed repairs, anything to keep his mind off how glorious it felt to be deep inside this woman. She continued moving slowly, driving him crazy. She was so hot and tight and wet around his cock, the need to take her swamped him. He had never been so dizzy with the desire to conquer and control.

She squeezed his ass and wrapped her legs around his waist.

He snapped.

One arm went under her waist, lifting her slightly for the perfect angle as he repeatedly thrust into her warmth. He lost himself in her sexy body, pounding into her with long and hard strokes, and groaning with pleasure. Together they danced in an energetic, erotic meeting of bodies, hands, and lips sliding over sweat slickened skin.

"Yessss," she cried out, spurring him on. "Harder, fuck me."

The words released him to take her the way he had fantasized. He slid out, flipped her over, lifted her into position and slid back inside, filling her completely. He grabbed her breast, loving the firmness of them as he took her hard from the rear. Asher was flying high on how good this felt. It wouldn't be long now.

Her walls tightened.

He wouldn't last much longer.

She shuddered beneath him; her sheath throbbed as she yelled her release. He leaned against her body and gave the last thrust, filling the condom with his release.

CHAPTER SIXTEEN

F IVE DAYS LATER, ASHER sat behind his desk reviewing job proposals. Most were from repeat customers who requested the same people to work similar security jobs as before. Days like today, he felt as if he owned a temp-service that sent in personnel to do short time work. With the news playing in the background, he took another sip of coffee and signed another contract for a job starting in two weeks.

"Good morning, everyone. This is Katy Meadows from Channel Six News in Denver. This morning, we're reporting on a story about one of our fallen heroes. Captain Colin Henry, Senior, served our country for nine and a half years. Three years ago, he gave the ultimate sacrifice, his life in service. Today, we honor Captain Henry for his service."

Asher stopped reading the documents on the monitor when he heard the name. He leaned forward and swore.

"Today, we have a Gold Star family member, Joshua Henry. The father of Captain Colin Henry is here in the studio to talk about his son." She turned to the man sitting in a nearby chair.

This was not the man in the photographs. Dark rings were beneath his eyes, and his skin looked sallow, as if he were sick or something. What had he done?

Dread grew in the pit of Asher's stomach as he snatched his phone and called Laura. She was in a meeting. He demanded they get her on the phone.

"What's wrong?" Laura asked moments later.

"Turn on Channel Six. Joshua Henry's on the news crying about wanting to see his grandson."

"What?"

"Turn it on. I have to call Mya. No, I'm going to pick her up from work."

"Sir. I understand you hadn't seen your son for a couple years before his last deployment," the News Anchor said, sounding sympathetic.

"No...no I didn't. He went to Tulsa to spend time with friends, you know how it is. I was supposed to meet him, but was detained and couldn't make it before he shipped out. That had to be his what? Fourth or fifth time going over there." He paused, stared at the camera as his eyes filled with tears. "You just never know when it's going to be the last time." He shook his head mournfully. "You just never know."

The Anchor touched his shoulder sympathetically.

"Son of a bitch," Laura said. "What did he do? Put on makeup or something? Hate to say it, but it's playing big on camera. If they come here, she might have to let the slimy bastard see the boy."

"He won't see sunset," Asher said, watching the television.

"No. You can't kill him. Not after this interview," Laura warned.

"I don't care about the interview. That fool is playing a deep hand by going on television with this." Asher's stomach clenched. This would be bad. He sensed it in his gut.

"Captain Henry died three years ago..." the News Anchor said.

Sniffling, Henry nodded. "Yes. Yes. He did. One of my greatest sorrows is not seeing him on that last visit. Later, I learned he had a son." He looked at the anchor as if she had pulled a rabbit out of the hat for him.

"A son? You never knew?" the Anchor asked, and Asher gave her points for that. If the man and his son were close, why didn't he know about the boy?

"No. He met my grandson's mother during that last visit and, well, you know. Those things happen. I've never met my grandson, flesh of my flesh. Before I die, I really want to meet him and get to know him."

"Why haven't you met him?" the Anchor asked.

"My grandson's mother doesn't want me to have anything to do with the boy. I took it to court, and the courts ruled in her favor. She does not have to allow me to meet him. Although I have a letter from the Judge with a request that she allow me a onetime visit with my kin," Henry said, looking pitiful.

"Damn," Asher said while grabbing his keys and half-listening as the anchor wished the old man well and promised to follow up.

He headed to the garage.

"Calm down, Asher. Calm down. Do not send anyone to take him out. Use that mind of yours to be strategic. Mya and Colin need you to think rationally," Laura said.

His phone beeped. *Mya.*

"Gotta go." He disconnected from Laura and clicked to Mya. "I was on my way to see you."

"That man was on television saying he wants to see Colin," she said.

Asher closed his eyes at the fear and terror in her voice. "He won't. Not if you don't want him to."

"He was crying, almost crying. Is this a game? What is he doing?" she yelled.

"Baby, calm down. I'm on my way. We'll talk about this alright?"

"What did you call me?"

He thought back and couldn't remember.

"You called me, baby."

"Yeah, calm down. I'm pulling out the garage now."

"We... I don't know what to think. You're..."

"I'm with you on this and everything else," he said, meaning it.

"Really? You're not just saying that because I'm freaking out?"

"I don't say things I don't mean."

"Okay."

"One day real soon we're going to have a conversation about why your default is to think the worst. We're going to open that box filled with BS and clear it out, so it doesn't affect you anymore. Something in your past is bleeding into your present, and that's not good."

"Do you think he's coming here?"

He let the change of subject go, for now, they had other things to deal with, but they would get to the bottom of her unreasonable fears.

"Yes. That news station is in Denver. Expect him to have a news crew or a cameraman." Asher had to give the old man credit. He played his hand well. Versteck Valley survived all these years unscathed as a haven for those who operated on the wrong side of the law. By going public, Henry ensured he could enter town unharmed.

"Hell." She paused. "Laura's on her way here, too. I've canceled my appointments. Should I get Colin from school?"

"Not yet. We don't have a plan of action. I'll meet you and Laura in your office." He thought about it. "Wesley will probably weasel his way in, so you might as well let him come too."

"Wesley?"

"Yeah, he's really good with a lot of things. Right now, I'm pissed and might not be thinking as clearly as I should. He'll be good to bounce ideas off of."

"Why're you pissed?"

"Because of the way this is affecting you," he said, as if it should be obvious.

"Oh."

Asher shook his head. They needed to have that talk.

"Well, alright. I'll see you when you get here. Thanks for coming."

He ground his teeth and didn't respond. Not yet. He would set things straight when he saw her. Although he hadn't slept over the entire night with her yet, they'd been in bed together for the past five nights. A record and commitment for him. No matter how breathless and boneless he left her each night, the next day she acted as if she wasn't sure of him, of them. He would make that clear as well.

He pulled into the parking lot of the Arms and drove around back to park next to her car. Dressed in a black and white suit with matching heels, Mya stepped outside and watched as he slid from behind the wheel. The moment he saw the bone-wrenching anguish in her gaze, he pulled her close and wrapped his arms around her.

"I'm scared," she said, holding him close.

"Don't be. We'll work through this," he said and placed a kiss on top of her head.

She leaned back and met his gaze. "Promise? I don't mean to put all of this on you, but--"

He jerked her close and stared down into her eyes. "Stop that shit."

Her mouth opened as her eyes widened.

"You laid the ground rules for this relationship, and this is a part of it. When you thank me for caring about you and wanting to help or protect you, I feel as if you're putting me in a friend only category or something. That's not who I am to you, so just stop it. You're my woman, and no one should scare you. No one."

Her tongue shot out as she licked her lips.

His gaze followed the action.

"I wasn't sure," she said.

"Are you sure now?" he asked, watching closely.

"Very. And I'm glad we cleared the air about that."

"Me too. It's time I met your son and spent the night," he said, holding her gaze.

She took a deep breath and stabbed his chest with her finger. "I agree, but you better not hurt me or play games with my heart. I'm taking a chance, and I don't want to get hurt again."

Her eyes filled as she stared up at him.

"I can't promise you won't ever get mad at me or become disappointed over decisions I make or things I do. That's a part of life and being two different people. If I don't like something you're doing, I'll tell you, and I ask you to give me the same courtesy instead of expecting me to guess. I hate that."

She nodded.

"This is uncharted waters for me. I've never had a woman that I've claimed as my own. Like I said before, it's never been necessary. I'll never deliberately hurt you. My word on that. I won't cheat either. If the fire dies between us and can't be resuscitated, we'll talk about it and go from there. Fair?"

She nodded. "Yes. Thank you for that."

He didn't like her thanking him for everything, but that was just her. "The rest we'll figure out as we go along." He placed his arm around her shoulder, turned her, and went inside.

Wesley, Connor, Mercer, Tombs, and the rest of the residents stood several feet from the door, watching as they entered.

"Is Ms. Burch your woman?" Tombs asked Asher.

"Yes, she is," Asher said, understanding what it meant to claim Mya publicly with these men, even if she did not. Staking a claim would secure her acceptance and protection from every man who lived here. She and her son would have a level of protection few in the world could match. But he couldn't explain any of that to her, not yet.

Most of the men nodded and seemed to relax.

"If you need us to help fix this problem, just ask. We take care of our own," Mercer said before turning and walking back toward the rec room.

"Kids are off limits. Everybody knows that," Connor said, his voice filled with disgust. The other men agreed.

"Is Laura here?" Asher asked. He hadn't explained Versteck Valley or the Arms to Mya and didn't want to do that now. One thing at a time.

"Just got here," Wesley said. "Go on in. I'll be there in a minute." When Mya walked slightly ahead, Wesley mouthed. "Does she know?"

"No," Asher said.

Wesley nodded, turned, and waved the men to him while Asher entered Mya's office behind her.

Laura sat in one chair and rose when they entered. "How're you holding up?" She hugged Mya, who accepted the embrace.

"Confused and angry." Mya stepped back. "If I didn't know the man never reached out to Colin before, I would've believed his sad tale. It's pathetic." She whirled around and looked at Asher. "Why's he doing this? There's got to be a reason he wants to see Colin so bad."

"Agreed. But I don't know the answer to that, yet. I've got a few contacts looking into it. Right now, we're dealing with a time issue. You've just received notice publicly that Joshua Henry intends to see Colin."

"Smart move," Wesley said, entering the room and holding up his hand when Mya started to respond. "Strategically, he let the world know he's coming to Versteck Valley without mentioning the town. He played the sympathetic role of a grieving father wanting to see his dead son's child. It was a brilliant move on the chessboard, one that'll be hard to defend."

Laura sighed. "By involving the news, if you say no, it becomes newsworthy and they hang around, start asking questions, dig into your background, all kinds of stuff. With him using his Gold Star status, it could get ugly if we're not careful." She looked at Wesley. "Damn, I hadn't thought of this. We were prepared for him sneaking into town, not with fanfare. This is harder to combat."

Mya wrapped her arms around her waist as she turned away from them. The idea of allowing that man to spend time with Colin pissed her off. She wouldn't do it.

Why not?

The question made her pause. She didn't know anything about the man, only that Colin Senior hadn't liked him and wanted nothing to do with him. But Colin was dead. She would never allow her son to be alone with him.

"Have you heard from the Trustee?" Asher asked Laura.

"I sent word. He's out of the country and will receive my message when he gets back. Hopefully, he can clear up a few things."

"What do you want to do, Mya?" Asher asked.

"What can I do?" she said without looking at them as a chill slid down her back. The old man wanted something from her son, but what?

"You don't have to allow him to see Colin. Legally, he can't force you. The letter from whoever doesn't mean anything," Laura said.

"But it'll turn into a media circus if I don't. Colin would be on TV, they'll follow him around, try to ask him questions?" Mya asked.

"Possibly. I think they'll do that to you more than him but can't rule out that some enterprising journalist will try to talk to Colin," Laura said, her tone somber.

"That's unacceptable. So, we set the ground rules and allow them to meet one time. I always have to be in the room, and Colin does not have to touch or talk to him if he doesn't want to. He's five. I won't pressure him to act obligated to a stranger." She turned and looked at Laura first, and then at Asher. "Agree on a time they can meet at the school or another public place, but not in our home. Never there."

Laura nodded as Asher moved closer and slid his arm around her waist. She leaned into him and took a deep breath. "This will be a meeting, not a meal or fun activity. Everything he brings into the room must be checked. I don't know what he wants with my son and don't trust him."

"I agree he wants something and would feel better knowing what. If you meet at the school, we'll have additional security there." Wesley looked at Laura. "Will Bonnie allow the press inside?"

"Only if Mya wants it," Laura said.

"I don't. Colin doesn't need to be in the news for this."

"On the other hand," Wesley said, drawing their attention.

"Colin is a very smart child. He's enrolled in a pre-school with some of the world's brightest children. Maybe the grandfather wants to show that off," Wesley said.

"Possibly. But if that's all there is, why make such a production out of it?" Mya asked. "Has he ever contacted Ms. Bonnie?"

"Just Bonnie," Laura corrected, gently. "Yes, his attorney contacted her and asked a few questions about the school. She forwarded him to the school website and hadn't heard from him since."

"Do you want to meet with him at the school or someplace else?" Asher said, looking down at her. "This is all about your comfort level. You're in charge here. He's asking a favor and will abide by your decisions."

Mya had to remember that. "If he's really interested in the school, then that's not a good place."

"He can come here," Asher said.

Wesley laughed.

"Can't promise he'll leave the same way he came, but we can put him in Chastity's office," Asher said.

"Not at my job. It's too personal, and he doesn't get that," Mya said. "I'll think of something."

Laura stood. "Asher's right. The ball's in your court. Joshua Henry made the first move, and now it's up to you. Legally, you don't have to play ball with him. But it's not worth the headaches of dealing with him and the press over this. Let him win this round. We'll build a case to make sure it goes no further."

"He won't get regular visitation?" Mya asked.

"No. Not unless you agree to it. He has no rights at all. None," Laura stressed.

Mya leaned into Asher again. "Alright, whenever we hear from him, we'll decide how to play it."

"You won't be alone," Asher said close to her ear.

Heat rose to her face as she recalled his earlier comments. She felt safer knowing he would be with them.

Wesley stood and nodded. "If you need anything at all, let me know."

"Thank you," she said, even though she had the impression he was talking to Asher.

Laura walked out with Wesley.

Asher turned her fully into his embrace. "You don't need to do anything you don't want to do."

"Thank you. That means so much." She placed a kiss on the middle of his chest.

"I came to take you home. Ready?"

She inhaled and released it slowly. "Chastity said I could leave early to deal with this. She's the absolute best boss. I haven't been here six months, and already so many things have happened, the break-in, dealing with the attorney, and now something else I have to take time off for." She grabbed her purse and slid it up over her shoulder. "I don't want to press my luck."

"How did you find out about the interview?" he asked as they walked out of her office.

"Wesley was watching it and came to get me. I caught the tail end when he had one last wish to see his grandson." She rolled her eyes, pressed the button to unlock her car, and slid behind the wheel. "Let's go to your place this time." Today was the first time she didn't have Colin to consider.

Asher nodded. "That's fine."

Surprised, she waited for him to get in his car. She'd never been inside his house before. She hadn't expected him to agree so readily, but didn't know why. It didn't take long to reach his home. Mya expected the house to be a replica of the one she lived in and was wrong. This one was much larger, more spacious, and tastefully decorated. She peeked into several rooms on the first floor. It was obvious he spent time in his office, the kitchen, and his bedroom. The other rooms looked untouched and unlived in.

"Come with me." He strode ahead of her into the kitchen and opened the refrigerator. "I don't have a lot of stuff to drink, but you need to get something to take with you to the room." He moved to one cupboard, searched it, and looked in another as she watched him, stunned.

He pulled out two liter bottles, rinsed them out and looked over his shoulder at her standing there watching him. "Seriously, what do you want to drink?"

"I'm not thirsty. Curious, but not thirsty."

"You will be," he said and filled the first bottle with cold, filtered water.

Her breath caught. In one of her stories, the hero had taken a case of bottled water and placed them in the room for his lover to keep her hydrated.

"What're you doing?" she asked, moving closer to watch.

He placed the top on the second bottle and placed both to the side. Turning, he pulled her close and kissed her hard, catching her by surprise. His hand slid beneath her blouse, squeezing and kneading her breasts as they kissed passionately. He fisted her hair, forcing her head back to look at him. "I gave you a chance to get something to drink. Now it's time to feed me."

She loved that idea. Her belly quivered at the look in his eyes just before he ravished her mouth again. He pinched her nipple. She shuddered and gasped for air. He massaged her scalp, stroked her face, and removed her jacket. Hungry for him. She shrugged out of it and kicked off her shoes.

He pulled her blouse over her head, stared at her breast as if he hadn't played with them several hours before and pressed his face between them.

She laughed at his antics.

He kissed each breast as he placed her shirt on the counter behind her and unbuttoned her skirt. "You always look so polished, polite, and professional, like a good girl. How'd you end up with a thug like me?" he asked, running his fingertip from her chest to the top of her lace panties.

Her belly shivered in anticipation. "Just lucky, I guess," she whispered.

"Ah, darling. I'm the lucky one in this room today. You're beautiful, cultured and all mine." He cupped her between the legs and took her nipple into his mouth.

Her legs shook, and she wrapped her arms around his neck. He lifted her and put her on the counter. Standing between her legs, his magical fingers played her like a master musician. Between sucking and teasing her nipples and stroking her with his fingers, she couldn't think, only feel.

"That's it, come for me. I love it when you fall apart on my fingers. We've got a few hours, and I plan to use every minute bringing you pleasure. Would you like that?" he murmured.

His words took her over the brink, and she shuddered her release. He made loud slurping noises as he licked his fingers while she caught her breath. The scent of her arousal rose in the air. He took a deep breath and grinned. "God, I love how good you smell."

"You... you are crazy," she said with a slight smile.

"Crazy about you," he said, and winked. He pulled her slightly, and she fell bonelessly against him. With one hand, he turned her around. "Rest your arms on the counter."

Tired and excited, she followed his instructions with anticipation. He pulled down her panties and rubbed his hardness against her ass. His fingers stroked between her legs again. She widened her stance for better access.

He slapped one cheek and then the other.

"Hey, why'd you do that?" she said, looking over her shoulder, pleased to see him naked as well.

"I like to see you jiggle. Sexy as hell, ruined me forever. I love the jiggle. I'm having tee-shirts made with "Give me the jiggle.""

She laughed and shook her head. He was a nut, but never boring. He slid a finger into her. She stopped laughing and purred at how good it felt.

"I've got to take you."

She shook her hips in invitation. He took hold of her, slid on a condom, and eased into her. This sense of fullness was always like this when he first entered her as if he was putting a size ten-part into a size eight sleeve.

"You're so tight, I love it," he hissed as her body loosened and accepted him.

The warmth of the stretch changed from pain to pleasure as he eased out and back in. She loved this dance, had always enjoyed it, but Asher mastered it in a way they both crested the top around the same time.

He slowly withdrew and surged back inside, plunging hard and deep. His hands dug into the side of her hips as his strokes became faster and faster. She held onto to the counter, pushed back into him, moaning as the fire burned and the itch in her belly increased. He knew what to do, knew how to scratch her itch, knew exactly how to hit it to take her over the edge.

"Yesssss," she screamed, almost there. Legs trembling, pleasure spiraling. It wouldn't be long. Her breath caught; she froze momentarily as wave after wave of mind-numbing ecstasy washed over her.

Blind with satisfaction, she slumped on the counter, barely aware of Asher holding her in place as he flew over the top. Both of them gasped for breath for several moments until he took her hand, kissed the back of it and spoke. "That's two. Shower and then we go for three."

Greedy for more of him, she took a deep breath and agreed.

CHAPTER SEVENTEEN

JOSHUA HENRY TOOK HIS time arriving in Versteck Valley. He hadn't tried to contact Laura or Mya in advance. Instead, he showed up, camera-man behind him, knocking on her front door on a bright Saturday morning.

Colin was still asleep.

Asher noticed the car pull into the driveway and called the Sheriff first and then Laura. He and Mya waited to allow the police and Laura to handle the negotiations. They all agreed there was no way Mya should talk to him like this.

"Stay inside. I'm going out through the back so I can listen."

"Call me so I can listen too."

He nodded.

Mya kissed him and left to go get into bed with Colin. She would remain with him until they decided what to do.

Colin had surprised them both with his easy acceptance of Asher. The same day Henry went on television, Mya introduced Asher to her son as her male-friend. She explained it was a grown-up boyfriend, which Colin understood.

After asking Asher what happened to his face and about the tattoo on his arm, Colin seemed alright with Asher spending time with them and sleeping in her room.

Jack was the first to arrive. He pulled up and got out of the car. He waved for Henry and the cameraman to leave the porch and come talk to him. Wesley, Beamer, Chastity, Maggie, and several others walked toward the house as the local cable channel van pulled up. Asher slipped out the back door, went through the newly installed gate, and walked through his yard to join the others.

Henry strode to Jack and went into character. "Officer, I've learned this is the residence of my grandson and have come to beg his mother to allow me to meet him. All I want to do is meet my son's son."

"First, you're on private property and need to stand on the sidewalk," Jack said, sounding aggravated. "Second, why didn't you contact her by phone and ask for a meeting instead of showing up at her house first thing on a Saturday morning?"

"I don't have her phone number," Henry said, sounding unruffled as the additional news camera set up behind them.

"You have her attorney's number," Jack said.

"Not with me," Henry hedged. "Is there a problem with me coming here?"

"There's a problem with strangers knocking on anyone's door first thing in the morning with a cameraman," Jack said.

Laura and Bonnie pulled up and stepped out of the car. Dressed in a black power suit, Laura marched forward with the light of battle in her gaze. The onlookers let her through.

"Mr. Henry, first off, we're grateful for your son's service and understand your grief as a Gold Star family member. My client, Colin Henry, Junior, lost his father and was never informed of his funeral or where he's buried. Why haven't you shared this information with him or his mother?"

"I had no way to get in touch with them."

Laura pulled out a piece of paper. "Perhaps you've forgotten the letter her attorney sent after you required a DNA test proving paternity. In the letter, you were asked about your son's funeral and burial location so that his only child could attend."

Henry's jaw clenched and smoothed. "It was a grievous time. I'm sorry I didn't respond and missed the request."

Laura nodded. "Most understandable. When did you want to meet Colin?"

Henry looked surprised by the question but recovered quickly. "Today?"

"No, not today. You'll need to make an appointment to meet him at my office when his mother and I can be present. What about Monday at noon? Will that work for you?" She handed him her card and sounded so reasonable. The only way Henry could object was to sound like a complete ass. After all, he had shown up out of the blue.

"That would be fine. Thank you so much, Ms.?

"Laura Williams. My name's on all the legal documents about this matter. I assure you I'm well-versed with your petition for visitation rights," she said.

He held her gaze a few moments longer, nodded and walked off.

The camera person from the local cable channel zeroed in on Laura. "As the attorney for both Colin Henry, Junior, and his mother, Mya Burch, they've asked me to make it clear Ms. Burch has never heard from Joshua Henry until he petitioned the courts for visitation rights one month ago. After requesting proof that Colin Junior was his son's child, Mr. Henry received that confirmation through the courts, who also gave him the contact information for his grandson. He's never contacted them in the past three years since the death of his son. Colin Senior talked to his son via the internet several times before his death. He was involved in making decisions regarding his son's medical care and school. If Colin's grandfather had expressed any interest in meeting the child in the past five years, two of which, while his son was alive, my client would have allowed it. Since so much time has passed and Mr. Henry filed a petition rather than reach out and ask if he could meet the child, my client was leery of his motives and said no, which was within her rights. For Mr. Henry to arrive at her home on a Saturday morning, again without reaching out to ask permission, was ill-advised. On Monday, both of my clients will be available for Mr. Henry to meet for the first time. There will be no cameras. Colin is only five years old, and we will protect his privacy. Thank you." She stepped aside and spoke to a few people before moving toward Asher.

Joshua Henry sat in his vehicle, watching and listening. When Wesley and several men from the Arms looked at him, he drove off down the street.

"I don't like him coming here like that," Wesley said.

"He came here big as you please, interrupting her life like that," Connor said, staring at the car before it turned the corner.

"Needs a lesson in manners," Mercer said.

"What we need is information," Asher said, pointing at Mercer. "I want the three of you to find out where he's staying and get everything you can. He's doing this for a reason. We need to know what and how big it is. No one goes through all of this for a small pay-out."

Tombs, Mercer, and Connor turned and walked back down the street toward the Arms. Like the rest of the Arms residents, they'd take a short-cut in town and go through the tunnels.

"Jack?" Wesley called the Sheriff over. When he stood closer. "Do you know where that fellow is staying?"

"No. I can find out," Jack said.

"No," Laura said. Her hand covered his as he went to speak into his mic. "You can't be involved at all in this, Jack. He can play it as a cover-up or brutality or invasion of privacy. You handled him just right. Just keep doing what you're doing."

He nodded, looked at the house and then at Asher. "How's she doing?"

"Not the best. She's concerned for Colin," Asher said unsurprised the Sheriff knew he and Mya were a couple. To keep the news quiet, a person had to be specific and say so. Otherwise, news traveled.

"I'll have someone watching the house until the meeting on Monday. He won't bother her again," Jack said and walked toward his car.

"How's she doing?" Wesley asked when the circle shrank to him, Laura and Asher.

"Pissed by his actions, still concerned for Colin," Asher said.

"Has she told him about that man wanting to meet him?" Wesley asked.

"I don't think she's been specific. But with the meeting date set, she'll do that now, I'm sure. He's a really smart kid, loves his mom, he'll be fine." Asher hoped so, anyway. From the looks on the faces of several men from the Arms if Henry stepped out of line, he'd wind up with a knife in his chest, or a bullet in his forehead or a lingering illness that would cause him months of pain and suffering before he died. They didn't like this stunt this morning any more than Asher did.

"You need to calm your men down," Laura told Asher without looking at Wesley. "At least for now. Let me get Mya and Colin through the meeting. When that's done, and things settle down with the media then hang him by his toenails for all I care. Just make sure nothing leads back to Mya or Colin. They've been through enough."

Asher glared at her. She was preaching to the damn choir. "Calm them down? Who told them Henry was here? I called you and Jack. I know this is a powder-keg, which is why I didn't tell anyone else about him strolling up here."

"Jack told me," Wesley said, stepping closer with his hands held up. "I passed the information along. Wasn't the best move given how helpless we're feeling, sorry about that. Allowing us to handle surveillance, to gather information to bring this asshole down, helps. We're doing something."

"Jack shouldn't have called you," Laura said.

"He always calls me to let me know what's going on in town," Wesley said. "I appreciate it, too."

"Then you shouldn't have shared the information. Did you see the look they gave Henry and the cameraman?" Laura asked, turning on Wesley. "We can't afford for them to be on camera or doing unauthorized hits," she hissed.

"They won't," Asher said, confident of the control he had on the men. "I'm going inside. Can you make sure everyone leaves? Looks like a convention out here." He looked at Laura. "What was the purpose for the cable station?"

"Henry's cameraman could edit their film to make it seem like we said anything. By having our own cameraperson, I let him know we would fight back on that level. Plus, I knew he was listening when I spoke into the camera. Now he knows I'll take it to his ass if he keeps pushing. It'll play later today, so it's a part of the record."

"I keep forgetting how devious you can be," Asher said and turned to leave. "Don't go to the front door. I'm going in through the back. Come with me if you want to talk to them." He walked toward his yard as the Deputy stood in front of the house, not allowing anyone to walk on the property. People started leaving.

Mya sat on the bed listening to Colin read. Asher and Laura would come inside soon, and they'd discuss Monday's appointment. When Colin woke, he'd been surprised to see her in bed with him. In true Colin form, he wanted to know why she was there and not with Asher in her room.

She explained what was going on and stood with him behind the mini blinds as he looked outside.

"Is that him?" Colin asked. "Is that Daddy's dad?"

"Yes, it is."

"He's short. The picture of daddy was tall. I mean, he was a lot taller than you," he corrected.

She nodded.

"How did he find us?" Colin asked.

"Good question." She assumed whoever had been following her gave him the address, but she didn't want to say that.

They stared outside for a few more minutes until Colin became bored and returned to bed. "Where's Mr. Asher?"

"Didn't you see him out there? He's listening to the conversation with the others," she said as she sat on the corner of his bed.

Colin ran back to the window, looked around, and nodded. "I see him now. He's taller than that man."

"Yes he is," she said, unsure if she should correct him on the "that man" comment. No matter what, Joshua Henry was his grandfather.

"Someone hurt him really bad, but he's not mad. I would be mad, wouldn't you, Mama?" He turned to look at her with those large gray eyes.

"Asher?"

He nodded.

"You're right, he's not mad anymore. I would probably still be mad, though," she said.

"You like him?"

She wasn't sure where this was going and nodded. "Yes, Baby. I like him a lot. He's a good man, and I trust him."

"Does he like me?" Colin asked, sounding like the five-year-old he was.

"Yes, he does. How can anyone not like you?" She teased to make him smiled.

"Why did he come over when I wasn't around?" he asked, looking at the floor and then at her.

Her stomach dropped as heat rushed to her face. Colin had known Asher was coming over. Hadn't he been asleep? Had she played this wrong? Should she have allowed Asher to meet Colin when they first started dating?

"This is new for me, baby. Mommy has never had a boyfriend since you were born," she said, trying to find the words to make everything better.

"Since Daddy?"

Sure, why not? "Yeah, since him. I didn't know if you would like Asher. Or if you would be mad because he wasn't your father. Or if I would like him the way I do. We were getting to know each other, and I didn't want you to like him a lot, and then I didn't want to be with him." She shook her head. "What I'm trying to say is I wanted to make sure I liked him enough to introduce him to you. When I realized I really liked him, I wanted you to meet him too. Does that make sense?" She watched him puzzle through her ramblings until he nodded.

"Think so. You wanted to like him first before telling me about him."

Succinct. "Yeah, that's about right. It was all me. He wanted to meet you right away. I made him wait. I hope that's okay?"

He looked up at her and nodded with a slight smile. "It's okay. The cut on his face scared me at first, but now I don't see it so much."

Her heart swelled with love for the miracle who was her son. He continued surprising her. "You know what? I don't either."

The back door opened.

Colin ran out of the room with her following. That had better be Asher, she thought and stopped short at the entrance to the living room. Colin was in Asher's arms. Both turned to look at her. Her throat tightened, robbing her of immediate speech.

"They set the meeting for Monday in my office," Laura told Colin. "You'll never be alone with Mr. Henry. We'll be there with you."

Colin looked at Asher. "Will you be there?"

Without looking at Mya, Asher spoke. "I'll be there." It was a promise given that she knew wouldn't be broken.

Colin nodded.

Asher put him down as Laura said a few more things about the meeting. Then she and Wesley left.

"I think we should spend the weekend at my house," Asher said. "If anyone comes looking for you, they won't find you."

"I've never been to your house, Mr. Asher."

"Call me Asher. And I know that. This is the perfect weekend to fix that, don't you agree? You can bring whatever you want with you. It won't take long to get there."

Mya smiled. The trip next door would take a few minutes.

"Can we go, Mommy?"

"Yes. Pack your backpack with your books and games. I'll pack your clothes."

"Yay," he yelled and ran to his room.

She looked at Asher with a soft smile. "Thanks. He had just asked me if you liked him." She gave him a brief version of the conversation. "I'll go pack a few things."

"We're not staying next door."

"We're not?"

"No." He smiled. "I have other places. We're going to the mountains to another one of my homes."

Frowning, she faced him squarely. "We're already in the mountains."

He patted her hips and stole a kiss. "Pack your bags. We'll come back Monday and head to the meeting. The sooner you're ready, the sooner we can leave. We'll take my car out through the back entrance. No one will know you're gone."

"This isn't something you had planned, is it?" She eyed him suspiciously.

"Does it matter?" He stared down at her.

She searched his face, couldn't read it, and let it go. "No, not really." She turned and went to her room to pack.

CHAPTER EIGHTEEN

THE DRIVE TO ASPEN took almost three hours because of traffic. Colin had been full of questions and held multiple conversations with Asher during the ride, leaving her alone with her thoughts most of the time. The boy acted star-struck and blossomed beneath the attention. Asher appeared to enjoy talking to him, answering, and asking questions. He complimented Colin often and gave a lot of positive reinforcement. It was all good, right? He understood they were a package deal and included Colin into their relationship, which is what she wanted.

So why was she uneasy? Was allowing Asher into their lives a decision she would later regret?

If it were just her, she'd hook her wagon to his train and hang on as long as she could without thinking about the future. But it wasn't just her, would never be just her. She had to think about her son.

Hands down, Asher was a great boyfriend. Kind, considerate of her and Colin, and a phenomenal lover. She couldn't get enough of him, and he appeared to feel the same way about her. The past few days they'd been like minks in heat, barely waiting for Colin to go to sleep before dragging each other into the bedroom.

Warmth filled her cheeks as she recalled the night he placed his cock between her breasts, moving back and forth slowly while she tried to suck the tip. It had been hard to keep most of the large mushroomed shaped head in her mouth, but she'd given it her best. He had looked so hot kneeling above her, moving his hips sensuously as his cock slid between her titties. She clamped her thighs tight and closed her eyes as her core clenched.

Past experiences taught her good sex wasn't enough to make a relationship work. There had to be more. The idea of Colin suffering rejection in the same way she had made chill bumps explode across her skin. Rubbing her arm, she admitted she hadn't dated Asher long enough to know how he really felt about Colin's latching on to him.

The whole thing seemed bizarre.

Had she assumed Colin was alright without a steady male influence? Colin's reaction to Asher made it clear her son wanted a man in his life. Second-guessing past decisions was a wasted exercise. This is where they were. She glanced at Colin, his face animated as he looked out the window, talking about the mountains, skiing, and what made the snow stay on top of the mountains.

Driving, Asher listened and responded appropriately. Occasionally, he covered her hand and smiled.

They pulled off Highway 82 onto Maroon Creek Rd, and Colin quieted. Mya looked at the ski resorts nestled near the mountains. It was beautiful and majestic. Asher's home was at the end of a cul-de-sac with unobstructed panoramic views of the mountains.

"That's Willow Peak and Tiehack Cliffs." Asher pointed before entering one of three garages.

"Wow," Colin said as they entered the two-story stone and wood house.

Silently, Mya echoed his appreciation as Asher brought in their bags.

"I bought it a few years ago as an investment. During the season, I rent it out. It has six bedrooms, seven and a half baths." Asher looked at Colin, who had been staring up at him with stars in his eyes. "Your mom and my room are on the first floor. There's one other bedroom on this floor near ours, one downstairs in the basement and three upstairs. I'd really appreciate it if you stayed on this floor with us instead of one of the other rooms."

Colin nodded. "Alright. I'll find it." He took off running.

Impressed by how well he handled Colin, Mya's concerns quieted. Moving through the kitchen, living, and dining rooms, she appreciated the elegant yet comfortable décor. "This is really nice. Do you come here a lot?"

He followed her gaze. "No. It's too far. If Colin really likes it, we can come more often."

Surprised by the offer, she spoke to cover the uneasiness that rose in her chest again. "I'll go check on him," she said.

"Wait." He held up his hand and opened a kitchen drawer. "We'll need to order groceries. The local store will deliver them within the hour." He handed her a small booklet along with his credit card. "Why don't you make a list and place the order? I'll go check on him. Once he's settled in his room, we'll go downstairs to the game room, play a bit."

Stunned, she watched him jog off in the same direction Colin had gone earlier, calling for them to go downstairs and play games. Colin's yelp of excitement, their footfalls on the stairs, and then... silence.

She glanced at the grocery list and shook her head. "Well, that's new," she whispered, uncertain how she felt about no longer being the primary object of her son's attention. Rather than dwell on all the things that could go wrong, she shoved aside the negatives and focused on the positives. They were in a gorgeous home in the mountains. Colin seemed happy and enjoying himself. She had the attention of a sexy man who made it clear they would be in bed together tonight.

Excellent.

She opened the large booklet, decided what to cook for dinner, breakfast, lunch, and dinner the next night. By the time she finished creating her menus, checked the empty pantry and placed the order an hour had passed.

The next day, the sun shone brightly, and they spent some time outside on the patio. Asher had been feeling uneasy all morning. As he stood on the patio gazing at the mountains, he silently cursed. Anyone could creep up on the house without him seeing them until it was too late. The house didn't have a fence, which worked well when snow was on the ground.

Colin had wanted to go to the nearby community pool, but Asher vetoed that idea because they hadn't brought the proper clothes. Later, he explained to Mya, the fewer people who saw her and Colin, the better.

"You don't think anyone knows where we are, do you?" she asked, glancing out the window and back at him.

"Laura and a few others know we're here," he reminded her. There was a 50/50 chance Henry's people knew they'd come here.

"They won't tell anyone," Mya said.

Asher nodded, wrapped his arm around her waist and changed the subject. He didn't mention Bryson had followed in the van with additional weapons and checked into a nearby hotel in case they needed him. She would only worry. He wasn't a hundred percent sure Joshua Henry would wait until Monday to see Colin. Even though he took precautions when they left, they could've been followed.

As the sun set, Colin went back inside to play on his mom's laptop. He had connected online with a few classmates who were researching something to do with biology. The kid amazed Asher. There were times he had to remember the boy was only five. The way Colin's mind worked to process information at an accelerated rate and recall the most mundane data was fascinating. No wonder Higher Dimensions had been excited to get him.

The house smelled wonderful, better than several of his favorite restaurants. He walked into the kitchen.

Dressed in snug jeans that showed her nice round ass, and a fitted top, highlighting her wonderful breasts, Mya stirred something on the stove. She smiled when he entered, her entire face lit with welcome.

He had to kiss her.

Moving closer, he placed his hand behind her head, pulled her close and took possession of her lips. She opened, and he plundered.

"Mmm, good," she said against his mouth when they broke apart.

"I've got something better." He rubbed his hard cock against her leg.

Her breath hitched, her eyelids lowered and turned sultry.

He loved how she always made him feel welcome with their love-making.

"What?" she frowned and stepped back.

He frowned. "Huh?"

"What did you just say?"

Had he spoken his thoughts aloud? "What did I say?" he asked, trying to remember the exact words.

"How I make you feel welcome when it comes to sex." She crossed her arms, staring at him with a narrow gaze.

"I'm not sure what I said to upset you, but I didn't mean anything negative." He watched her body language and cursed. She wasn't angry, more hurt, vulnerable. *What was going on?*

"Forget it. Never mind." She turned and walked to the refrigerator.

"Remember, I asked you to tell me what's on your mind instead of expecting me to guess?" he said, remaining in the same spot, watching her.

She stopped, looked over her shoulder at him. What was that look? Embarrassment? Fear? Pain? Possibly all three. Why would she be experiencing any of those over what he said?

"Turn off the stove and talk to me. It's time for you to come clean about what's going on in that sexy, smart head of yours," he said, crossing his arms as he straightened.

She opened her mouth, looked at him, and then closed it. "It's not important."

"Good, then you shouldn't mind sharing it with me. Talk." He wondered what had her in such a state. She looked as if she wanted to run out of the room. "Mya?"

Misery filled her gaze as she looked at him.

"Whatever is bothering you, whatever is or was wrong, we can fix it and move forward. Isn't that how relationships work? I'm here. I'm trying. You have to do your part and it's more than fantastic sex." He could've shot himself in the foot when tears filled her eyes. It took everything within him to remain firm and not cave. But something from her past kept creeping up and coloring their relationship. That had to stop.

"Mya?"

Her head snapped up, and she stared at him for a few moments. "My ex said I was a nymphomaniac."

Not what he expected to hear, but his response was immediate. "He was a fool and not the man for you."

Her mouth gaped open. Her eyes widened as she looked at him.

Seriously? Did she believe that crap? "You don't have sex with a lot of men. As tight as you were, I'd say it's been years since you've been with anyone. That's the opposite of a nymph. Since you've started having sex again, I'm the only man you've wanted to be with." He tried not to sound smug, but failed miserably.

She leaned against the granite counter-top and told him about her marriage. She shared how her ex-husband bashed her for enjoying sex, blamed her for killing their son, and how he told other men his wife was a nympho. Asher's fingers itched to punch the jerk in the face. Now he understood why, after losing her first child, she was so protective of Colin. Why she pushed to maintain a professional image and the reason she struggled to simply let herself go sexually without guilt.

"How old were you?" he asked.

"Just 18 going on 19. He was my first. Things got so bad we moved to Tulsa to get away from all the rumors and guys coming on to me. I worried that Colin's grandfather would talk to my ex and use what we're doing against me in court. If Ahmed told the judge I was some sort of sex freak --"

"He would have to prove you were the same woman at 28 that you were 10 years ago, and he couldn't do that." Asher moved to her and held her close in his embrace. "Baby, that's over. You're an exceptional mother and a good woman. No one can take that from you. I bet your ex tried to find you over the years when he realized how rare it is to find a woman who truly enjoys sex."

She stiffened, but he held her tight.

"Not all women do. It's one reason men don't want to commit to one woman." He leaned back and met her gaze. "Some women just want to nurture a man, keep a home, have a family and be good friends with him. There's nothing wrong with that, but in all honesty, his mother can do that, or he can hire staff to meet those needs. What he needs from his woman is to feel needed. To feel as if he's the only person in the world who can meet her sexual needs and that what they do in bed matters to her."

Her brow rose in skepticism.

"Women have no idea how much of a turnoff it is when we realize they're only having sex with us because we want to. To know you woman wants you as much as you want her... that's the shit. To see her enjoy what you're doing to her, know that you're bringing her pleasure... it's a serious high."

"You're saying men cheat to get high," she said dryly.

Appreciating her wit and pleased that she'd relaxed against him, he tried to explain something he hadn't articulated before. "When I see you, my dick gets hard, period. I control my desire to push you over the chair, pull down those tight jeans that make your ass look so tempting because now is not the time."

Her breath hitched. Her eyelids lowered as she placed a hand on her chest.

"See? That excites you, and because it does, I want you more than anything or anyone else. When I get that kind of reception from you, coupled with the fact I find you extremely sexy and intelligent, it's a total package that makes me want to stay, to be around you, to come to only you. Understand?"

He held her gaze for a few moments until she nodded. Her hand moved and rested on his crotch.

He hissed as she squeezed first and then stroked his turgid length.

"When I see you, my titties get hard, my stomach clenches and my panties get wet, but I don't drop to my knees, zip down your pants, and fill my mouth with your hard, delicious cock, because now is not the time. I work around men every day, and no one else causes a reaction from me, so I wait until I see you. You're handsome, smart and did I mention sexy? A total package."

Need slammed into him as her words hit his fertile imagination. His already hard cock leaked and left a spot. She gave as good as she got.

"Touche. Well done," he said, moving his hard-on to the side as he took a few deep breaths. "Just so you know, I really, really, like that you enjoy sex."

"It's better when you care about the person," she whispered.

He kissed her again. "I care, Mya. I do. Never doubt that."

"I know." Mya leaned against his chest and took a deep breath. "Is Colin too much? Since we've been here, he's spent a lot of time with you. I know you aren't used to having a child around."

"I want to get used to having him around." He leaned back and stared down at her. "I don't play games. You made it clear that if I wanted you, I'd have to accept your son. What you didn't say was how amazing Colin was. I enjoy talking to him and he's a beast in video games. I'm scared to teach him how to play cards... come to think of it, maybe I should. We could challenge Moses and Drake, clean them out." His gaze narrowed as he thought about it. "That would be fun."

She laughed.

Surprised, he looked down at her.

"No, you will not teach him to cheat at cards."

Since he was thinking along those lines, he smiled. "Cheat is such a strong word."

She grinned and stepped back to turn off the stove. "Food is ready. Get Colin. We'll eat and then see about taking care of that." She patted his hard cock again.

"Like last night?" He leaned forward and whispered in her ear. "God, you tasted divine. I can still taste you now. How many times did you find release by my mouth?"

She shuddered.

He felt like Superman.

She pushed his shoulder. "Stop, go get Colin." Her voice wasn't as strong as it had been before.

"Three times? I want to break our record tonight. I want you weak and wet when I slide into you. I plan to plunge into you so hard you'll yell my name in your dreams." His cock throbbed in pain. His plan to make her horny and wet trapped him as well.

"Go. Go," she said, stepping backward.

He followed, snared her waist with one arm and bent close to her ear. "Maybe in the shower before bed. I'll bend you over, taste your sweetness first, and then take you against the wall. Would you like that? Would you take me deep into your tight --"

"Asher, please, stop." Breathing deeply, as if she'd run a mile, she leaned her forehead against his chest.

"Alright, I'll get Colin. But after dinner, after he goes to sleep, I want you."

She took another deep breath and met his gaze. "I want you more."

He smiled at the need he saw and brushed his lips against hers. "I don't know what I did to find a woman like you, but I'm not going to question it."

"I write erotica," she whispered.

He stilled. "What?"

She took a deep breath, wrapped her arms around her waist, and straightened. "I write erotic stories under another name. It started when my therapist suggested I write about my feelings. There was a lot of anger, confusion, research and finally acceptance. I didn't and don't want to ever experience what I went through after my divorce, so dating was out. I had so many questions about sex, how to do it, what felt right, and pleasure, I started reading."

"You learned the answers through research?" He didn't try to hide his skepticism.

"No. What I learned was people are different and like different things. Some like to watch, others like to be watched, some like pain in various degrees with their pleasure, others like more words than actions, some liked more than one at a time, various positions... all kinds of sex, none better or worse than the other."

Now was a good time to tell her he had read her stories online, tell her he had been in her home and that he owned it, tell her the truth of his business in Versteck. "What's your fake name?"

Laughing, she shook her head. "That's personal. Since I shared the other, figured I'd come clean about it all. Now go get Colin." She pushed his chest.

He stepped back, uncertain how much to tell her later tonight about him and Versteck Valley. Some secrets weren't his alone.

Mya took advantage of Colin wanting to show Asher what he and his classmates had been working on to take a nice, hot shower. The trip had started rocky, especially last night when she saw Asher's weapons. What had the man been thinking about bringing so many guns? He hadn't bitten his tongue, not that he ever did when he told her she hadn't been thinking clearly to think they'd travel anywhere without protection.

The idea of guns had never crossed her mind. She didn't have much of an opinion about them. But she didn't want her son around them and protested when Asher offered to show them to Colin. He insisted guns were tools for protection and only deadly when misused. It wasn't until he asked how far she would go to protect her son that she realized she would use a gun to save him, and it would be better if she knew how. When they returned to Versteck, he promised to teach her how to shoot and care for her gun.

Feeling refreshed and looking forward to a bit of time for herself, she applied lotion and spritz in preparation for a night of lovemaking. *Correction*, sex.

A real romantic. She wished they could call what they were doing making love. *Correction, again*. She wanted Asher to fall in love with her, wanted him to always want her the way she wanted him.

Just thinking about the way he stroked her body made her toes curl. His tongue was lethal and should have a warning label. He was game for anything and even allowed her to ride him without moving. She loved watching him strain and try to maintain his control, to no avail. Deliberately, she would tighten her muscles around him and tease his nipples with her fingernails. So far, he hadn't been able to hold out against what he called, "double trouble."

The door opened.

Asher looked at her and smiled. "Smells good in here. Give me a second to hop in the shower." He pointed at her. "Don't move."

She smiled and continued applying the lotion.

He moved across the room, pulled her up, and kissed her hard. "You're so fucking sexy, I love seeing you like this. I'll be right back. Do not put on any clothes."

"Do I ever?" She smiled at his pleased look.

"Good point." He headed to the shower.

There was a faint rumble in the distance. Colin had become accustomed to the fast-changing Colorado weather. There were more thunderstorms than they were used to. Most occurred while he was in school. Since Ms. Jenkins and the other instructors were aware of his phobia, they handled it in a way that didn't single Colin out.

She turned down the lights and slid beneath the covers.

Lightning flashed, followed by the boom of thunder. The house shuddered. Mya jumped out of bed, scrambling for her pajamas. If Colin didn't wake, it'd be a miracle.

Thunder rolled again.

Colin's scream pierced the air. Dressed in one of Asher's tee-shirts that hit above her knees, Mya threw open the door and ran across the hall to Colin's bedroom. Wide-eyed with tears rolling down his face, shivering as if frozen in place, he lay huddled and whimpering in the middle of the bed.

Lightning flashed, followed again by raucous thunder.

Colin screamed again and shook so hard it was difficult for Mya to pick him up. He turned into her arms and buried his face into her shoulder. The lights flickered off. The room went dark, causing him to cry harder.

Asher stepped into the room wearing nothing but his jeans and looked at them. He checked the window and returned to the hall. "Lock this door, don't open it until I come back."

"Alright," she said, struggling to hold Colin. "When will the lights come back on?"

"Soon. Lock the door, Mya."

There was something in his voice that had her lifting Colin, moving to the door and locking it.

"I'm scared, Mommy."

Thunder rolled again, but didn't sound as close this time. Colin held her closer and closed his eyes.

"I know, baby. It's going to be alright." She lay on the bed next to him, holding him close as the storm continued outside. Her thoughts wandered to Asher. He hadn't returned, and the lights were still off.

There was a crack that sounded like thunder, but not quite. Colin cried. She held him close, making soothing sounds as fear slid up her spine. Had someone followed them here? Had Asher made her close the door to keep someone out? Were they in some kind of danger?

She heard footsteps. Tense, she moved so that Colin would be hidden. There were more sounds. Lightning cracked the sky at the same time she thought she heard someone yell, but wasn't sure. Colin's continual screaming and crying didn't help.

By the time the storm quieted, Mya was worn out. She had heard the thunderstorms in the higher elevations were fierce, but this was the worst they'd ever experienced. It had sounded as if the lightning and thunder were close. Sleep tugged at her.

"Mya?"

She heard more tapping.

"Open the door."

Colin's even breathing had lulled her asleep. She glanced at the clock. It was after three in the morning. Wait, the alarm clock? The power had returned. She rolled off the bed and went to the door just as another knock landed.

"Mya, are you and Colin alright?"

"Yeah, I must've fallen asleep."

"Open the door."

She opened it and looked at him. His hair was wet, like he'd just showered. She frowned, trying to make sense of it.

Asher walked into the room, picked up Colin and carried him across the hall to their bed. Sleepy, Mya followed and climbed in behind them. After depositing Colin in the middle of the king-sized bed, Asher locked the door and joined them.

"Get some sleep," he told her.

Mya yawned and did that.

CHAPTER NINETEEN

T HEY LEFT THE MOUNTAINS Monday morning, intent on heading to Laura's office to meet Joshua Henry. Earlier during breakfast, Mya whispered Colin had a terrible fear of thunderstorms to Asher. He nodded, but didn't say anything. In fact, he hadn't said much at all this morning.

Laura called around 10:30 to find out where they were. She sounded a little off, but Mya hadn't known the woman long enough to mention it.

"Tell Wesley I want him at your office with a full team," Asher said into the phone.

Mya looked at Asher first and then over her shoulder at Colin, who was reading in the back seat. When Asher hung up, Mya looked at him and asked in a low voice. "Why is Wesley going to be at the office?"

"Just in case," Asher said.

When he didn't explain further, she pressed. "In case of what?"

Asher looked in the rear-view mirror, smiled and didn't answer her question. She glanced at Colin, saw he was listening and understood.

"Are you sure he wants to meet me?" Colin asked for the millionth time.

"Yes. He came across the country to meet you," Mya said, trying to keep the irritation from her voice.

Asher frowned at her, which made her more cross.

"Sorry," Colin whispered.

Mya closed her eyes, counted to ten to bring her emotions under control. "No. I'm sorry, baby. I'll just be happy when this is over, that's all. It's not you, I'm nervous."

Colin looked at her for a few moments. "Alright. But you don't have to be nervous. I'm his grandson, not you."

She smiled. "True. I'll remember that." She glanced at Asher. "Still want to know what's going on, though," she said. "If there's any problems I want to know before taking my son into that building."

Asher glanced at her and nodded, but didn't speak.

The three of them walked into Laura's lobby area with 12 minutes to spare. Laura took Colin into her office while Asher and Mya entered another, smaller, empty office.

She whirled around with a narrowed gaze. "What's going on? Why's Wesley here and not at the Arms? Why do we need a security team for a 10-minute meeting?"

"Last night during the thunderstorm when the lights went out, that wasn't because of the storm."

She jerked as if he struck her. "What?" She searched his face for an answer. "Someone turned out the lights?"

"Someone took advantage of the storm and shut down the power in the basement," he said.

"From inside the house? How'd they get in?" she asked in a horrified whisper as her imagination kicked into high gear. What if Colin hadn't woken up screaming? They would've been caught unaware in bed. Nausea rolled in her stomach. This couldn't be happening.

"That house is used as a rental property and doesn't have the same security either of us has on our homes. I thought it would be alright for two days. I was wrong and that almost cost... I'm sorry."

"Sorry? For what?" She was still processing someone had broken in and turned off the lights in the midst of the storm.

"You or Colin could've gotten hurt. I should've taken you someplace safer. I won't make that mistake again," he said, sounding as if making a vow.

"What? That wasn't your fault. Please don't make one of the best weekends in our lives into a dramatic mistake. We had a great time."

He stared at her for so long she wondered if she missed something.

"Alright," he said. "Anyway, that's the reason for additional security. Just in case someone attempts to take you or Colin."

"Or you," she said, although her heart knew he was right.

"True, but doubtful," he said.

When he didn't smile or laugh off her comment, she suspected something more was going on. "Asher, have you told me everything?"

He looked at her and shook his head. "No. I've never told anyone everything."

Frowning, she grabbed his arm as he walked toward the door. "Wait. Why do I feel something's changed or is changing between us? You're cold, almost indifferent. Tell me what's going on?"

He cupped her chin. "A lot depends on what happens in the next two or three hours. If Joshua Henry is being honest and simply wants to meet his grandson, then no problem. But if he thinks he's going to take Colin, then expect to see hell on earth because that's what will rain down on the man." He didn't smile when he delivered his prediction.

She shivered with fear. "He can't take Colin."

"No, he cannot," Asher said, and it sounded more like a vow. He opened the door.

Mya had no choice but to walk out and head toward Laura's office. Her heart fell as she realized Asher hadn't addressed her concern over their relationship. Colin's safety was a priority, but afterward, she would press for answers. Plus, he never mentioned what happened to whoever broke into the house.

Joshua Henry was as slippery up close as he'd been from the distance when he stood in Mya's front yard two days ago. Not only did Asher take an immediate dislike to the man, he knew Henry's real interest in Colin had nothing to do with familial love. Greed rolled off the man as he stared down at Colin.

This was about money. That was a motive Asher understood and sent a text to Mercer. "Dig deeper into Henry's finances."

"Colin Junior, I'm so happy to finally meet you. I'm your grandfather, Joshua. Your daddy was my son. I've brought a photo album of him while he was younger to show you. Would you like to see it?"

"Yes, that'd be good, thanks." Colin glanced at Mya.

She smiled as the old man opened an old photo album and placed it on the table. With each turn of the page and explanation of each picture, Colin moved closer and got caught up with memories of his father.

Asher didn't blame him and fought the bite of jealousy. Colin wasn't his son, but that had nothing to do with his feelings right now. Over the weekend, they bonded, which surprised and pleased him. No one would hurt the boy. When this situation was settled, he planned to explain everything to Mya, admit his misdeeds, and ask for her understanding. In his opinion, there was a lot on the line. She could break up with him or leave town or tell someone his secrets. His gut clenched at all three negative options.

She could also see things from his perspective and forgive him and forgive all the people she had met so far for deceiving her. Others had. He rubbed his forehead while standing in the corner, watching Henry try to worm his way into Colin's affections.

"You remind me so much of your father. He was a good man. A good son," Henry said with emotion. "Much better than I deserved."

"He never mentioned you to Mama or in any of the letters he mailed me. I still have them. Were you friends?" Colin asked.

Henry's cheeks pinked. "He was my son."

Colin stared at the older man for a second. "Why didn't he want me to meet you?"

"Why do you ask that?" Henry glanced at Mya, Laura, and back at Colin.

"Because we would've met you when I was born or before now if my dad had asked. He had a lot to say. Mama has the videos he made for me for when I grew older, and he never mentioned you or anyone from his family, just some of his friends," Colin said seriously.

"Are you sure you're just five? You talk well for someone your age. Is it because of the school you're attending?" Henry asked.

"You didn't answer my question," Colin said.

Joshua Henry laughed. It filled his eyes and softened his face. "You're so much like your father it's amazing. He sounded and looked just like that when I avoided answering him. I can't answer why he didn't want us to meet. He never mentioned you to me, either. I didn't learn about you until after he died."

"And now you wanted to meet me?" Colin asked.

With a slight, almost nostalgic smile, Henry nodded. "Yes. You're very smart, like your father. Gosh, I can't get over how much you're like him."

"Did he win a lot of awards in school like Mama?" Colin asked, looking through the photo album and then up at his grandfather.

"Erm no, but he was really smart," Henry said, watching Mya.

"Oh." Colin sounded disappointed. He continued flipping the pages until he came to the end of the album and pushed it aside.

"I enjoyed meeting you, Colin. You've made me very happy." Henry glanced at Mya before speaking. "I hope we can do it again. I'll bring more photo albums next time. Would you like that?"

Laura stood.

Mya's jaw tightened.

Asher placed his hand on the butt of his weapon.

"I don't think so," Colin said, surprising everyone as he pushed the photo album toward his grandfather and stood.

Joshua Henry wasn't the only adult astonished by Colin's response. "Why not?" Henry stuttered, clearly flustered.

"I have videos of my father whenever I want to see them. He had a lot to say about what he wanted for Mom and me if anything ever happened to him. One thing he wanted was for Mama to be happy and for me, too. She wasn't happy when you came around."

Asher's estimation of the kid rose in leaps and bounds.

"It doesn't matter that I won't be happy if I don't see you again?" Henry gave it another shot.

"I don't know you," Colin said and walked over to Mya. He took her hand. "My daddy's been dead a long time. He wanted me and Mama happy. You don't make us happy."

"You don't want me to be a part of your life?" Henry asked, standing slowly, his gaze on Colin. He sounded genuinely hurt. Asher gave the man a star for a brilliant performance.

Colin shrugged. "You haven't been so far."

"I want to change that, I really do," Henry said, sounding painfully desperate.

Colin looked at his mom.

Mya leaned forward and kissed Colin on the cheek. She whispered something in his ear.

"Mama said it's up to me," Colin said.

Henry looked relieved and smiled.

Colin shook his head.

Henry's smile dropped.

Colin turned and placed his face on Mya's shoulder. "No."

Laura stood. "Mr. Henry, you've made your case against our expressed agreement, nevertheless my client has decided to continue his life without you in it. Respect both of my client's wishes and the response of the court and stay away from both of my clients. Security will see you out." She held up her hand and pointed to the door.

Henry looked ashen with disbelief and pain for a moment before turning. "I'm sorry to have bothered you, child. Truly, I only wanted to meet you. You're so much like Colin and more." He left without a backward glance.

The moment the door closed behind Henry, Colin left his mom and ran to Asher. Surprised, Asher picked him up and held him close while watching the shock fade from Mya's gaze. She stood, walked over to them, and rubbed her son's back.

"Seems he made a choice to go forward instead of living in the past," Laura said wisely from the other side of the room, watching them. "Always knew he was a smart one."

Mya almost asked Laura what she and Colin talked about during the time they were in the office alone, but didn't. Colin had done a great job, and she was so proud of him.

"Am I going to school or are we going home?" Colin asked.

"Do you want to go to school?" Mya asked.

He nodded.

"Alright, we'll take you to school," she said. "Guess I'll go to work."

Asher shook his head. "Tomorrow. Chastity knows."

Laura smiled. "Go out the back to the parking lot. I'll let Bonnie know you're on the way. Bryson's already at the school."

"Thanks for everything," Mya said as she hugged Laura. "I can't tell you how relieved I am that this is over."

Laura's smile slipped as she nodded. "We love you and Colin and want you to stay here in Versteck. Anything you need, we're here to help." She looked at Asher, nodded, and then at Mya again. "Call me if there are any problems."

Mya nodded. The three of them left and headed to the school.

CHAPTER TWENTY

MYA AND ASHER LEFT Colin with his teacher, Ms. Jenkins, and headed to the house. Asher's nerves had him on edge. Since Mya and Colin would be a part of his life, he had to explain Versteck Valley and the Arms to Mya.

Asher wasn't sure what Laura and Colin discussed, but he was sure it was along the lines of Colin having a family, a father in particular. No doubt she picked up on Colin's affection for Asher and used it, not in a bad way, but to make sure they could move forward without Henry's shadow dogging them. He wasn't sure how he felt about her interference and would deal with that later.

Right now, he and Mya had to talk.

He wasn't sure if he should tell her everything about last night. As common as storms were in that area, the power shouldn't have gone off. Immediately, he'd grabbed his weapons and sent a text to Bryson for backup.

After checking on Mya and Colin, he insisted she lock herself in before moving into the alcove in the hall to hide, secured the silencer to his weapon, and waited for intruders. It hadn't taken long.

Fortunately, the storm was loud and Colin's screams louder. Otherwise, Mya would've heard when the first man dropped on the staircase with a bullet in his head. Since the two men had separated, the chances of taking the second as quickly as the first were slim. Asher didn't want the intruder anywhere near the bedrooms. Assuming the second person had gone to the basement, Asher laid on the floor near the basement entrance in the shadows to wait.

Moments later, a small beam of light crept up the basement stairs and went out. Asher had stilled and went to that place in his mind of utter calm, void of emotion. One of them would survive the night. Asher decided it would be him. The bullet whizzed by his head and went wide.

He had returned fire, heard the man fall, but that didn't mean the person was down. Inching forward, he moved deeper into the shadows and listened. The storm continued raging, making it hard to hear the ragged breathing coming from the area of the basement entrance. The man had been hit but was still alive.

A car pulled up out front. Bryson wanted everyone to know he had arrived. As the van door opened, Asher heard movement. Lightning flashed, and he saw his target. Asher pulled the trigger. The man fell to the hardwood floor. Moving quickly, he reached the fallen intruder, kicked his gun aside, and checked for other weapons. The man had two more guns, three blades, knuckles, and a cell phone.

Asher checked his pulse. It was light. The man wheezed, trying to breathe as blood flowed from the corner of his mouth. Asher unlocked the front door. Thunder boomed in the background as Bryson entered, carrying bags over one arm and a Glock in his other hand.

"One on the stairs and this one," Asher told him as he locked the door. "I'm going to turn on the power. I locked Mya and Colin in that room." He pointed to the door. "I don't want them to see this or you, if possible."

Bryson nodded and headed for the body on the stairs while Asher returned to the man near the basement entrance. "Why did you break into my home?"

The man grimaced but didn't answer.

If Mya wasn't in the next room and the storm wasn't abating, Asher might have pressed the issue. Time wasn't on his side. He knocked the man out with the butt of his gun and began putting the man's legs inside the bag.

Bryson hefted the first bag on his shoulder and placed him in the garage. Then he returned to help Asher finish placing the second man in the bag. He took him into the garage as well and made sure he wouldn't wake to escape.

Asher had turned on the power.

The two of them cleaned the hardwood floors to remove the blood as best they could. It took over an hour before Bryson was satisfied and left with the bodies.

Asher had taken another shower.

When Mya had opened the door all sleepy-eyed, he realized he would've done anything to keep her and Colin safe. They belonged together. He remembered the knives and metal knuckles the intruder carried. Those men came to torture or kill, possibly both. The night could've ended differently. Grateful Colin had calmed down, and Mya had felt safe enough to fall asleep, he'd moved Colin to their bed without a second thought. In his mind, he killed to protect his own. She might not see things that way. Might think him a monster or worse. Should he tell her about last night?

"Hungry?" she asked.

"I could eat something," he said, marshaling his thoughts. "Want to head to Denver for a bite and come back to pick up Colin?"

Her gaze widened as she looked at him. "Denver? That's over an hour away. We can grab something local and head to the house. We've been gone since Saturday."

He nodded, turned, and headed towards town. It didn't take long to grab two plates of fish tacos, with salsa. They saw a few people who nodded, waved, or spoke. Then they drove the few blocks to the house.

Inside, they ate in companionable silence. Asher's thoughts were filled with how to explain everything without sharing personal secrets of anyone else and keep her in his life.

"So what's on your mind?" she said.

He looked across the table at her. "What?"

"You haven't tried to get in my panties since we dropped Colin off, which means you're thinking about something else really hard. What's going on?" she said.

"Can't argue with your deductive reasoning," he said. "I need to tell you some things, and I'm concerned about how you'll handle the information. It's not just me, well, some of it is just me, but it's a lot."

She held his gaze. "Why do you need to tell me this now? Has something happened?"

Smart lady. "Yes, something's happened. My feelings for you have grown, not just you, Colin, too. I want... I want us to be together. Like a family." There. He said it, got the words out in the ozone. That word, "family" had been branded on his mind since last night when he placed Colin in bed with them. He wanted this.

Her mouth dropped open. She moistened her lips with her tongue. "When you say your feelings have grown... what do you mean?"

His brow furrowed. "I like you a lot more now than before. It's not the same as when we first started talking."

She nodded. "Because you're falling in love with me. You think you need to tell me more about yourself?"

Love? He hadn't mentioned love. Hell, the closest thing he could call love was his feelings for Moses and Drake, possibly Laura. It was all mixed up with loyalty, honesty, fairness, fidelity, and things like that. Chances are that was love. How would he know?

"Yes." It was easier to go along with her than pick at things.

Visibly, she relaxed her shoulders and swiped her tongue across her lips again. "You're concerned I'll get angry?"

"You probably will. I ask that you hear me out to the end before passing judgment. There's a lot going on."

She stared at him for a few moments, took a deep breath, and nodded. "Alright. I can do that."

"Best start at the beginning. Me, Moses, and his brother own Versteck Arms."

"What?" she yelled as she sat straight in her chair, staring at him in disbelief.

He nodded.

"No wonder Chastity never gives me grief when I can't make it to work," she murmured.

"That's not fair or true. She just found out about us a short while ago. She's really a great boss and wants you to succeed there," he said, watching her relax.

"True, she was great even before I met you," Mya said.

"You already know I own a security company. I also own a few smaller ones. Real Estate, investments, and a talent agency of sorts," he hedged.

She frowned. "What kind of agency?"

"Remember, I told you the history of Versteck Valley? Von Mark's Robber's Roost?" She nodded slowly. "Yeah."

"Versteck Arms is a modern version of that. The men who live in the Arms have checkered pasts and have retired from an active life of what some would call crime."

Her eyebrows shot up. "What? Some would say? Like who? Would the cops call it a crime? Or a judge?"

"Most have never been in front of a judge or police," he said, sidestepping her question.

"Answer me."

"We've all committed crimes," he admitted and leaned back in his seat. Heart racing, he watched several emotions cross her face. Disbelief. Shock. Disappointment. Pain. Sorrow.

No. No. No, don't stop with sorrow, he thought. Get angry. I can fight your anger.

"You're a criminal? The men at the Arms are criminals?" She sounded as if someone sucker punched her and stole all the air.

"I'll only discuss myself," he made that clear.

She swallowed hard and nodded.

"I've committed crimes, mostly in self-defense or in defense of someone close," he said, watching her.

"Like your cousin?"

He nodded. *And you and Colin.* Based on her reactions so far, he would never tell her about last night.

"Colin... my son adores you."

"He knows a good man when he meets one," Asher said. There was more to say, but it might not be necessary if she couldn't move past this.

"This town is made up of criminals?" Doubt played heavy in her voice.

"No. I didn't say that. Some are, most aren't and don't know of the rest of us. If I weren't falling in love with you, you would never have known," he said.

"Lucky me."

His jaw tightened as if she'd slapped him. "Would you like me to leave?"

She looked at him for a few moments. "I don't know how to handle this. It sounds like some kind of movie or novel."

Deflated, he pushed from the table, stood, and walked to the back door. A hundred thoughts flew through his mind. *You shouldn't have told her. You should've told her upfront. Stay and fight through this. Let it go before things get worse. Never put your heart out there again.*

"But I want us to talk it through. I don't want you to go. Colin's not the only person who knows a good man when he meets one," she said from the table.

He turned to face her as she stood and walked slowly to him. "You've known all of this for years. Be patient with me. I need time to digest things and learn about the place we call home," she said, extending her hand to him.

Relief overwhelmed him as he took her hand and pulled her close for a quick kiss.

Mya leaned into him, loving his strength and honesty. She didn't like the criminal thing, especially around Colin, and had several more questions about that, but she wanted to hear and learn more.

He took her hand and led her to the sofa.

"Talk to me," she said once they were seated.

He shared his dream as a teen to reinvent a modern-day Robbers Roost and how it came about. Fascinated, she listened intently as he spoke with pride about how he and his cousins built the business and his managerial role.

Stunned by the magnitude of it all, she sat back and stared at him. "Is this one of those "if I tell you I'd have to kill you" moments?" She tried for humor instead of tears or screaming.

He didn't smile. "No. This is me trusting you with my secret. Me wanting you to know something very few people in the world know. Me wanting you to accept me as I am. Is that possible?"

Her heart melted. How could she say no? Her heart was all in, but her mind balked. "Will my son be in danger?"

She would never cross that line.

"No more than if he lived anywhere else. Nobody messes with our own. You've seen how we rally around those who're a part of our community," he said.

Mya leaned forward. Her forehead rested on his chest. His fast heartbeat was at odds with the placid look he wore.

He was afraid.

She wanted to be with him, but wasn't sure. "I really, really like you," she said, glad he hadn't used her attraction to him as a bargaining chip. "How do we make this work?" She wasn't ready to let him go.

His hand rubbed her back. "We continue the same way as before, except now you know there's so much more to this sleepy town than you first thought. This kind of relationship is new to me. I want to spend more time with Colin so we can get to know each other better. We won't move in together or take the next step until he's ready, okay?"

She wasn't sure about the shacking part and marriage had left a nasty taste in her mouth. "Next step?"

"Whatever that is, we need to bring him in so that he doesn't feel excluded. I don't want him to ever feel that way again," Asher said.

"Agreed. He likes you."

"I know. He chose me today over his father's memories. That was a deep, special moment," he admitted.

She had wondered if he'd picked up on it and should've known better.

"My experiences with family aren't great, but you're an expert. I'll lean on you to help us merge or blend or whatever it's called," he said.

"I like that. And I'd like to put this out there. You know more about family dynamics than you think. You're great with Colin."

Again, he kissed her breathlessly.

"Take me to the tunnels. I want to see them," she said when they broke apart.

He placed her hand on his hard cock. "Now? You want to see them now?"

She giggled as she stood, ready for a new adventure. "Yes, now. If you hurry, we'll get back in time to take care of that before going to pick up Colin." She pointed at his groin.

He grabbed her hand and stood. "Alright, but we have to go to my house."

Pleased he had given in, she nodded and followed him out the door. They entered his home, headed toward the basement, and stopped at a wall. He touched a panel that blended so well she hadn't seen it before. He completed a palm and retinal scan, then keyed in code before the door opened. He held her close as they walked in. The door closed behind them.

Mya gasped as they stood on the short landing and started walking down. The temperature was much lower, and chill bumps rose on her arms. "Should've worn a heavier jacket," she said.

"Didn't think to tell you it's cooler down here," he said, taking off his lightweight jacket.

"No, keep it on. I'll be fine once we're walking."

"You're sure?" He held it out to her.

She shook her head. "I'm warmer already. Put it back on." Her head swiveled back and forth. "This is wild."

He grinned. "Been called a lot of things. First time I've heard it called that."

Once they reached the bottom of the stairs, she looked left and then right. "How long is this?"

"Several miles," he said, taking her hand. They walked side-by-side in some places and other places single file. It was quiet. She ran her palm against the rough-hewn walls. "What's this?"

"Earth. Stone. We busted through tons of rock to make these. Then reinforced the passageways with steel," he said.

"Hard to believe we're walking underground. I mean subways do it all the time, but this is a lot more primitive. Know what I mean?" she said, awed by what they had accomplished.

"Yeah, I do."

When he turned and assisted her up another flight of stairs, she was shocked to be in a house near the center of town, and it hadn't taken them long to get there. The house was furnished but dusty. No one lived in it, probably hadn't for a while. They walked outside and eventually reached Main Street.

"Speechless?" he said.

She nodded.

"They're dangerous if you don't know the codes or how to navigate them. We have a system in place that keeps people safe. I'll teach it to you, but for now, don't go in the tunnels or the caverns, especially the caverns without me," he said.

"Promise. No worries on that front. I wouldn't know how to find the entrance," she said.

His phone rang. He looked at the caller ID. "Laura." He answered and listened for a few moments. Mya felt a chill waft off him as he stiffened. "Where does he want to meet?"

She frowned and wished he had placed the call on speaker.

"We'll be there. Can you keep this quiet? Thanks." He looked at Mya. "Joshua Henry called Laura; he wants to talk to you. He says Colin could be in danger from the man who hired him."

CHAPTER TWENTY-ONE

M YA AND ASHER CROSSED the hotel lobby to the elevator. The ride to the third floor was done in complete silence. Asher hadn't said much since Laura's call. After speaking to Ms. Jenkins at the school and hearing her assurance that Colin was fine, Mya, and Asher headed to the hotel to meet Henry. On the phone, Henry sounded scared and insisted they come to his hotel for a face-to-face meeting.

Neither Laura nor Wesley liked the setup and advised against it. Mya over-ruled them and made it clear she wanted to hear whatever the man had to say. She agreed to give Asher's team time to get in place in case things went wrong.

They knocked on the door of room 312.

Henry opened it, looking worse and smelling musty as if he had been running and hadn't showered. Mya stepped inside, crossed her arms, and stared at him. "What did you want to tell me?"

"Did you tell the boy not to see me again?" Henry countered.

"No. He made up his own mind," Mya said. "Now, who hired you and why does he want my son?"

Henry released a long sigh, placed his glass on the table and held out his hands. They shook badly. "I'm dying."

"Alright," she said, unmoved. This piece of trash took money to harass her and Colin.

"I had a son and a daughter. Neither wanted anything to do with me. Not that I blame them. I was a horrible father, a bad example. Colin despised me and Meghan hasn't spoken to me in 12, no 13 years. Not even at Colin's funeral." He ran his hand through his hair and walked toward the lone sofa in the room.

"I don't have to tell you I've never been interested in your son. I proved that. But it cost me nothing to go along with the plan, and they paid me well." He snorted as he slumped in the seat. "Very well. He tries to act like he's got limited funds, but he always has money. I think someone else is bankrolling his operation, which makes things worse for my grandson." He chuckled. "I liked the little tyke. He's got spunk, smart, and still has manners." He met Mya's gaze. "Most kids don't these days. You've done well with him."

Should I say thank you? "Who's after Colin?" she asked instead.

"Greg Parson is the person I dealt with, but I don't think he's the one in charge. I researched Parson, and he shouldn't be able to pull off the things that've been happening."

"Like trying to kidnap Colin?" she asked.

Henry looked surprised and then thoughtful. "Didn't know about that. Which means there's a plan B and C in place."

"Why do they want Colin?" Mya asked, growing pissed and frustrated with his trips down memory lane.

"Colin, my son, was approached to participate in a series of tests, more like experiments Parson's company was handling. It was government sanctioned, all above board. Colin started and then dropped out once he realized what they were about." He narrowed his gaze at her and pointed. "This is me reading between the lines of what Parson told me."

She nodded.

"Parson's trying to get a new government contract and needs to prove his tests work. His research pulled up my son, his death, and his son, your son, Colin Junior. Once he checked into things, he learned the little one is a genius."

Icy dread slid down Mya's back.

"He plans to use Colin Junior as proof that his experiments work so he can continue his project and get funding. We're talking millions of dollars," Henry said.

Mya's stomach plummeted. "Is it true? Was Colin a test subject?"

"No. Do you know Griff?"

"The name sounds familiar."

"It should. Major Griffin Thomas is the trustee for your boy and my son's best friend. He swears Colin was never in the program and was making sure the records were correct. Parson's scamming the system, but he's doing it with someone else's backing." He held out his hands again. "As I said, I'm dying and a loose end that'll be snipped soon. I knew that when I accepted the first check and rode the high life for a few months. The kid meant nothing to me... not until today." He peered up at her. "He looks like my son. Had I seen a picture of the boy, I never would've asked for proof. He doesn't deserve to be anyone's guinea pig, and that's in his future."

Mya shook her head as calm, yet brutal, determination filled her. "No, it's not."

He looked at her for a few moments. "They've already paid someone to take a sample of his blood. That's what they wanted me to do." He shook his head. "But it won't stop there. Once they run tests on his blood, they'll want something else. Maybe test scores or a trip to parade him around in front of the brass to show what the drug can do."

"No, they won't she said," confidence in her tone. No one would hurt her son.

"If you get in the way, they'll just remove you," Henry warned.

Asher spoke for the first time. "No, they won't."

Henry looked at them both for a few seconds. "Once Colin said he didn't want to see me again, he signed my death warrant." He waved his hand. "Prolonged it. I don't expect to make it to the airport tomorrow, which is why I wanted to tell you this today. Trust is a commodity you can't afford. These guys have deep pockets, and everybody has a price." He stood with some effort. "I wish things had been different. Wish I had a relationship with my kids so I wouldn't be alone when I died. Wish I had the courage to take the boy and hand him over--"

"That would've cost you your life," Asher said in a low voice.

"Which has very little value, anyway." He took a deep breath. "Who knows? Maybe I'll see my son in the afterlife and be able to tell him I did this one thing for his kid, gave him a small window to prepare for what's coming at him. Maybe we'll be even. What do you think?"

"Sounds good to me," she said, although she didn't care.

He nodded toward Asher. "This one's much better than the other one. Your ex-husband. Totally useless and blaming the world for his misfortune. I could buy and sell him all day if he had anything worth selling. Glad you've got someone with balls of steel in your corner. My grandson will need him, and so will you."

She glanced at Asher. He remained standing slightly behind her, watching the room and listening to the team through the earpiece as they patrolled the hotel for signs of trouble.

Henry waved them to the door. "That's all I have to tell you. I'll have a meal, watch some television... and who knows? Will I see the sunset or sunrise tomorrow?" He shrugged dismissively.

Mya took a step back. Once she passed Asher, she turned to open the door.

"Tell my grandson, meeting him today was the singular, most pleasurable event in my life and worth everything."

Mya opened the door, saw Connor in the hall, and stepped out. Asher followed. Quietly they took the stairs to the first floor with Asher in the lead, Mya in the middle and Connor bringing up the rear.

They reached the first floor, crossed the lobby, and headed toward Laura's dark SUV in the parking lot. Once inside, they waited for the all clear and then pulled out.

Mya's emotions were all over the place. "Do you believe him?" she asked Asher.

"Parson's name came across my desk while searching for Moses. I've got a file on him, and Henry's correct. He shouldn't have the finances to pull this off."

"Have Mercer dig deeper," Laura suggested as she pulled into the parking lot of her office.

"I did. This is based on his information," Asher said.

"Which means he has a silent or not so silent partner," Laura said.

"Who helped them get blood from Colin?" Mya asked, confused. "When did it happen? How could I not know about it?"

"Ask Colin," Asher said.

"If it happened during nap-time and they drugged him, he probably won't remember," Laura said.

"You think it happened at school?" Mya asked, shocked.

Laura nodded. "Had to. Otherwise, you'd know about it. Asher can look at the classroom security cams to determine if anyone messed with them or not." She looked at Asher. "We need to know who's been bought off before Colin returns to school."

He nodded. "I'll get my car and head over there now."

"I'm coming with you," Mya said. The whole thing seemed unreal, but if there was a kernel of truth in what Henry said, she would do whatever was necessary to protect her son. If that meant joining a group of older, seasoned criminals, she would pack her morals in a trunk and ship them to Timbuktu. She wasn't losing another child.

CHAPTER TWENTY-TWO

WHEN MYA ARRIVED AT the school, Ms. Wails met her and Asher in the lobby and took them to her office. She showed them a picture of Colin's arm where there had been a small puncture mark.

"When I asked Colin about it, he didn't remember but said it was sore. I asked when his arm started feeling sore, and he said a couple of days ago. That would be Thursday or Friday, Wednesday at the most, don't you think?" she asked Mya.

Mya looked at Asher. "He didn't mention anything to me this past weekend, and I couldn't tell there had been a problem. You?"

"He used his right arm to play air hockey, winced a couple times when he used his left but never said anything," Asher said.

"Now that we know blood was drawn, we need to find the miserable bastard who did it," Ms. Wails said angrily. "There's been no new staff in that class or on this campus, which means someone we know and trust around our children sold him out. I want them."

"If it happened here, I'll pass that information on to you," Asher promised.

"Laura promised to help," Ms. Wails said, surprising Mya.

"Good. We'll start looking at the tapes, and then we'll take Colin home. He won't return until the breach is repaired," Asher said.

"Understood." Ms. Wails led them down the hall and opened a door. "Since you designed this room and the security for the school, I'll leave the two of you alone."

He nodded, removed his jacket, hung it up, and walked toward a large console filled with several monitors displaying different areas of the school.

"Felt like you guys were speaking in some sort of code," Mya said taking a seat next to him while looking at the library on one screen, cafeteria on another, students in classes, the playground, lobby, the front of the school, parking lot, there were cameras everywhere.

"What happens when we find out who took the blood sample?" she asked after finding the camera in Colin's class. She watched him working on his laptop and talking with Ms. King, one of Ms. Jenkins assistants.

"We tell Bonnie. This is her business. She'll handle it."

"Why didn't you say we'll call the Sheriff? Isn't that the next logical step?" she asked, watching as his fingers flew over the keyboard.

"I won't lie to you, not even to make you feel better," he said, sounding distracted.

She had no response for that and sat quietly watching her son as he did his thing. "Am I being hypocritical?"

"About?" He continued looking at surveillance tapes.

"This whole criminal enterprise thing. On the one hand, it goes against everything I know and was brought up to believe in. Yet, at the first sign of Colin being in trouble, you and your people were the ones, the only ones I trusted to help protect him. Not once did I consider calling the Sheriff or police?"

"In that case, maybe," he said.

"Maybe I'm being hypocritical?" she asked for clarity.

"Yes. Look at this." He pointed to the screen. "She moved Colin out of camera range, why would she do that? Why separate him from the rest of the class? Was he sick one day or something?"

"No. He's very healthy. Who separated him?" she asked, trying to see more.

"One of the adults. I don't know which. Then they leave, all three of them, and Ms. Jenkins is alone in the room. See her at her desk working?

Mya nodded.

"The kids fall asleep. The assistants return 30 minutes later, and Ms. Jenkins goes to lunch. This is the only time I cannot see Colin," he said. "I'll send this feed to Bonnie and have her ask them about it."

"Is that the only day you couldn't see him at all times?" Mya asked.

"The only time last week Wednesday through Friday. Want me to check further back?"

She nodded. "Check the entire week, to be sure."

"That was the only time," Asher said 23 minutes later. "Someone either came in and drew blood or an instructor did it."

Heart in her throat, Mya took several deep breaths as he continued typing and stood. "Who do you think?"

"Like the old man said, money buys people. I think it's one of the staff. Either they were lax and allowed someone else to do it, or they did it. Laura and Bonnie will know before the end of the day," he said as they left the room.

Bryson met them in the hall. "Bonnie wants you to stop by her office before you pick up Colin."

Asher nodded, and they headed to the office. Bonnie sat on the corner of her desk watching the monitor. "Was this the only time he was separated in class?"

"The only time in the past week," Asher said. "Have Bryson or Mercer do a complete scan if you want to know if her actions went further back."

Ms. Wails looked tired as she nodded. "I'd have bet my last dollar none of the people working in that class were involved in this. I can't believe I've missed this." She inhaled deeply and looked at Asher, her gaze a mixture of misery and anger. "Who do you think did this?"

"If Laura hasn't already, have Mercer check the finances of all your personnel to see who's had a recent financial boost. If they're savvy and didn't put it in the bank, he'll still find it. Before you approach anyone, make sure you have the answers to all the questions before you ask." he said.

She nodded. "Laura's on it and will be here as the school's attorney to press charges. We'll call Jack in for this."

Mya was surprised but didn't said anything.

"Sounds good. If you need me, call. We'll be taking Colin now," he said as her phone rang.

Bonnie answered and looked at him. "Yes, he's here and has been here for the past hour." She paused. "Alright, I'll tell him." She hung up.

"That was Jack. He just received a call from the Lakeshore Hotel. The maid found Joshua Henry's body; they shot him in the head. The security cams show you and Mya as his last visitors. He wants you to stay here until he arrives."

Asher shook his head. "Amateurs." He looked at Mya. "We'll let this play out for now."

Nervous, she nodded. "Alright." She didn't know what Asher meant or what he planned to do. She swallowed hard and placed her trust in him and his team.

Joshua was dead?

Although he predicted it, she still found it hard to believe. Her stomach rolled. She closed her eyes and inhaled. "*You will not be sick. You won't be sick,*" she repeated the words in her mind over and over until her stomach eased.

"You okay?" Asher asked as he placed his hand beneath her elbow and escorted her to a chair.

She sat and placed her fingertips to her forehead. "Yes, hard to believe. We just talked to him recently."

"Take a deep breath. Put your head down and breathe," he said.

"Want something to drink?" Bonnie asked.

"No, thank you." The idea of eating or drinking anything made her stomach clench. *Good Lord, the man was dead?* It must have happened right after they left. Did the police think she killed him? Or Asher?

She leaned further down to stop the rising nausea. He rubbed her back, calming her.

When she could swallow, she lifted her head slowly and met Asher's concerned gaze. "They think we did it?"

He shrugged. "Doesn't matter what they think, we didn't. That's what's important."

She wished she could be as confident as him. "What about the news? He'd been on the news."

"Don't worry about that. It's covered," he said. "How're you feeling? Better?"

She didn't feel one iota better. "Where's Colin?"

"In class. You want me to get him?" Asher asked.

She thought about it. "After we hear what the Sheriff has to say."

He nodded, placed his arm around the back of her chair, and leaned back as if he didn't have a care in the world. "Why are you so calm about this?" she whispered.

"Ever feel like you were being tested? Like someone wants to know how much or how far they can push your buttons to see how you handle yourself?" he asked.

"No, not really."

"That's what this feels like. There's no way we would've gone into that room without a genuine record of what happened and covered ourselves once we left. Only amateurs do that. Whoever shot the old man is living on borrowed time because we have a video of him entering the room and leaving. It's not connected to the hotel security system because, once again, that's amateurish. My team has the person entering and leaving the hotel."

Stunned, she looked at him.

He placed his finger beneath her chin and closed her mouth. "This thing with Henry is escalating and should come to a head soon. I would never put you in danger like that."

"I'm glad to hear it," she said when she could talk. "What does the Sheriff want to talk to you about?"

"We wait and see." He stroked her cheek with his thumb. "Bryson is watching Colin on the cam and will alert me if anything happens before we pick him up."

"Thanks." She took a deep breath and released the tension slowly. "His death is going to be on the news, isn't it?"

"Probably."

"What do I tell Colin?"

"The truth is always good."

She looked at him. "Is he ready for that?"

"Honestly, I don't know," Asher said.

They sat in silent contemplation until the door opened and Jack entered the room.

Asher stood. "What's going on, Jack?"

"Lakewood's not in my district. Brighton's the Sheriff. We get along and he called me with the information regarding the shooting. He's concerned it's going to turn into a media circus with everything that went on before. I told him about the old man showing up at Mya's place Saturday morning and the meeting at noon today. Laura has it on record. Henry called her office demanding a meeting to tell Mya who paid him to grab Colin." He nodded. "Heard the tape myself, handed a copy to Brighton. Henry admitted he'd been paid to search for Colin and wanted to come clean, which is why you went to his hotel room."

Asher nodded.

Mya listened in disbelief. Stuff like this didn't happen to normal people. Joshua Henry had been an opportunistic old man who had no problem wrecking people's lives. Still, he didn't deserve to die that way.

"Brighton wants you and Mya to come down and give a statement regarding the meeting with Henry. He says you were the last to leave his room," Jack said.

"No, we weren't. Whoever shot him was the last to leave his room. Once they have the hotel security cam checked professionally, they'll discover someone tampered with it and won't show what happened in the hall after we left his room. He was alive but expected to die before morning."

"He tell you that? Knew someone would kill him?" Jack asked, not nearly as surprised as Mya thought he should be.

Asher nodded and looked at his watch. "It's getting late. Can we give the statements tomorrow?"

"I'll check." Jack stepped aside and placed a call. After a few moments, he returned. "Someone will come to the house to talk to both of you this evening."

"Thanks, I appreciate that." Asher shook Jack's hand.

"I'm sorry you're still going through all of this, Mya. Versteck Valley isn't normally like this. We live nice, quiet, peaceful lives. Joshua Henry wasn't a very nice person. Still, no one should be gunned down like that. Sheriff Brighton and his men will search for the killer."

Mya had no idea if he was serious, reciting a speech or trying to placate someone he thought was upset over Henry's death. Rather than say something inappropriate, she nodded.

The sheriff left.

"Ready?" Asher asked.

She stood, leaned into him, and said. "He could've told us that at the house or on the phone. Why make us wait?"

"Good question," Asher said as they left the office and headed to the front where Bryson, Ms. Jenkins, and Colin waited.

"Mommy," Colin's face lit up when he saw them. "Asher."

"Hey there," Asher said, stooping down to hug Colin as he ran over. "Did you have a good day in class?"

"Yes, we had a lot of fun. We learned about the ocean and all the things in it," Colin said, stepping back to take his mom's hand.

Mya waved goodbye to Bryson and Ms. Jenkins as they headed toward Asher's Hummer.

During the ride home, Asher's thoughts perched on the things he needed to do. He'd placed a hold on rentals of the Aspen house until Bryson oversaw the replacement of the hardwood floors.

There were a few jobs scheduled this week. Tombs would complete a job tonight and would return as a ghost through the tunnels. Asher would have Wesley manage them just in case he was unavailable. He still hadn't heard from Moses, and that concerned him. Not to the point he would make noise, but if he didn't hear from him soon, he or Drake would contact Senator Bing to get some information.

"What do you want for dinner?" Mya asked, breaking into his thoughts.

"I'm easy," he said.

She smiled, turned in her seat, and looked at Colin. "Spaghetti?"

"And meatballs?" he said, grinning.

"Yep. Lots of meatballs," she said, turning back around and taking Asher's hand.

He squeezed hers.

"Thanks for a wonderful weekend," she whispered.

Asher nodded. "We're staying next door at my place tonight after the detectives leave and tomorrow."

She looked at him and nodded slowly. "Alright. Will we have that conversation tonight or tomorrow?"

He didn't know when a good time was to tell a kid the person you met earlier today was dead. "Whenever you think best."

She exhaled and bit her bottom lip. "Okay. Is Laura coming over? Or is it alright to talk to the police by ourselves?"

Laura's primary concern was that Henry was a pawn. She believed they would pay the locals off to botch the investigation and convict Mya so she lost custody. Henry mentioned a Plan B or C, and Laura jumped on it. She had the tapes and recordings from the meeting in Joshua Henry's hotel room. She and Wesley were engaged in planning a release strategy. She'd been adamant that they handle the release a certain way. Asher wanted to be a part of the meeting, but Mya and Colin came first. Since it wasn't a good idea for either Mya or Colin to be a part of the planning session and Asher wouldn't leave them, he had to trust his friends would come up with the best plan.

"I don't think so. You can call and ask how she wants us to handle it."

She pulled out her phone and made the call.

Asher's thoughts returned to the men who helped them today. Connor had placed the additional camera in the hall just outside Henry's door while waiting for Asher and Mya. Mercer had been monitoring the small camera Asher had pinned to his jacket and the one Asher left in the plant on the table near where he stood.

Laura had been in the SUV listening, watching, and recording the entire conversation. There was another camera in the lobby that tagged the time they arrived and left, as well as who else entered the small hotel.

Mercer and Connor were still on site at the hotel monitoring the sheriff's inquiry. He would check in with them soon. People rarely paid older men attention, especially when they blended in well.

"She said it was okay to talk to them. If we needed her, she'd come over after she left the meeting at Higher Dimensions," Mya said, pulling him from his thoughts.

They pulled into the driveway. She took the garage door opener from her purse and pressed. Asher drove inside and parked.

"Thank you," he said, leaned over and kissed her cheek.

Smiling, she opened the door and stepped out. Colin did the same, grabbed his book bag and went inside.

"You know what, Asher? I bet you don't know what this is," Colin said over his shoulder as he ran to his room and came out holding the white cardboard box.

Mya patted Asher's shoulder and rubbed her finger between his brows. "Good time to get to know him better and ask a few questions, man to man." Smiling, she headed toward the kitchen.

"What is it?" Asher asked as he removed his jacket and followed Colin to the living room sofa.

"Look and see. We made it in class." He held the box up in his hands.

Asher took the box and looked inside at the various colors. After several moments of back and forth, Asher looked at Colin. "Did someone stick you with a needle?"

Colin frowned. "Needle?"

Asher took Colin's left arm, rolled up his sleeves and pointed to the small mark on his arm. He leaned forward, whispering. "Is it a secret?"

Wide-eyed, Colin shook his head, glanced at the kitchen and back at his arm. "I was sleep."

"Who stuck you with the needle?" Asher whispered.

"I don't know who it was, I was sleeping."

"Did it hurt?" Asher asked.

Colin nodded.

"Did you wake-up?"

Colin nodded.

"Did you see who hurt you?"

Colin frowned. "I think so."

"Who?"

"One teacher."

"Which one?"

Colin shrugged and looked at the box again.

Asher didn't push or show his frustration. At least they knew it was someone who worked at the school.

When they sat for dinner, Mya told Colin about the death of his grandfather and their visit to his hotel room. She let him know the police were coming over later to talk to her and Asher about that visit.

Asher wouldn't have told Colin that much, but it was Mya's call. Colin seemed to take it well. "Does this mean I'll never see him again?"

"Yes, baby," Mya said.

Colin seemed to think about it and nodded. "Okay. How did he die?"

"I don't know yet," she said.

"Will it be on television?" Colin asked.

"I don't know that either. Are you alright?" she asked as she rubbed his arm. "He was your grandfather."

Colin shrugged. "I didn't know him." With that pronouncement, the conversation changed to spending the night next door and what he could take with him.

After dinner, Detectives Wynn, and Vinson arrived. They were cordial, asked a few questions, and listened intently as Asher and Mya repeated what happened in Henry's hotel room.

"Someone tampered with the hotel's camera. Any ideas about that?" Detective Vinson, a smaller version of the former movie star Telly Savalas, asked.

"Other than they wanted to make it look like we were the last ones to enter the hotel room, none," Asher said.

Vinson nodded and stood. "If we have more questions, we'll be in touch. Is this the best place to find you?" He looked at Asher.

"Yes, this is fine." Asher stood and walked toward the door.

Both men left.

Mya remained seated, staring at the floor.

"You okay?" Asher asked.

"No. This is such an ugly mess. I wish Joshua Henry never started any of this. Now he's dead, and it's a shame, but he started this ball rolling, and I hate that more," she said and covered her eyes.

He pulled her up and wrapped his arms around her. "It's been a long day. We left the mountains late, then the meeting with Henry at Laura's, coming here instead of resting, we left again to meet with Henry. The day dragged on and on. Let's get some sleep. Tomorrow will be brighter. We're both tired and operating on fumes."

She nodded, took a deep breath. "Alright. In the morning, you're making breakfast. I want to sleep in."

"Deal."

CHAPTER TWENTY-THREE

T WO DAYS LATER, ASHER listened to the news while clearing out his email. Mya was still in bed asleep. He smiled in remembrance of what he termed his early morning appetizer. He swiped his tongue across his lips, still tasting her sweet essence. Nothing beat early morning sex, late night sex was a close second. But waking her in the morning either with his mouth on her mound or his cock filling her sweetness were the best moments of the day.

Colin sat on the sofa in Asher's office, doing something on his mom's laptop. The two of them had eaten peanut butter and jelly sandwiches earlier before coming to his office.

His phone rang. He looked at the caller ID. *Laura.* "Good morning."

"You haven't heard the news, I take it," she said.

"Probably not," he said, glancing at Colin.

"Sheriff Brighton found the man who killed Joshua Henry. Found him last night, went to his hotel to arrest him, claimed he fired at the Deputy and was killed avoiding arrest. Guess what they found in the room where he was staying?"

"Colin, you want something else to eat or drink?" Asher said.

"No, thank you."

"Ah, I see. No wonder you're so slow this morning. You've got company. In that case, no guessing," she said.

"Much appreciated," he said.

"They found the murder weapon, photos of the deceased, Henry's itinerary, everything except a huge neon arrow pointing at his back," she said with heat.

"Cover-up?"

"In capital letters. Don't get me wrong, I'm sure that guy pulled the trigger and took the fall. But only because they realized the plan against Mya wouldn't work and went to Plan C," she said.

"I thought that was Plan C." He didn't think Henry's death ranked all of this behind the scenes plotting, but Laura was rarely wrong with her conspiracy theories.

"Possibly. Things are moving fast. Something must have happened."

"Has any of this hit the major news?" he asked in a lowered voice, turning from Colin and turning off the television behind him.

"Not yet. Expect it to happen. Wouldn't be surprised if some reporter dug a little deeper," she said. "By the way, the three assistant teachers in Colin's class are on administrative leave during the investigation. No extra money in their bank accounts or recent expenditures. Nothing that points to any of them being involved, plus they swear they had nothing to do with it. I believe them," she said.

"If not them, who? Ms. Jenkins?" He couldn't see her doing it either, but stranger things happened.

"No, I don't think so. Could be another teacher or staff. We're still investigating."

"It was hard keeping him home from school yesterday. Mya had to explain several times why he couldn't go. We promised to go to the park later today, maybe a picnic or something." He watched to see if Colin was listening. When there was no response, Asher leaned back in his chair. "Weather should be nice today."

"Sounds good, but it should be okay if he returned to school." She paused. "Bonnie's really upset by all this, leaves a stain on the school, and that's her baby. She's not going to let this rest. Eventually, she'll find out who took the bribe and drew his blood. You can count on that."

"Much appreciated," he said, unsure if Mya would allow Colin to return to school before they found the person. "Thanks for keeping me in the loop."

"Of course. Talk to you later." She hung up.

Laura might be on to something with this new theory. The question was, how did it impact Mya and Colin? He looked across the room at the boy. "What's wrong?" he asked. "Why're you frowning?" Asher stood, walked over, and sat on the arm of the sofa, waiting for an answer.

"Atoms."

"Huh?"

"We've been working with atoms and making models in class. I'm missing working on my model with everyone else."

Asher's brow rose. "You're upset because you're not in school?" He'd never heard of a kid wanting to be in school for academic reasons.

Colin nodded, but didn't look at him.

"Tell you what, go ask your mom if you can go and we'll take you. But only if she says you can go."

"Is the problem fixed?" Colin asked, looking up at him.

Their gazes met. Asher read Colin's trust and acceptance of whatever he said. His chest constricted and expanded. "There's an investigation going on. Ms. Jenkins' is working in the class by herself today." He didn't want to say too much and cross the line into lying.

Colin nodded, slipped off the sofa, leaving the laptop, and ran out of the room. Asher pulled the laptop closer to see what Colin had been doing. Sure enough, there were images of atoms, hierarchies, splits, and stuff that would give Asher a headache.

He returned to his desk to finish dealing with his email. Mya and Colin entered the room a few moments later. She wore a confused look and one of his tee-shirts that hit mid-thigh. Maybe after dropping Colin off at school, they could return for some alone time and inspiration. She hadn't released any new stories since they met. Maybe he could help fuel her imagination with a few toys he kept in his room.

"What happened?" she asked as Colin returned to the laptop after giving him a pleading look.

"They found the guy who knocked off Henry."

Her eyes widened. She placed one hand on her chest, the other on the corner of his desk. "What? When? How'd they do that so fast?"

In a lowered voice, he told her what Laura said.

"That's... I don't know what to say behind that." She shook her head. "Colin wants to go to school. Did Laura say anything about that?"

"Yeah, she did." He shared that information as well.

Mya's lips pursed and brows furrowed. "They still don't know who did it."

"No, they don't."

"What do you think?"

"I don't know. Bryson's there and will be in the room during nap-time until they sort this out. Security's good. But it's always been good, and someone found a way around it." He shrugged. "It's your call. I'm down with whatever you decide."

She looked at Colin. He sat slumped in the seat, looking as if his world had collapsed. Asher wasn't sure if it was an act or real. Just as he was about to ask Mya, she moved to the sofa.

"Colin, do you understand why we kept you home from school yesterday?"

He nodded. "Because someone took my blood without permission, and no one knows who did it."

His mom nodded. "No one should ever do that."

"I know."

"But you want to go back to school, and we still don't know who did it," she said, frustration ripe in her voice.

"Maybe they're gone and won't come back. Ms. Wails and Ms. Jenkins won't ever let it happen again. I think it's alright to go back to school, Mommy. I want to finish my project," he said.

Impressed by the short speech, Asher knew before Mya nodded she would let the boy return to school.

"Alright, go get dressed. I'll get dressed too. I've missed work most of the week, might as well go in and earn my check." She stood and looked at him. "We're going next door to get some clothes."

This was not how he envisioned their day going. "I'll come with you, and you can dress there."

She smiled and nodded.

His dick hardened. He cursed beneath his breath as he stood. With Colin bouncing with excitement, no way would they be able to get in a quickie. He'd have to be satisfied with last night and this morning's wake-up call.

CHAPTER
TWENTY-FOUR

M YA STEPPED INTO HER office and stopped. Maggie and Chastity stood in the outer office, waiting.

"Haven't we done this already?" Mya said, happy her assistant wasn't around for this awkward moment.

Chastity moved closer and took her hands in hers. "This time we want you to know we're so sorry for everything that's happened since you've been here. Versteck's not usually like this. We look out for our own, we have to, but for the most part we live quiet, peaceful lives."

That's what everyone keeps telling me. "Which is why I feel so bad about bringing my problems here. Granted, I'd never had them before, but that doesn't matter," Mya said. "The last thing I want to do is draw attention to the Arms or the town. People should be able to live the way they want without interference, as long as they aren't hurting other people."

Maggie stepped closer with outstretched arms and hugged her. "I'm so glad you're a part of our community and staying here. I've been worried you would leave once you found out about the Arms. They're good people who want to live quietly in peace. We give them that."

"And my man is the boss." Her brow rose when she said that.

Maggie looked embarrassed. "We can never talk about that. Not to anyone. But I'm glad the two of you found each other. I've never seen him with anyone before."

"Never seen him settled or content. He's happy with his cousins," Chastity said. "You'll meet Moses and Drake. Real hunks, fine and good looking. Still single."

"Drake and Beamer are close friends, went to school together," Maggie said.

Chastity nodded. "Drake's a trip. I can't wait to meet the woman who reels him in. She'll have her hands full."

"More like he'll have his hands full," Mya said, thinking of Asher. "Men don't always fall for the women they think they want, more like the woman they need to be with to feel whole, complete. That's different for each person."

The two women looked at her for a few seconds and smiled. "You're right," Maggie said as she walked to the door. "Welcome to Versteck Arms. Now you'll really get to know us, and I'm happy I can be free around you."

Touched, Mya nodded. "It's a bit much to take in. Soon as I get some time and the world slows down. I'll do more research about the "Robber's Roost" and the wild west. For now, I'm taking it one day at a time."

"Best way to digest everything," Chastity said, coming to stand in front of her as Maggie slipped out. "How's Colin? He found and lost his grandfather the same day."

"He seems to be alright. He wanted to work on a project at school, Bryson's going to shadow him most of the day, so we let him go. Yesterday was hellacious, and I wasn't looking forward to a repeat of whining, complaining, arguing and sulks over not going to school." Mya shook her head. "Only my kid would throw a fit over staying home from school."

Chastity laughed. "Well, I'm sure things will work out. Like Maggie, I want to welcome you to the real Versteck Arms. For us, Versteck Valley is the safest place in the world and the best place to raise a family. For our enemies, it's a nightmare of gigantic proportions. Don't let their ages fool you. These men are sharp, with years of experience and still at the top of their game. They'll treat you as their daughter and the "Boss' Lady." They have their own code of ethics and self-police really well. You're safe here."

"Thanks, Chastity. You're the absolute best boss, hands-down. Thanks for being so understanding about all the time I've taken off."

Chastity waved down her comment. "We do things differently in Versteck. You're family and have been for a while. The men adopted you before Asher got his hands and everything else on you." She winked and left the office.

CHAPTER
TWENTY-FIVE

Wesley was Mya's last client before lunch. She planned to return home and have a long break with Asher. Just thinking about the things he would do to her made her nipples hard, core clench and panties damp. Lord have mercy, she was addicted to that man.

"I'm glad you're back, and things worked out," Wesley said, standing and moving toward the door.

Mya stood but remained behind her desk. "Me too. Should I still discount everything I hear?" She had been wondering about that after her first appointment. Had Kelly really assembled a home-made bomb?

"Yes. Most of its fantasy mixed with bits of truth. You're a precious resource where we can freely clear our minds of toxic ideas, dreams, and desires. Nothing should be considered truth or something you can testify in court about," he said.

Relief swamped her. "Thanks, Wesley. I appreciate that. Enjoy the rest of your day."

He waved goodbye and left.

With a quick look at the clock, she grinned. "If I leave early, I can pick up something from the drive-through, head home, and do a striptease. Wonder how far I'd get before he pulls me down?" She loved Asher's sense of sexual adventure, things were never boring in bed. Grabbing her purse from the drawer, she picked up her phone just as it rang.

"Hey, I'm leaving now," she told Asher.

"Stay there for the moment," he said.

Dread rolled down her back at the chill in his voice. "What happened?"

"Bryson was shot by Ms. Jenkins when she took Colin from school--"

She screamed and dropped the phone.

Moments later, the door opened. Wesley and Chastity took her hand.

Mya couldn't stop shaking. "They took my son. My baby. Lord, please help me."

Chastity wrapped her in her arms.

Wesley picked up the phone and took a few steps to the side.

Misery swamped Mya. "I should've kept him at home. I'm the parent. I should've made him stay home until this was all over." She stared at Chastity. "This is my fault."

"No, it's not your fault. Whoever took him, it's their fault," Chastity said.

"His teacher. Ms. Jenkins took him," Mya said, still finding it hard to believe. "I thought she liked him."

"Jenkins took him?" Chastity sounded just as surprised.

"She shot Bryson."

"They were sleeping together," Chastity said, appalled.

"What? And she shot him?" Mya couldn't process that or most of this. Sorrow weighed heavily on her chest.

"He never would've let her take Colin, no matter how good she was in bed or whatever kind of relationship they had. Like I told you, these men have a code of ethics. Asher is their boss. Beamer made that clear before we married. There are lines they won't cross no matter what," Chastity said, tugging Mya gently to sit down.

Tears ran down Mya's cheeks as she wrapped her arms around her waist. "I can't just sit here while he's out there. I have to look for him. Have to help him. I should've kept him home, he would be mad, but he'd be safe," she murmured as a weight of despair dropped on her shoulders. "They'll take him away, far away, and we won't find him."

"We'll find your son," Wesley said, his voice strong, confident. He held her phone to her. "Asher needs to talk to you. He's in motion, so is everyone else. He wants me to stay here with you so I can take you to him once he has Colin."

She took the phone. "Asher."

"I'm so sorry this happened. It's not your fault. We'll find out why Jenkins turned and get Colin back. Can you stay there while we search? It'll make it easier to focus on finding Colin and not both of you," he said.

"I can't just sit here doing nothing. I can't. I have to help," she pleaded for him to give her something to do.

"We're looking for a white male with dark hair, light-colored eyes driving a late model black Suburban. If you and Wesley can check that out, it'd help."

"Who is it?" she asked as she moved behind her desk to make calls.

"The man waiting in the car that drove off with Jenkins and Colin. Several people saw him waiting."

"What?"

"Jenkins took Colin through the playground. When Bryson stopped her, she told Colin she was taking him to you. Something about you'd called and wanted them to meet you."

"Oh God," she said. Colin would've gone without a second thought.

"Bryson tried to stop her. She told Colin Bryson was one of the evil men. She'd protect him and shot him. Bryson's got this thing against hurting women, almost got him killed," Asher sounded disgusted.

"Plus, they were sleeping together," she said.

"There's that too. It's a cluster-fuck of epic proportions. He's in the hospital in surgery, and we've set up a net to find her. I want them all. This needs to stop now. Colin won't be looking over his shoulder the rest of his life."

"I know you hate it when I say this, but thank you. I needed to hear you say that."

"Stay there, so I'm not distracted and let me work."

She didn't like it, but he was better than her at this. *What about the tunnels?* "Does Ms. Jenkins know about the tunnels?"

"Doubtful, but I don't know for sure. It'd be difficult for her to access them even if she knew about them. Why?"

"If she takes Colin into the tunnels, they could get lost," she said.

He cursed. "Can't ask Bryson, he's in surgery, and he'd be the only person who might've talked about them to her or taken her down." He cursed again. "Good point. I'll have a sweep of them."

Feeling she'd been of some help; she took a deep breath and released it slowly. "I'm trusting you, Asher."

"I know how difficult this is for you and appreciate you trusting me in this. Talk to you soon." He disconnected.

Mya and Wesley worked for the next 20 minutes searching for information on the person who drove the car Ms. Jenkins left with Colin in. With each passing second and no word from Asher, her nerves tightened to the breaking point.

"We need to go check the tunnels," she told Wesley. "Asher said he would have them checked, but everyone's above ground. We need to make sure they're clear." She grabbed her purse and headed to the door.

"You can access the tunnels?" he asked.

That stopped her. "No. I've been below once with Asher, but I can't. You can." Teary-eyed, she stared at him. "I've got to do something. I can't just sit here. Please help me. Let's clear the tunnels. If she took him down there and they're lost or can't get out... he's just a little boy, no matter how mature he sounds. He's my little boy and I have to help find him. I can't just sit here... I can't lose another son... I have to look for him. He could be lost or hurt or..." She broke down crying and covered her face as visions of her son calling for her ran across her mind. He would be scared by now, especially since they hadn't come to find her.

Wesley patted her shoulder. "It's alright. I'll help. We'll check the tunnels. Should've thought of it myself. Pull yourself together. I'll let Asher know what we're about and we'll go down. Just give me a minute to get a few things."

Too grateful to be embarrassed, she nodded and went to the bathroom to fix her face. Moments later, her phone rang. She wasn't surprised it was Asher.

"Have you found him?"

"Not yet, but we're closer. Can you wait for me to go into the tunnels?"

"I have to do something now," she said firmly. "I'm going out of my mind sitting here thinking, wondering... Ms. Jenkins would only fool Colin for a short while before he realized something was wrong. I'm going with Wesley."

"Alright, thanks for your patience so far. Take down this code."

Stunned by his quick capitulation, she went to her desk for a pen.

"Type it in your phone. You can't leave it lying around."

"Alright." She pulled up the notepad on her phone and typed in a code.

"This won't get you in the tunnels. You're not set up for that yet. Wesley will take you down. Use this code to leave through any door in the tunnels otherwise, none of the doors at the top of the stairs will open. Once you go through a door, you can't go back down, understand?"

"Yes, thanks." Relief with a sense of purpose filled her. "If we find anything, we'll let you know."

"Can you shoot a gun?"

"No. I've never seen one until you showed me yours."

"You realize Ms. Jenkins shot Bryson, right?"

She nodded, realized he couldn't see her. "Yes. I hope she won't shoot us."

"Wesley's not Bryson. He'll shoot first and ask questions later, which is why I'm not shitting bricks about you going into the tunnels without me. He's steady and will be a good person to handle the search. I can't send anyone down to help right now, but after we get Colin, I'll let you know."

"That's if they aren't in the tunnels," she said.

"Right, that." His tone said he didn't think they were in the tunnels. He disconnected.

Were they on a fool's errand? Maybe, but if there was a chance, no matter how slight, they should check it out. She would be doing something to help.

When Wesley returned, he wore a long gray coat and waved her forward. They entered an area of the Arms she had never seen before. The security panel was unnoticeable unless you knew where to look. After completing the scans and entering the code, the door opened.

Wesley ushered her in first and followed close behind. The door shut behind them. Lights turned on, illuminating the stairs. She held onto the rail.

"Me first," Wesley said as he passed her.

It didn't take long for them to enter the tunnels. As they reached certain sections, lights turned on, allowing her to see long stretches of carved rock. They walked single file in silence.

"Stay here. I'm going to check this exit." Wesley walked a short distance and disappeared from sight.

Mya looked behind her into the darkness and shivered. The light had turned off once they left that section, and it looked spooky. Suddenly, being in the tunnels no longer seemed like a good idea. She took several deep breaths and started shaking as the walls closed in around her.

"Wesley?" she called and moved in the direction she'd seen him walk. The light went out in the area where she'd been standing.

She whirled and cried out. "Wesley?"

She tried to find him. Lights came on and she took a deep, shivering breath. "It's okay. It's okay," she murmured looking around. Where was she? She didn't want the lights to turn off and kept moving in the direction she'd seen Wesley go.

Minutes later, she tripped over her foot and broke her fall on the wall next to a staircase. The lights went out. Without a second thought, she scrambled up the stairs, typed in Asher's code and opened the door into a room of an old abandoned house. Chilled, she rubbed her arms as she stepped fully inside and closed the door. Her phone rang.

"Why'd you leave Wesley in the tunnels and enter the house on Fairmont?" Asher asked.

She knew Fairmont Street. After taking a deep breath, she told him what happened with the lights turning on and off and her fear.

"I thought I told you about the lights," he said.

"No, you didn't."

"That's my fault. I'll let Wesley know. When you go outside, I'll have someone come to pick you up." He hung up before she could asked questions. She went up the stairs. The place smelled musty and rank. Moving through the kitchen, she headed toward the living room and stopped.

There was someone in there.

CHAPTER TWENTY-SIX

T HE MOMENT ASHER RECEIVED the call from Bonnie that Ms. Jenkins had taken Colin, he had been in motion. Within minutes, he had men at every checkpoint to stop her from leaving Versteck Valley.

They had spotted Jenkins less than five minutes after leaving the school with Colin. She and the driver had separated not long after. Alone, she ran to an all-terrain vehicle and drove off across the mountain pass. If successful, she would reach a highly populated ski area, but the terrain was brutal, which is why few ever tried to cross.

Asher wasn't interested in her reasons or feelings for betraying the school and sent Tombs to get her. He didn't believe in hurting women, but assured Asher he would do whatever was necessary to protect himself after learning what she did to Bryson.

The driver continued to the edge of town, stopped, and carried Colin into a large cargo van with other men and weapons.

Connor shot out all four tires when they tried to drive off. The van moved a few feet, but with the weight inside, it couldn't go far or at any speed, which allowed Asher's men to completely box them in.

They remained at a standstill for a few moments when he heard the helicopter in the distance. After a few shots were fired from the copter, Connor shot the gunner. The helicopter flew off.

"They may come back, stay low and hidden," Asher advised his team through their communicators.

When Wesley called, Asher knew his luck had run out. Mya had been patient a lot longer than he'd expected. No way would he tell her what was going on down here, she'd be there in five minutes flat making the perfect hostage because she would go to that van and snatch her son. He didn't like her going to the tunnels without him but going with Wesley, who didn't have the same qualms as Bryson or many of the others when it came to dealing with women in a fight, he let it go. She would be safe down there. Wesley would be watching her, and it would keep her mind off what he was doing up here.

Minutes later, Jack and his deputies arrived. It had never occurred to Asher to contact the Sheriff. Apparently, it didn't cross Bonnie's mind either. Someone must have seen the helicopter or heard the shot and called it in.

"What's going on?" Jack asked.

Asher explained the kidnapping and the man meeting the van. "He's got Colin inside." Since his company provided security for the school, Jack wasn't surprised by the firepower Asher carried.

Jack frowned. "I thought all of that was over since the old man died and his killer caught. There's more to all of this than we knew."

Asher nodded.

"I can call in some help, some backup. Brighton would be glad to assist."

"Go ahead. "We need Colin out of there as soon as possible," Asher said, willing to go the legal route for the moment. If things went south, they would do whatever was necessary to save Colin. One thing was certain: Colin was not leaving with anyone other than Asher or one of his men.

Jack stepped aside to make his call.

"I've got Jenkins," Tombs said. "Someone should tell the little lady that all-terrain doesn't mean mountain climbing. Her truck's stuck, wouldn't move. She started walking. Being the gentleman I am, I let her tire herself out before picking her up. Got her nice and tied in the back and taking her to Laura for the time being."

Asher could only imagine Ms. Jenkins' reception when faced with Bonnie and Laura. As far as the law would be concerned, Ms. Florence Jenkins escaped the long arm of justice, never to be heard or seen again.

"Jack's recruited the help of Sheriff Brighton. I think they plan to negotiate with the kidnappers now that they can't move and are surrounded."

"Duh," Tombs said. "Can't wait to see how that pans out. Soon as I drop off this package, I'll be headed that way."

"Sounds good," Asher said, watching Brighton step out of his car. Had the man been on his way? How'd he respond so quickly?

Brighton and Jack talked for a few moments. Jack stepped back as Brighton retrieved a megaphone from his trunk and spoke into it. "This is the Sheriff, send out the boy."

Asher didn't respond to the snickers or snide comments he heard over his communicator. Nor was he surprised when there was no response from the kidnappers. It had to be hot inside the van even with the engine running. He wondered what the Sheriff would do next.

After a few minutes, he motioned Jack over. "Get Colin out of there now. He's been in there too long."

Jack looked at him and nodded.

"I'll go with you," Asher offered and noticed the look of relief on Jack's face as he walked over to Brighton, talked to him a few moments. The two of them unholstered their weapons and headed to the van. They split up, one going to the driver's side, the other to the passenger's side.

Glock in hand, semi-automatic on his back beneath his long jacket, Asher walked slowly behind them and stood where he could cover them both. He wasn't as good a shot as Connor. Few people in the world were, but he was accurate and steady. Brighton talked to someone, nodded, and after a few moments of conversation, backtracked to Asher. Jack joined him.

"They've agreed to let the boy go, but they want to leave. They were hired to take the child away and aren't vested in him at all. I say we let them go," Brighton said, looking at Jack and then Asher.

"Getting Colin back safe is the most important thing, right?" Jack asked.

"Yes, that's what's most important. Did you see him? How's Colin doing?" Asher asked.

"No. He's in the back. I didn't get a good look at him," Brighton said, almost defensively.

Asher nodded, rather than yell and call them names. These men had retired to low-crime areas to deal with jobs that required minimum fuss and exertion. Their hearts weren't into asking questions like, what if they come back for Colin with more men and weapons? Who hired them? Where did they plan on taking Colin? Someone in that van had answers, and Asher intended to hear them. His team would do what the law was too lazy to do.

"So, we're agreed? I'll tell him they can go as soon as they release the boy," Brighton said.

"How do they plan to leave?" Asher asked, looking at their van.

"Copter's coming back to pick'em up. Just got to be sure your men don't shoot at 'em." Brighton's brow rose in question.

"We want the boy back. The rest will be dealt with later," Asher said. "This was a kidnapping, he was stolen from school. They can leave for now."

"Now's all I care about," Brighton said with relief.

Jack held Asher's gaze for a few moments and nodded. "We'll get Colin to safety first; the rest can come later."

Asher nodded.

Brighton was already at the van talking. Asher sent a text to his team explaining what was going on. No one liked the idea of the kidnappers going free. They'd taken a child, and that held a penalty. The men wanted to make sure was paid in full.

Three men stepped out the van. Tall, pale, armed. They stood near the vehicle as the sound of the copter drew closer.

"Where's the boy?" Connor yelled.

The three men immediately looked around trying to find him but wouldn't unless he wanted them too.

"They'll release the boy once they're on the copter," Brighton yelled.

"No, release the boy first. We have to make sure he's alright," Asher said, glaring at Jack for this punk-ass move. Who the hell did they think were in charge? The kidnappers?

The three men started moving back toward the van.

"Stop," Jack said.

Asher's phone beeped. "Beamer, what you got?"

"Just as you thought, Gregory Parson was staying at a hotel in Denver under another name. Once I verified his identity, I picked him up, and we're on our way to you. Figured you'd like to have a chat with him," Beamer said.

"Most definitely. That's welcome news. Place him in a cage as a guest of the Arms Mecca." He referred to the second building behind the Arms that belonged solely to him.

"Will do. Should be there within the hour. Anything else?"

He shared what was happening with Colin and the kidnappers. "They expect us to let them go."

Beamer snorted. "I'll be happy to be on the round-up team to teach them some manners. I think Parson's the one who ordered the pickup, I'm sure he'll be happy to explain all the reasons when you talk to him later."

"No doubt," Asher said, watching Brighton. His phone beeped, and he looked at the message. "Good job. Gotta deal with this." Mya had just used his code to access the door in the house on Fairmont. Their conversation had been brief. He'd been wrong in not telling her about the lighting system and would make it up to her by taking Colin with him to pick her up. He sent Wesley a quick text to let him know Mya was alright.

"Stop right there, don't move," Jack yelled, finally finding his voice, and acting like a Sheriff. "Send the boy out first."

Brighton left the driver's side of the van and headed toward Jack.

"I'm going in," Asher told his team and walked toward the van ignoring the three men who watched him but didn't move. When he reached the driver's door, he opened it and looked inside.

A pale complexioned man with a military cut sat holding Colin.

Asher pulled out his weapon and pointed it at the man. "What happened to him?"

"The woman gave him something to make him sleep when he started fighting her and yelling for her to take him to his mother."

"Who are you?" Asher demanded.

"That's not important. Are you here to help him or give him to the other side?"

"Don't know anything about sides. I'm here to take him back to his mother. She'll hurt every one of us if anything happens to her child." Asher met the man's gaze. "Seriously, she'll go after anyone who tries to hurt this one."

"And you and your invisible men will assist her?"

"Abso-fucking-lutely. Every time and any time." Asher wanted to be clear on that point.

They continued staring at each other for a few moments. The man nodded.

"Good. All we wanted was for him to be safe and cared for." He waved. "Those men have nothing to do with this. I hired them to help me take him away to safety. They know nothing. Take me and let them go."

Asher had so many questions, but now wasn't the time. He had to get Colin to Mya before she set the town on fire, searching for her son.

"Alright. They can go after we've left. You're coming with us. Hand me Colin. If you don't want a bullet in your forehead or heart, don't make any fast movements," he warned the kidnapper as he holstered his gun.

"You and I want the same for him." He placed Colin in Asher's arms.

Asleep, he looked peaceful and calm. "Do you know what she gave him?"

"No, sorry I don't. It was some kind of shot and done before I could stop her," he said, following Asher.

"Let them go after we leave," Asher told Jack as the helicopter came closer and the men below waited.

"Is he alright?" Jack asked.

"She gave him something to make him sleep," Asher said, more for his team than Jack. He looked at Tombs and motioned him close. "Take him to Mecca, place him next to the guest Beamer just brought in. Make them comfortable. We'll talk to them later tonight, after I get Colin and Mya settled."

Tombs nodded and walked the kidnapper to his truck, looking like two buds on a stroll until the door opened. Tombs frisked the prisoner, took his weapons, and secured his wrists with plastic ties.

"We'll see you later," Tombs said, letting Asher know everything was alright. Two other team members slid into the back seat next to the prisoner and they drove off.

CHAPTER TWENTY-SEVEN

M YA JERKED TO A stop. Her eyes widened. She had to be seeing things. The man on the ground in front of her looked suspiciously like... no, it couldn't be. He was dead. She was upset and scared, in need of rest and fresh air, that's all.

Still, she couldn't look away. His face was bruised, eyelids half-closed. She wasn't sure if he was awake or asleep, but she needed to move past him to get outside to meet Asher's man.

She took another step.

He grunted or maybe snarled, she wasn't sure, but she stopped. Shaking, heart in her throat, she watched him for a few moments, looked around the living room, saw a large blanket, food wrappings and when she inhaled, the odor of piss. Had he been living here?

She moved forward. He got up.

Barefoot, he stood several inches over her. His unbuttoned shirt gaped open, displaying a well-defined chest and arms littered with tattoos. The top button of his dark jeans was loose. The pants fit snug over thick, muscular thighs, and hips.

His tattoos jarred a memory. Her breath hitched as she looked at him closer. Leaner, rougher, but he could be.

"Colin?" she whispered, afraid she was seeing a ghost and losing her mind.

He didn't respond but continued looking at her with those weird half-closed eyes. Then he shifted on the balls of his feet. Her breath locked in her throat when she saw his eyes and battered face.

"Who did this to you?" she whispered, looking at him differently. "Where have you been all this time?" Distrustful over who stood in front of her, she could either cry, shriek in fear or ask crazy questions.

He grunted and shook his head. The military hair cut heightened his high cheekbones and now gaunt features. "What's going on, Colin?" If this was him, she hoped he would answer her. Otherwise, she needed to get out of there right now.

"Mya?" the word sounded guttural, confused.

Fear latched onto her with a parasitic grip as she nodded and looked around the small area. "What happened? They said you were dead. Your father thought you were dead. No one told us about the funeral. Did you do that? You didn't want Colin there?" *What did any of that matter?* She had to think rationally but couldn't get past the point of seeing the dead raised.

"Colin," he said and closed his eyes as he staggered back.

She reached out to steady him and was surprised by how solid he felt. He stopped and looked down at her hand before looking at her face.

"Mya?"

She removed her hand and fought the instinct to move back, to run. Something was really wrong. Colin was dead. But he wasn't. "Are you Colin Henry?"

"Colin?"

"You look like Colin, but I need to be sure. Are you Colin Henry, Senior?"

He shook his head, took several deep breaths, and exhaled. "Mya?"

Frustrated, she nodded while staring at him. "I'm not going crazy. You're not Colin. He's dead. He's been dead for three years. The military gave my son a flag. He's dead." She crossed her arms to stop shaking.

"Wait a minute. It's...it's the drugs. I can't always think clearly. Wait."

She swallowed hard. Did he know what happened to her son? Did he know where Colin was?

"I don't have time to wait. I'm looking for Colin, my son. Someone took him. We know who took him, but she gave him to someone else. We need to find him before it's too late," she said, watching his eyes clear.

"She gave him to me, gave him to --"

Mya screamed and swung at his face, knocking him back. Tears blurred her vision as she kept swinging and kicking and yelling. "You gave them my son! I'll kill you! How could you give them my baby? He's just a baby!"

He grabbed one arm, then the other, and grunted when she kicked his leg.

"Stop. Stop and listen," he growled close to her ear.

"No, you listen and tell me where they took him. Where did they take my son? I swear I'll kill you if he's hurt," she yelled, seeing red.

"I'm dead."

Suddenly cold, she stopped struggling and stared at him.

"You're not crazy. Legally I'm dead. A part of a testing program. There's another group who wants to copy what we're doing. They want my son. When I saw... saw the old man on television, I knew what was going on. Griffin's helping me. I sent Griffin to take Colin and keep him safe until I fix this."

His face may have been gaunt, but his hands were like steel cuffs around her wrists. She couldn't break free. "Let me go."

He released her.

She stepped back, sending him a hate-filled look. "This is all your fault. Why're you doing this to him? How could you do this?" she asked, wiping the tears from her face.

"If the old man hadn't gone public, we wouldn't have known where they would strike next. They gave me a short window to clean this up. They used the female to draw his blood, to take him from the school. We had to step in, take him to keep him safe." He shook his head. "There are moments when I can't remember anything, blackouts, but ... doesn't matter. I'll never be able to live with regular people and had to give up everything." He shrugged. "I made sure Colin was well taken care of."

"Only financially, and you didn't answer my questions," she snapped as the realization hit. *Colin was alive.* He was alive and talking to her. She couldn't wrap her mind around it.

"A good financial future was all I could give him." He paused, shook his head as if he would said more, and thought better of it. "For the moment, he's safe. I plan to eliminate the threat to him, at least the current threat, and destroy his records so they can't continue operating." His words became clearer and more coherent with each passing second.

"Were you in the program when we met? When I got pregnant?" she asked, afraid of what that meant for her son.

"I'd taken a couple shots, that's all. When I realized it was about altering more than I'd been originally told, I quit and went back to my unit. Didn't notice anything initially. The symptoms didn't show until a few years down the road, and they placed me in the program. It wasn't a choice but an order. The blackouts were worse then, and so were my actions. When I saw a tape of what I had done during a blackout, I agreed to die and join the program. You got the letter about my death and Colin was taken care of."

Mya's mouth dropped open. She waited for the punchline, for him to say "just teasing" or something equally insane. But he looked serious. She swallowed hard and prayed he wouldn't kill her for sharing his secret. This was so much worse than Asher's secrets. She would never give him a hard time again.

"That's why they drew his blood to see if he was affected by what happened to me. From what I was told, he's clean." He paused, closed his eyes tightly, as if in pain. "But that won't stop the men who want to copy our program."

"If he's clean, why do they want him?" she said, so afraid she had to whisper the question.

"Exactly." He opened his eyes. Their gazes met, and she saw Colin, the father of her son, discussing what kind of school he wanted Colin to attend, the sports he planned to teach him, and the results of their son's physical. That man loved his son and would do whatever was necessary to keep Colin safe.

"What can I do to help?" She said, sensing she had a partner with the same goal, keeping their child away from the bad people.

He released a long, ragged sigh. "I'll remove the head or the known head. Something like this goes deep into rival governments, corporate enterprises, or various militaries. Everyone wants to be first, on the cutting edge of every new weapon, toy, or life-altering drug." Sweat ran down his temple. He swiped at it. "That should buy him some time, enough to grow older, stronger, wiser. But they'll always watch him and in time will try to woo him to work for them. Colin's too bright a star to keep hidden for long." He rubbed his forehead. "I promise to do my best to get him back to you soon."

Not good enough.

"Why didn't they breed you to have more kids?" She was being sarcastic.

"They did. Colin has a brother and sister, twins."

That knocked the wind out of her, but she recovered. "Uh, no he doesn't. You're dead, remember?" she reminded him. Obviously, those two weren't public knowledge and safe. Lucky them.

He nodded. "True. They'll never be introduced as such. Look, right now Colin's in danger because Parson's group thinks he can help them in their program. He can't. Parson knows this, but is too greedy to admit it. He'd sacrifice my son to win a contract. That's not going to happen. We made sure he wouldn't receive another contract. In the meantime, Colin must remain hidden to be safe until I clean the nest of Parson's backers. Give me a month or two, and then Colin will be returned."

"Hell no. You've lost your mind if you think I'll wait 30, 60 or 90 days for him to come home. I won't do that," she said, thinking of Asher and the men in the Arms. "We'll find my son and deal with whoever's trying to take him," she said with a stubborn tilt to her head.

They locked gazes for a few moments. She read his sorrow and pain over what happened, but couldn't allow it to matter. If he were telling the truth, he would never be an active part of Colin's life. That fell to her and, hopefully, Asher. Which meant his thoughts and feelings weren't a priority.

"Go before I pass out again. It's getting hard to think, soon I won't be able to talk. You shouldn't tell anyone you saw me, especially Colin. This was a blip that never should've happened and if you make a big deal out of it, well, remember I work for the government, and they'll mess up your life."

He didn't have to tell her twice. She walked past him.

"Thanks for doing such a good job with him. I'm proud of him," he said.

She looked back over her shoulder. He stood with his head down, hands curled in fists and the veins rising on his neck. Every vampire and shape-shifter story she ever read raced across her mind, prompting her to move faster.

She started running.

Disoriented, but desperate to leave that house, Mya got turned around a few times until she found the front door. She would've sworn she'd circled back to the area where she'd talked to Colin, but there had been nothing there, not even a wrapper.

Once outside, she ran down the middle of the road from the house, no doubt looking like a crazy woman. She didn't care. The dead weren't dead. Tunnels were dark and cold. A woman she trusted had taken her son. The world had turned upside down. At the end of the street, she stopped and took several deep breaths while looking over her shoulder to make sure Colin hadn't followed.

God, what was happening to her? Both Colin's gone? Bone deep, agonizing pain ripped through her and came out in a howl of despair. Body shaking with the force of her loss, she collapsed onto the ground and covered her face with her hands. She wasn't sure if she cried for all Colin's father had gone through, the waste of a good man and father or herself. Her son was missing and despite her big talk, she didn't know how to get him back or where to look.

Heartbroken, she wanted her son.

When she heard a car coming down the road, she didn't look until it stopped. Asher stepped out and ran to her side.

"Baby, I'm so sorry," he whispered.

"They took my baby, Asher. They took him for no reason. It's all a mistake, and they took him," she babbled against his shoulder.

"No. He's in the car. I'm sorry I should've called and told you immediately. I'm so sorry," he said, lifting her.

She half heard him, and it didn't fully register until she saw Colin lying on the back seat and screamed. "Colin!" She threw open the door, lifted him and wrapped him in her arms, placing kisses all over his face.

Asher returned behind the wheel and drove to the hospital.

CHAPTER TWENTY-EIGHT

Later that evening, Asher, and Mya sat in the living room of Mya's home with Colin and several others. Maggie and Chastity had come over with their kids to check on Mya and Colin after he'd been released from the hospital. The kids were upstairs playing video games. Now and then Asher heard one of them complain the other had cheated or cheer over a move.

"The doctor cleared him?" Chastity asked while moving over so that her husband, Beamer, could sit comfortably next to her.

"Yes. They gave him an IV, and he woke up a short while later upset that Ms. Jenkins had hurt Mr. Bryson. There was some serious hero worship over Bryson that Ms. Jenkins could never touch. We had to go see him before we left the hospital," Mya said.

"I checked on him too," Maggie said. "He's doing better and swearing he won't work at a place with a lot of females again."

The others laughed.

The doorbell rang.

Asher opened it to let Laura, Wesley, and Bonnie in.

Mya placed her drink aside and went to Wesley with her arms outstretched for a hug. "Please forgive me for being so scared and leaving you in the tunnels like that. I'm so sorry and promise I won't do it again," she said.

He accepted her hug and apology. "Of course, I forgive you and it won't ever happen again, I assure you. From now on, Asher will take you to the tunnels, not me."

She grinned good-naturedly, stepped back, and offered them refreshments. Bonnie went upstairs to talk to Colin while Laura accepted a glass of sweet tea and a seat.

"The dust is clearing a bit," Laura said. "Jenkins had no real excuse for what she did, other than the need for money. She placed the money in her mother's account. At least she had the comfort of knowing she helped her mother. When I asked if she really believed shooting Bryson was necessary, she broke down. Seems shooting him was the only thing she truly regrets."

No one said anything or asked questions. The subject of Ms. Jenkins was officially closed.

Less than ten minutes later, the pizza delivery guy arrived. It took three trips to bring in all the boxes of pizza, wings, and soft drinks to celebrate Colin's safe return. The kids came down, grabbed food, and went to the patio to eat.

Mya smiled as Colin, who had never liked pizza before, took part in a dare from one of the other kids to see who could eat the most slices. He didn't win, but he ate the pizza.

Another car arrived. Tombs, Connor, Mercer, and Kelly came in, grabbed some food, checked on Colin, talked for a bit, and left within 30 minutes.

During the food fest, Mya received a call from her mom and decided it was a good time for Asher to meet the woman. He posed for the picture of him and Mya that she planned to send to her mom and tried to hide the scarred side of his face. No need to scare the woman. Mya kissed him on his cheek, revealing part of the scar and ruining his intentions. Oh well.

"Mom knows nothing about anything that happened," she told him before putting him on the phone.

Asher had never talked to the mother of a woman he dated before and stuck to answering questions.

Beamer smiled at his discomfort.

Laura laughed outright.

Asher didn't mind because Mya glowed with happiness, and that was all that mattered. He and Beamer stepped onto the patio to watch the kids as they ate and ran around the backyard with a ball.

"Little league?"

Asher looked at him.

"Are you going to sign him up for sports? Chastity's after me to do that with the boys. They seem interested. Growing up, I never did anything like that and don't know what it's about. Some days I feel like I need a manual to deal with them, but they seem to like everything and forgive me when I mess up and forget something. Mostly, it's cool being a dad. Think you guys will have more kids?"

Asher looked at Beamer as if he spoke a language he had never heard before. *More kids? Being a real dad?* He hadn't thought that far ahead, but it was something to think about. "I don't know about anything you're talking about. We've got a ways to go before dealing with any of that." He looked at his watch to change the disturbing subject. "Now's a good time to talk to the guests at the Arms while everyone's here. I don't want Mya or Colin alone."

Beamer nodded and didn't bother hiding his grin.

When they returned to the living room, he pulled Mya aside. "I've got to run to the Arms for a bit with Beamer. We'll be back soon. Laura, Chastity, and Maggie will stay here with you and Colin until I get back, alright?"

Leaning forward, she brushed her lips against his. "Alright, be careful." She had told him about seeing her dead ex in the house on Fairmont and their conversation. She'd been scared and unsure if it really happened.

"Will do." He waved to Laura and nodded. "Be back soon."

"We'll stay here until you come back," Laura said.

Asher nodded and waited for Beamer to finish talking to Chastity.

"Watch the kids in the backyard," Beamer told her. Chastity and Maggie stood and went to the patio while Asher and Beamer left through the front door to take the tunnels. It would be faster.

Asher had asked Wesley and Mercer to check the house on Fairmont to see if anyone had been staying there. He didn't share Mya's story, but wanted to make sure their security measures hadn't been violated. No one should be able to access the doors or windows of that house without an alarm alerting Asher, Beamer, or Wesley.

Using the tunnels, they made good time and reached the basement access of the Mecca Building in half the time it would've taken to drive.

Upstairs, on the first floor, Wesley, Connor, Mercer, and Tombs waited for them. Beamer checked on the two prisoners in the lock-up section while Asher headed to the conference room for a debriefing. When he entered, the others sat around the table with cups and remnants of the food they'd taken from Colin's celebration.

"This shouldn't take long," Asher said. "Someone we trusted took Colin from school this morning." Step by step he laid out for everyone what happened once he got the call from Bonnie. The strategy employed, risk factors, complications, and wrap-up. When he finished, he looked around the table. "Did I leave anything out?"

They shook their heads.

"One thing," Wesley said. "I found one food wrapper caught under a baseboard in the house on Fairmont. Still fresh, pliable. Can't say if one of our own left it at some point or not."

Asher nodded and looked at Mercer. "Run a full security analysis on that building. We need to find the problem if there's one and fix it." He and his cousins spent thousands of dollars to remain on the cutting edge of security features and were constantly updating their systems.

"I'll get on it first thing tomorrow," Mercer said.

Asher's phone beeped. He looked at it, cursed and jumped up. "Run a security scan now. Someone just left through the roof vent." He ran toward the lock-up while calling Beamer's number.

No answer.

Tombs and Connor followed Asher. It took a few moments for the steel gate to open that led to the lock-up corridor. Once inside, the gate closed automatically. The three of them ran down the hall to another gate. Asher entered his information. The gate opened. Asher drew his weapon, held it in position and crept toward the corridor, holding the prisoners.

Beamer lay on the ground in front of a cell. Asher ran forward, noticed the cell was empty, and checked Beamer's pulse. He was breathing steadily.

"This one's still here. Seems we have one runner," Connor said with his weapon drawn and pointed at whoever was in the cell.

Tombs helped Asher with Beamer. Other than a minor cut on his forehead, probably from when he hit the ground, there didn't seem to be anything wrong.

Asher stood and looked at the man in the other cage. Gregory Parsons. Of the two men, Asher would've preferred to talk to the other man who'd been in the van. No doubt he was long gone now. It would be interesting to watch the cams to see how he dropped Beamer and escaped.

"Get dressed and take him to the room," Asher told Connor as he pointed to Parsons.

Connor nodded and left for a few moments. He returned dressed in black, wearing a black ski mask. He threw Asher and Tombs masks as well and one for Beamer, although Parsons had already seen him.

Connor waved a small bottle of smelling salt beneath Beamer's nose. He woke coughing and pushing the offending odor away.

"Easy. Easy, Big Guy," Asher said as Beamer sat up, taking small sips of air and snorting to clear his nose.

"What the hell happened?" Beamer said, holding his head. "Feels like someone's hammering inside my skull."

Asher placed his hand beneath Beamer's arm. "Let's get you up and someplace comfortable until you're feeling better. We'll talk about what happened later or look at the cams."

Beamer stood slowly with help, almost lost his balance, and swayed drunkenly. "Something packed a punch," he said. "Can't remember what, though." They moved him to a room down the hall.

"We'll be in the chat room talking to Parsons," Asher told him while walking out.

Beamer waved and nodded as he lay down.

Connor left to bring Parsons to the chat room where they'd ask him questions.

Parsons was still out of it when Connor sat him in the chair and placed the shackles on his ankles. The room was dark, with a spotlight on the chair and its occupant.

"Wake him up," Asher said from the other side of the table.

Connor waved the small bottle beneath his nose.

Frowning, he jerked backward, turned his head, and coughed. "What? Stop." Parsons blinked several times and covered his eyes with his hand. He wasn't a big man or anyone that would leave a remarkable impression. He reminded Asher of George Costanza, the short guy on Seinfeld.

"That light... what's going on?"

Asher said nothing.

"I already agreed with your plan. What else do you want?"

No one answered.

Parsons closed his eyes, took a deep breath, and spoke. "Look, I told you I'm not the only person with the notes or formulas from the project we ran when Henry enrolled in the project. I lost that contract. The government brought in new people to handle it.

Whatever they did with it, I have no knowledge. We don't have that information. What I've sold, shared with my backers, is my work which, as you said before, is incomplete and possibly dangerous. Your people already killed my chances of receiving a new contract."

"The boy," Asher said.

Parsons released a long-suffering sigh. "We talked about this. Henry messed up, over-played his hand when he thought the boy would want to spend some time with him. When that didn't happen. We pulled back. Henry knew the job was over. I never au-thorized a kidnapping. That wasn't me. When I realized there was a problem and the boy wouldn't accept Henry, I wiped the child's file and created another one, so he's not a target. But I told you I did that the day Henry met the boy. I lost my backers and the contract the same day."

Either the kidnapper had talked to Parsons, or Colin Henry had somehow gotten to him. Asher hoped it was the kidnapper, otherwise building security had been badly compromised.

Sweat beaded on Parson's face. He swiped it, wet his lips, and spoke while looking at the table. "You said if I cooperated, told you about the others, I could go home, return to my family." He held out his arm, and there was a red mark on it. "I even agreed to the damn shot so you could find me if I renege on my end of the deal. I've held up my end of the bargain and don't know why you brought me here." His voice rose at the end.

"Where do you want to be taken?" Asher asked.

Parsons stilled. "Who are you? You're not Griffin. Where'd he go? Did he leave me someplace else? What about our deal? We had a deal."

"Where do you want to be taken?" Asher repeated. Parsons was guilty of several things but not kidnapping, which was the violation that concerned Asher and the others. It seemed someone else already had their foot on Parson's neck and would break it if the man stepped out of line. There was no need to draw more blood. Parson's day would come soon enough.

"Fairway hotel to get my things and then the airport," Parson said, his gaze narrowed, searching to see across the wide table.

"Take him back to his hotel," Asher said.

Connor and Tombs walked from the shadows. Parson's startled gaze stared up at the masked men. "I kept my end of the bargain," he said, showing his arm again.

Asher said nothing as the men left the room. Once they left, he checked on Beamer and went to review the security cams. Had Colin Henry infiltrated this building? If so, how?

After completing both a retinal and palm scan, he entered the control room and sat at the console. Moments later, he pulled up the cameras in the lock-up sector to around the time the kidnapper was placed in the cell. Asher watched as the man walked in, said nothing, and took a seat. Once Tombs left, he continued sitting on the twin bed, staring at the floor.

Asher fast forwarded and stopped. The kidnapper and Parsons were talking. He turned on the sound to listen.

"I came to Denver because of Henry. My backers didn't think he could get the blood sample and bribed the teacher to get it for them. I changed the reports to show the child had none of his father's attributes."

"Why didn't you call off the kidnapping?" the Kidnapper asked.

"I never planned a kidnapping, knew nothing about it. They went around me with their own agenda for the boy. I had nothing to do with that."

So Parson's had been telling the truth about that, Asher thought.

"Is he alright? The boy?" Parsons asked.

"He is safe, I believe." The Kidnapper looked at the camera as if speaking to Asher.

"When we learned the teacher had taken a sample of blood and had been bribed to turn over the boy to the other side, I replaced the driver and hired a team to take him to safety. What we didn't know or factor in was his mother had friends and resources in place to fight against the kidnapping attempt. The boy is in excellent hands, and we're satisfied they'll keep him safe."

Asher paused the tape and watched it again. *Who was this guy?*

The conversation between the two men ended, and there was no movement again until Beamer entered the area. The camera glitched, static filled the screen.

"Damn it," Asher cursed. Nothing he did returned the footage. They had wiped five minutes of tape clean. When the camera came back online, Beamer lay on the floor, the kidnapper's cell was empty, and Parsons lay on the floor in his cell.

"What the hell happened?" Asher murmured and spent another 15 minutes trying to recover the data from that camera without success. He sent the file to Mercer to see if he had better luck. Next, he pulled up the camera on the roof and caught the flash of white as the Kidnapper ran across the roof and jumped, yes jumped down from a two-story building. The cameras on the side of the building showed nothing. Asher searched every ground camera twice. None showed when the Kidnapper hit the ground or ran in the distance. Stumped, Asher sat back in his seat staring at the images.

There was something going on that was much bigger than anything he wanted to get involved with. He might never know everything that happened tonight. He'd seen the shadowy part of the government enough times to understand that.

Colin was safe, which was the most important thing. Colin's father had taken measures to make sure his son didn't have to look over his shoulder the rest of his life. Also, a good thing. As far as the other stuff? Asher had no clue. Moses might make sense of some of it. Asher would show him the videos whenever he returned home.

He reset the cameras, left the room to collect Beamer, and headed to the tunnels.

CHAPTER TWENTY-NINE

THREE MONTHS LATER, ASHER and Mya held each other close as they moved around the dance floor at the Charity Ball, which was held in Von Buck's manor. People in formal and evening wear filled the room. Laura told her this was the one night of the year gowns and tuxedos were mandatory. She, Chastity, and Maggie had spent an entire day shopping in Denver last month for their outfits.

Mya wore a shimmery, rust colored, fitted gown with a long split up her thigh and matching heels. Colin said she looked like a princess in one of those girl's books. A high compliment from him. Asher hadn't said much, other than "wow." But the look in his eyes made her pick up her purse and move quickly out of the house. Higher Dimensions provided babysitting for the event, and they dropped Colin off on the way.

Maggie waved from across the floor as she and Bryson danced to another song. Since the kidnapping, Bryson had been scarce, especially after asking to be reassigned to another post. Asher placed him at a factory just outside Versteck.

Chastity and Beamer stood near the food table talking to Laura and Bonnie, who opened the ball with a dance.

"There's the Sheriff, be nice," Mya said.

Asher grunted. Things had been chilly between him and Jack since the kidnapping attempt. Connor wanted the man removed from his position, but cooler heads prevailed, as well as a lot of groveling from Jack. He kept his position with a warning that if he let down the citizens of Versteck again, he would be gone.

"Asher, Mya," Sheriff Jack said when he and his wife danced close enough to speak.

"Hello," Mya said politely.

Asher nodded, but remained quiet.

"This is really nice," Mya said, looking at the twinkling lights and elegant decorations.

"Yeah, they normally go all out for this. They should for the money they take in," he said.

Mya frowned. "What charities benefit from all this?"

"Von Buck's Robbers' Roost," he said, with an evil grin.

"What?"

"The legend lives on. The money takes care of this house, the grounds, taxes, staff." He shrugged.

At the end of the song, Laura introduced the guest who would present the check to the Von Buck Trustees.

"Imani and Theo Barnes aren't strangers to most of us here. At least Theo's signature isn't if you've looked at your last bonus check," Laura said. "Robert Von Buck was one of the first people who invested in Theo's grandfather's company and has been receiving dividends ever since. Proving Europeans stick together."

People laughed, some clapped, others whistled as the gorgeous dark-complexioned woman walked to the middle of the stage holding hands with a guy who could've been a linebacker on any football team.

"They're here tonight to present the check from tonight's proceeds to the Von Buck Memorial fund." Laura clapped and stepped aside as an older woman in a wheelchair was pushed to the front.

"That's Laura's grandaunt, Maude," Asher whispered, as Theo presented the woman with the check.

The crowd cheered as Maude kissed the check and waved it in her hand as she was wheeled back to her table. The music started playing, and Asher held her close. "Your mom's coming tomorrow."

Smiling, she nodded. "Can't wait to see her. It's been over four months. We've never gone that long without seeing each other." For the past two and a half months, her mom had been dating Alan, a guy from the church who had been around for years, which caused another delay in her mom's trip. Alan wanted to come with her.

"Hi, Carol. We really enjoyed the presentation at the school yesterday," Mya said to Colin's new teacher. Ms. King had been Ms. Jenkins assistant and had done a great job with the kids.

"I'm so glad, the kids were great," she said with a wide smile and nodded to Asher before continuing on her way.

"How much longer do we have to stay?" he asked, near her ear.

"We haven't been here an hour," she said. "I don't get the chance to get dressed up like this often."

"I'm more interested in getting you out of that dress," he said.

Unsurprised, she chuckled. The fire hadn't gone out of their relationship. Quite the opposite. Asher's imagination matched hers, and they always tried new things. She loved that about him.

"What I really want to do is reenact a scene from this incredibly hot, sexy story I read online. It's about this guy who ties up this woman, bends her over and pounds into her --"

She gasped and covered his mouth. *Had he read her story? How?* She had only published two stories since they'd been dating and had never told him her pen name. "Asher, don't talk like that here."

He grinned and nipped her palm.

She removed it.

He moved closer to her ear. "The guy had a long, jagged, sexy scar on the right side of his face. She actually thought he was sexy."

Her core clenched as she met his gaze. "When did you read my books?"

He grinned. "I'll tell you my secrets tonight when you let me explore yours. Deal?"

Just thinking of what he had planned made her panties wet. With a look or touch, he got to her on so many levels.

"Deal," she said, accepting a brief kiss filled with the promise of more to come later that night.

When she moved across the country to start over, she never imagined she would find someone like Asher, a man with his own convictions and a heart larger than the Rockies. Thank you, God!

About Author Erosa Knowles

U SA TODAY'S BESTSELLING AUTHOR, Erosa Knowles has a love for the written word. Originally from Miami, Florida, Ms. Knowles now lives in North Carolina. Her three adult children live in North Carolina as well. An avid reader since college, Ms. Knowles is one of those people who keeps her books as old friends and has re-read all of them at least once. Many have been read more often.

Please visit her website: http://www.erosa-knowles.com for other titles.

Also By Erosa Knowles

Reclamation – Murder at the Beach

Reclamation – Lies in the Morgue

Reclamation – That's Not My Baby

Reclamation – I've Got Your Six

Letting Go

Lyon on a Leash

Promises Kept

Secrets

Special Forces

Nikki's Challenge

The Ultimate Breed

Have I Told You Lately?*

Ready for Love*

Where There's Smoke*

Not This Time*

Run to You *

Double Trouble *

Loving a Bad Boy*

Lawked Flame

Jaleesa's Pleasure

Jones Girls – Sabrina

Jones Girls – Melissa

Jones Girls – Angela -

Asher – Men of Versteck Valley

Moses – Men of Versteck Valley

Drake – Men of Versteck Valley

Desperate Measures

Protect the Seed

Legacy of the Seed

Children of the Seed

Arrowheart – Quinton

Arrowheart – Maxwell

Arrowheart – Harrison

Corset Diaries

The Midnight Ball- Books 1,2,3

Race for the Senate

* denotes Men of 3X CONStruction series

www.ingramcontent.com/pod-product-compliance
Lightning Source LLC
Chambersburg PA
CBHW020410210626
46816CB00006BB/2207